Books by Amy Dressler

How to Align the Stars: A Novel (Shakespeare Project)

The Best Advice: A Novel (Shakespeare Project)

THE BEST
ADVICE

SHAKESPEARE PROJECT

THE BEST ADVICE

a novel

AMY DRESSLER

 EGRET LAKE BOOKS
SEATTLE

Egret Lake Books
www.egretlakebooks.com

Excerpt from Shakespeare, William "Sonnet 23" Shake-speares Sonnets
(1906). This poem is in the public domain.

Library of Congress Control Number: 2025935390

978-1-956498-12-7 ISBN (paperback)
978-1-956498-13-4 ISBN (epub)

First Edition
1 2 3 4 6 7 8 9 10

Mom.
If I could have a single wish, it
would be one last conversation
about a book with you.

Chapter One

Roz

R oz slipped out one of her earbuds, keeping her eyes on her phone so it wouldn't be obvious she was eavesdropping.

"Did you watch the show last night?" The young woman in a polka-dot dress to Roz's left asked the latest arrival at the bus stop, a nerdy-cute guy with a leather messenger bag strapped across his chest.

"As soon as the episode went live. I can't believe that plot twist."

"I didn't see it coming either."

Although Roz listened with great interest, she had no idea what they were talking about. What caught her attention was their enthusiasm, which she was convinced had more to do with each other than a TV show. Roz had been rooting for Messenger Bag and Polka Dots to get together for weeks. Listening to them was so much better than being alone with her own early morning thoughts. She guessed they were a few years younger than she was, perhaps recent college grads with their first professional jobs.

On Fridays, they each wore jeans and graphic tees. Last week, they'd both shown up wearing a shirt with characters from the same series and had such an animated conversation through the whole bus ride, she felt sure they'd finally exchange phone numbers. When they didn't, she felt as let down as she did when her own flirtations didn't pan out. More so, actually — after all, she had far too much on her plate right now to worry about dating.

She buttoned her jacket against the chilly fall morning, adjusting the strap of her bag. According to the transit app, the bus was running late. Roz looked up from her phone and broke the silence. "The bus is still twelve minutes away," she said. "Does anyone want to grab a coffee across the street?"

"I'll go," said Polka Dot Girl.

"Why not?" said Messenger Bag Guy.

"No thanks, I've already got a thermos in my bag," said the only other person at the bus stop.

Of course you do, thought Roz. She had secretly nicknamed this woman Mary Poppins because of her capacious, comprehensive tote bag. Every morning, Poppins ate a balanced breakfast, applied a full face of makeup — contouring and everything! — and did an actual pencil-and-paper Sudoku puzzle on their twenty-minute ride into downtown Seattle.

"Let's go," Roz gestured at the coffee shop across the street from their stop. "It doesn't look like there's a line."

When the crosswalk signal changed, she pretended to read her phone again. "Damn," she said. "I have to answer this email right away. You two go." No need to be a third wheel.

"Want us to get you anything?"

She'd been up early to take her dog, Bowie, for a long run and was starting to feel the tendrils of a caffeine-deprivation headache creeping around the back of her skull, but Roz declined. She wanted them to focus on each other, not her coffee order.

Roz turned back to the bus stop, watching the pair go into the coffee shop. Messenger Bag opened the door for Polka Dots, she smiled, they walked inside and his hand drifted toward the small of her back, then he pulled it back as if having second thoughts. Roz watched through the window as they ordered their drinks; he asked her something with a nervous look on his face. She burst into a grin, nodded, and handed him her phone. He gave her his, and they punched in each other's numbers.

Warmth bloomed through Roz's chest. As an advice columnist, it was her job to help people sort out their problems, but she seldom knew how things turned out for her anonymous letter-writers. It was immensely satisfying when she could see the results of her work up close. All these two had needed was a teeny, tiny push. Not that it was difficult; a Hollywood casting agent couldn't have done a better job picking a pair with obvious chemistry. They were adorable, and the signs of how attracted they were to each other were crystal clear.

Maybe someday she would have her own meet-cute, but for now, she'd settle for living vicariously through others; the stakes were too high at work for her to risk dividing her focus. And deep down she suspected she wasn't ready to put her still-healing heart on the line.

The enamored pair crossed the street with their coffees. She'd better look busy. She opened her work email for verisimilitude.

The contents of her inbox killed her matchmaking-induced buzz immediately. "See me the moment you get in. E.O.M. -F.G."

Only Frederick George would initial his subject-line-only emails in addition to the "end-of-message" acronym. She'd known a showdown was imminent with her boss (ugh, she still wasn't used to calling him that, but she'd also never felt comfortable calling him her stepfather and had stopped the second her mother signed the divorce papers), but she'd been hoping to have a little time to organize her thoughts about the matter Fred undoubtedly wanted to discuss. The company attorneys had worked through the weekend to prepare a memo with options and talking points, but it hadn't arrived until late last night and she hadn't read it thoroughly yet.

Fine. If Fred could come in on the offensive, so could she. Not only was she unambiguously right, she was a sentimental favorite with their readers and she knew it. It was in Fred's best economic interest to see her side of reason.

"Hey!"

Roz looked up to a welcome distraction. Celeste, her ex-step-sister, favorite coworker, and housemate joined her at the bus stop. The craftsman bungalow Roz had spent her early child-hood in and inherited after her mom died had turned out to be much lonelier than her one-bedroom apartment. Companionship helped, especially Celeste's. With her calm, kind nature, Roz had never fully been able to believe she was related to Fred.

"Morning." Roz returned the greeting. Celeste had run for the bus and was out of breath. Though they were occasionally mis-taken for biological sisters, it was only because of the way they acted, not because of appearance. They both had pale skin that flushed in the cold, but that was where the physical similarities ended; Celeste was petite and curvy, with flyaway blonde hair, delicate features, and blue eyes. Roz was tall, with an athletic build, freckles, red-brown hair, and an angular face accentuated by strong eyebrows.

Roz had heard Celeste come in after midnight; no wonder she was scrambling this morning.

When the bus finally came, it was standing room only, as usual. They found a handhold with space for both of them near the front. Celeste wordlessly reached for Roz's bag, holding it while she unbuttoned her jacket. Roz gripped a bit higher on the pole because Celeste's shorter arms couldn't reach as far. They'd known each other so long, sharing space was second nature. Whenever anyone commented on how well they got along, Roz credited Celeste's easygoing personality, which smoothed out her own rough edges.

The bus lumbered through their neighborhood, slowing even more when it reached downtown traffic. Roz filled Celeste in on the email from Fred.

"What do you think he wants to talk about?"

"The Unconvertible letter, I'm sure. The parents know their kid wrote in and they're pissed."

Celeste blew a wisp of hair out of her eyes. "I don't think you need to worry. You definitely did the right thing."

"I doubt your dad sees it that way. I'm not looking forward to the lecture."

"I don't blame you, but I'm sure this will all work out."

Maybe, but the bigger problem was Fred micromanaging the content of her columns, and that wasn't going to let up. One of Roz's favorite things about her column was the opportunity to help marginalized letter-writers understand they weren't alone. With Fred's interference, she'd be restricted to answering questions about wedding etiquette by spring.

Roz was going to be too tense to see straight by the time they got to the office. She changed the subject. "You had a late night."

Celeste's cheeks turned pink. "We sat talking until our server asked us to leave so they could go home. Then we had a glass of wine at her place. I think I got home around one."

Roz gave her a gentle slug on the arm. "Way to go. Are you going to keep seeing her?"

"I don't know." Celeste's face was turned toward the window

and Roz could barely make out her words over the rumble of the engine. "I had a great time but getting serious might just be too much of a change. I can't imagine what it would be like to meet someone so special she's worth shaking up my life over. This definitely isn't it."

Celeste had been doing this for years now and Roz was sick of being a bystander. Time after time, she had a promising first date, an exciting second date, and then...fizzle, retreat. Though she would never say it in so many words, Celeste was nervous about how her father would handle being introduced to a girlfriend. Roz's own avoidance of romantic entanglements was sensible, at least for now, but she knew Celeste's hesitation was rooted in a desire to avoid conflict. Although Roz sympathized, she hated seeing Celeste get in the way of her own happiness. Maybe there was still time to prevent this latest love interest from falling victim to the same pattern. Celeste deserved to be unreservedly happy. Roz began, "Celeste—"

"I'm just going to hop off here and get some tea!"

Stuck in rush hour gridlock, the bus was only a few blocks away from their office building but moved at an excruciating crawl. Celeste reached up to pull the cord to request a stop and had swung down the steps and into the closest café before Roz could say anything more or follow.

Roz shifted her bag to the other shoulder and tapped the toe of her pump against the floor of the bus. The irresistible impulse to repair someone else's love life had provided a vital diversion. Without it, anxiety about the workday ahead inched toward the front of her consciousness. She had the moral high ground, but the impending confrontation was going to be ugly. The icing on the cake was that there shouldn't be an argument at all. It was a gross injustice for her content, her column, to be subject to the whims of Frederick George in the first place.

On a dreary Tuesday evening a week after burying her mother, Roz had found herself sitting outside the NWC Magazine conference room, waiting to hear the outcome of a vote. She picked at her cuticles, an old nervous habit she thought she'd long outgrown. The board chair, Margaret Olson, a family friend who'd known Roz since she was four years old, came out and sat beside her.

"I'm sorry, Roz. You're doing great work here and I know your mom wanted you to fill her shoes someday, but the majority of the board doesn't believe you're ready for leadership yet, even if we created a deputy editor role for you."

How could it be possible to be unsurprised and gut-punched at the same time? "Did Fred vote against me?"

"The individual board member votes are confidential." Margaret lowered her voice and glanced behind her to make sure the hallway was clear. "Frederick made a strong case for continuing as solo editor."

"I see." Roz gathered her things to go.

Margaret placed a hand on her arm. "If it's any consolation, we are all thrilled to have you on staff and feel, Frederick included, that it's right for you to take on permanent authorship of the "Kate Knows Best" column. We all miss your mom so much and the readers miss her too."

Roz tried to swallow the lump in her throat. At least this was something. Her mom had built this magazine from the ground up — with financial backing and some input from Fred — and Roz always expected to take over someday. No one had expected Kate's seat as co-editor to be vacant so soon, but it didn't seem unreasonable for Roz to expect a spot at the table. Apparently,

Fred had other ideas. He now had full control of NWC.

Still, the column was important to Roz. "I'd be honored to write 'Kate Knows Best,'" she said.

Ever since, she'd poured her broken heart into her work. Her mother's readers provided a sense of community. They'd felt connected to Kate, and they were grieving along with Roz. The letter writers' individual sadnesses made Roz feel less alone with her own sorrow.

Roz was sure the board had swung against her on Fred's say. They were supposed to provide neutral governance but sandwiched as they were between the shareholders and company management they had been in a tough position. Fred held the largest number of shares even though Roz had inherited her mother's stake in the company. It would take something major for the board to go against his wishes. Reliving that evening only increased her agitation, and by the time the bus doors finally hissed open at the stop in front of the skyscraper that housed NWC, Roz felt like a teakettle about to come to a boil, on the verge of shrieking. She couldn't lose control of her column to Fred. She'd lost too much already.

Chapter Two

Roz

Celeste caught up to Roz at the door of the building, a paper cup in each hand. Roz's hopes for coffee were dashed when she saw the pastel tags of herbal tea bags dangling from both lids.

"It's going to be fine. Relax. Drink some tea." Celeste waved a cup at her. Roz gave her a small smile, heartened in spite of herself by Celeste's well-meaning but misguided attempts to wean her off caffeine. She didn't take the cup, though. She had her principles.

Roz stepped onto the elevator and jabbed the button for the twenty-third floor as Celeste hopped in behind her.

"In the twenty years you've known me, have you ever seen me drink herbal tea voluntarily?" Celeste's expression dropped into one of genuine hurt, and Roz relented immediately. "Okay, fine, give it." Principles compromised, she took a sip and emitted an exaggerated blissful sigh. Although the tea didn't work as intended, Celeste's laughter reduced her agitation from a boil to a simmer.

The other elevator arrived at their floor at the same time, as if they'd been racing. Its doors opened to reveal their office manager, Barry Santos. Barry was dressed in one of his trademark dapper outfits; a black and white checked shirt with a fire-engine red bowtie and slim trousers in the same shade, his thick black hair slicked into a shiny pompadour.

"How are my two favorite writers this morning?" He held a latte from the downstairs café in each hand, handing one to Roz. "Triple shot, oat milk. Drink it fast, Fred's waiting in your office, and he doesn't seem inclined to be patient."

"How did you know how badly I needed this?" Roz smiled and grabbed the coffee from his hand.

"You'll need caffeine courage to deal with Fred today. Good luck."

Of course Fred would ambush her in her own space before she had a chance to settle in for the day. She zipped down the corridor: depositing the unwanted tea in the break room, dabbing irritably at a bit of coffee foam she'd already managed to spill on her blazer. Celeste followed as if by moving calmly herself, she could slow her sister's frenetic pace.

The NWC Magazine offices consisted of a handful of individual desks with tasteful, frosted glass privacy walls ("Not cubicles," insisted Celeste, who had used her artistic eye to lend class and warmth to the recent remodel) for staff writers to use when they weren't working from home. A few senior writers had offices around the perimeter. Roz shared a window office with a view of Elliott Bay with Celeste, who wrote a style column. If they looked all the way to the left on a clear day, they could see past the groups of cranes at the shipping piers to a stunning vista of Mount Rainier. To the right, they saw the Olympic range and ferries crisscrossing Puget Sound. Today the city was crisp, golden, September perfection, but Roz didn't expect to enjoy the view.

"Rosalind!" Fred barked. This was not necessarily a bad sign on its own—barking was Fred's typical mode of speaking. Combined with his meticulously coiffed white hair and less-than-average height, he evoked a well-groomed but poorly trained Pomeranian. "We need to talk about your answer to *Unconvertible*."

His bluster put Roz on edge, even though she ought to have been used to it by now. Fred had been a presence in her life since she was a baby. Roz's mom started NWC with Fred when she was pregnant. A decade later they'd married, and although they'd divorced while Roz was still in high school, they stayed in business together. Roz could never understand how her mother, a woman of otherwise impeccable judgment, had been able to remain cordial with Fred after his cheating ended their marriage.

"I'll step out," said Celeste.

"Stay, Celeste." Fred's command was more suited to a pet than his daughter, and Roz wanted to slap his domineering face. "I'd like you to hear this."

In Roz's view, the only good thing about Fred was that he'd brought Celeste into their lives, but even that was a point of friction. Roz had never been able to measure up to Celeste's sweet disposition and had endured countless tirades from him about her clothes, her mannerisms, her proclivity for organizing protests against injustice. With her mother gone, they were in regular conflict about work. When Fred co-edited with Kate, NWC's content had been balanced between high-quality investigative journalism, social justice-oriented editorials, smart culture criticism, and pieces with what Fred called "middle American appeal." The latter used to be things like TV reviews, but lately had been a lot of trashy clickbait.

Without Kate, the balance had faltered. Roz had stopped reading most of their output because it upset her too much. She'd been asserting control in the one place she could. Even though "Kate Knows Best" was only one column, it was their most popular regular feature. It was syndicated in regional publications nationwide and shared across social media, which meant it was also their biggest earner of ad revenue. Roz was proud of the column's success, but she was most proud of what it represented. It was gratifying to know so many others understood how special her mother was, and Roz endeavored to fill the void Kate left for the readers. In a strange way, writing the column filled the void for herself, too, by keeping her close to Kate. It made her feel like she could keep a little piece of her mom. Roz knew it irritated Fred when she chose letters that allowed her to make a social statement, and so she did that as often as she could. This, too, was part of Kate's legacy; she had never shied away from butting heads with Fred.

Many of the letters the column received broke Roz's heart, but none quite so much as the one from *Unconvertible.*

> *Dear Kate,*
>
> *I, 16, AMAB (assigned male at birth), am from an evangelical Christian household. Six months ago, my parents looked through my phone and found out that I had been questioning my sexuality. They pulled me out of school and sent me to a camp where we spent days in humiliating group therapy sessions, with worse activities for the campers who didn't cooperate. I pretended to be "better" because I just wanted to get out of there. I didn't want to go back to the way things were at home, but I thought things might be okay if I just did what they wanted me to. Since I've been back, I am not allowed to leave the house without my parents or an elder from our church accompanying me. I am frequently reminded that I am going to hell unless I "stay away from sin." I am suffocating. I don't really believe I have done anything wrong,*

but when you are told every day your feelings are sinful, it starts to feel true. I don't know how to make it until I turn 18, or even what I will do then. I feel miserable, alone, and hopeless. My parents say they love me and are doing this for my own good, but I can't live like this.

So lost. What can I do?

-Unconvertible.

Dear Unconvertible,

Your parents may believe they love you, but they aren't treating you with love. Some people — I am one of them — would classify the way they are treating you as verbal and emotional abuse. It sounds like the camp you were sent to may have upped the ante to physical abuse. In fact, what happened to you is illegal in many states. First, I need you to understand that none of this is your fault and you don't deserve it. Say it out loud to yourself, in the mirror, every day. "This isn't my fault. I deserve to be loved unconditionally. I am going to be okay." Then, I want you to contact someone local to you who can help you. I am linking information for The Trevor Project. They can put you in touch with a local advocate. If you have any other trusted adults (someone like a former teacher or a friend's parent), reach out to them for help as well.

In your corner,

Kate

The letter-writer had taken her advice and then some. He'd spoken to a reporter at a local TV station in Boise and was pursuing emancipated minor status. Roz was collaborating with an investigator in Idaho to produce a follow-up article about the camp, and conversion therapy in general. She believed it was one of the best things she'd written in years. She knew she'd have to fight Fred to get him to publish the article, but it would be worth it.

"Yes, I've gotten a lot of positive feedback about that letter." She hoped she'd smoothed her voice out enough to hide her nerves.

"I haven't. Certainly not from the boy's parents, who are threatening to sue us for libel."

"They can go ahead and threaten. Our attorney says there isn't even a whisper of a solid case because we didn't name them. We didn't even name the city they're in. You know damn well my mother would have written the exact same answer if she were here, and she'd stand behind it, too."

"Your mother's style of idealism won't keep us out of court. You shouldn't be answering letters from minors at all, Rosalind. You don't understand what it's like to have children and you need to stay out of other people's parenting decisions."

Heat flared in Roz's cheeks. "Some of these kids have been gaslighted by their parents their whole lives. It takes a lot of courage to reach out for help. I might not be a parent, but I sure understand that."

Fred waved a hand as if trying to clear a bad smell. "That's ridiculous."

"Think so?" she replied. Fred would never be able to see his own hypocrisy unless someone pointed it out to him. It was high time someone did.

"I'm surprised you're taking issue with this. You said donating to Pride was good for business. And my advice column is the top revenue earner here."

"This is different. This time you went too far."

"Says the man who barely reacted when his daughter came out, then later said it's okay to be gay as long as she—how did you put it? — 'doesn't get too dykey.'"

The last bit was something Roz overheard Fred say to Kate after Celeste came out. Celeste had waited until she was twenty-two to tell her father because she'd been so afraid of his reaction. Roz had never forgotten what he said after Celeste was out of earshot. Until now, she'd kept it to herself because she'd done the emotional math and knew it would hurt Celeste much more than it hurt Fred. But in the heat of the moment she'd let it slip out.

"Oh." It was the first thing Celeste had said since the argument started. One small syllable that spoke volumes.

But Roz wasn't ready to back down. Now that it was all out in the open, the only thing to do was keep going in the hopes that she could shame Fred into seeing reason.

Celeste

Celeste was used to being in the middle. It had been that way her whole life. One of her earliest memories was sitting in her car seat while her mother screamed at her father on the way home from a party. Her parents finally divorced when she was in third grade, but soon after, her dad married Kate and then there were an endless configuration of strong personalities for her to mediate between: Roz and Fred, Fred and Kate, Roz and various friends and boyfriends. Even Roz and Kate, who'd welcomed Celeste under the wing of their close mother-daughter relationship, had butted heads with each other on a semi-regular basis.

It wasn't as if she didn't know her father accepted her sexuality on a purely theoretical basis that would be tested the minute he had to confront the reality of it. It was a balance beam she'd been accustomed to living her life on, pirouetting between moments of conditional love from her dad and living her life the way she wanted to, never pushing the envelope too far lest she stumble. But now Roz had voiced it and Celeste was going to have to deal with it.

And Roz wasn't finished. "You write a check to the Pride Foundation every June, Fred, but if your daughter brought a girlfriend to Thanksgiving, you'd be horrified."

Celeste felt all her energy pull in toward her core, her body trying to protect itself from what was happening in the room. "Roz," she said, but her ears rushed with blood and she could barely hear herself.

Roz finally turned in her direction and Celeste could see remorse on her face, but she wasn't sorry enough to stop. "You were never going to say it on your own, Celly. And if he knows how this behavior impacts you, maybe he'll finally care."

"Celeste?" Fred's voice was unusually small. Now they were both looking at her. She would do what she always did: mediate, smooth things over, keep everyone calm.

"She's right, Dad. It's almost like you didn't hear me when I first told you. I've tried to talk to you about it a couple of times, but you changed the subject so quickly I knew you didn't want to hear it." His refusal to engage had been hurtful enough, but now thanks to Roz she had confirmation of how he really felt. Agreeing with Roz right now, given how careless she was being, hurt almost as much, but honesty was her only choice.

"Honey, it's simply difficult to imagine. You're so feminine."

Celeste was so focused on bracing for Roz's reaction, she barely had any time to absorb the words for herself, much less formulate a reply. Across the room, a deep flush crept up Roz's neck to her cheeks. "Oh my god. Are you kidding me with this? How can even you be so clueless?"

Fred's composure returned as if a switch had been flipped. It was easier for him to butt heads with Roz than relate honestly to his own daughter. Sometimes she liked it that way; she could fly under the radar. Right now, she was keenly aware that they were arguing about her feelings while neither one of them had taken a second to see how the tension in the room was impacting her.

"Rosalind," Fred said, "it's clear we're at an impasse. The board won't allow me to terminate your employment here, but I do have complete control over your assignments. I'm giving 'Kate Knows Best' to someone else, and we will find other content for you to work on."

This was catastrophic. Roz was deeply attached to the "Kate" column. Celeste wasn't sure she realized it was a final shred of her mother that she was hanging on to with white knuckles. Most days, Roz seemed like she was coping, but she'd put a lot of emotional stock into writing the column, connecting with Kate's fans and the letter-writers who sought Kate's advice. Without that, Celeste was afraid she would crumble.

Roz squared her shoulders and set her jaw, as if she knew what Celeste was thinking and was determined to prove she wasn't crumbling anytime soon. "Absolutely not. If I can't write 'Kate Knows Best,' there's no reason for me to stay here. I have the contacts and name recognition to find another job, and this way I won't have to watch my mother's magazine turn into mindless, heartless crap."

Celeste felt like she was watching a contentious tennis match. She looked back to her father for his reaction, but he seemed ready for this. He was studying his nail beds, looking bored while Roz ranted. "That's fine. I'm sure once you relinquish your shares in NWC, you'll have plenty of offers."

Roz stared at him. "I beg your pardon?"

"You inherited your mother's shares in the business and as a shareholder, you're not allowed to work for a competitor. Our bylaws prohibit it."

"I'm not giving up Mom's shares."

"Then I hope you enjoy being a barista. If you change your

mind, I'll be happy to buy you out at a fair price."

Celeste held a small number of shares herself, and was aware of this bylaws rule, but she wasn't worried about on her own account because she wasn't interested in writing for anyone else. Lately she'd come to realize she was barely interested in writing for NWC. It was something she'd fallen into because it was the family business. When she left, it wouldn't be for another writing job. In fact, she was already considering a new path but hadn't spoken to Roz or her father about it yet.

When she encouraged Roz to familiarize herself with all the technicalities of holding company shares, Roz had said one of the perks of working for family was not having to worry about being screwed over by petty red tape.

Roz's eyes darted around, as if seeking an escape, but Fred was standing in front of the door.

Roz said, "Well, but Mom—"

"With your mother gone, these matters are at my discretion now. If you want to take your chances, you're more than welcome, but you might not find a new employer who's willing to take the risk along with you. Competition in this business can get ugly; look what happened to Jeff."

Since he'd taken editorial control of NWC, Fred had taken to using backchannel connections to sabotage the careers of any staff who left, shareholder or not. Their sportswriter, Jeff, had left NWC when he'd been offered an on-camera job with one of the local news stations, but something had fallen through with his deal. The last Celeste heard, he was teaching journalism at a high school in Tacoma.

Celeste had tried to believe that this was all just a series of unlucky breaks, that her father wouldn't be so vindictive, but now he was practically admitting it. She hated the position she was in, torn between loyalty to a parent and her own ethics, and was angry at her father for putting her there.

This was it. This was their breaking point. Even with the divorce, Kate, Roz, Celeste, and Fred had remained familial, all four working together after both girls graduated from college. But Celeste's father was drawing a line in the sand.

Roz had stepped over it immediately. Celeste didn't want to choose a side, but there were only two options. Stay or go.

Staying here without Roz would feel too much like choosing her dad's side. Everyone else would certainly interpret it that way. It might hurt him, but it would hurt Celeste to stay. This was her out and she was going to take it. She could only hope he would get over it eventually.

"I quit, too," she said.

Her voice must not have come back to her yet, because Roz and Fred both snapped their attention to her and said, "What?" in unison. It would have been funny if the situation weren't so fraught.

"I'm resigning, too." Celeste made eye contact with each of them in turn. "I don't think this is the right path for me anymore."

"Sweetheart," Fred said, in the be-reasonable voice she'd grown to hate. "You don't want to do this. Where else would you work? I'm sure we can sort this out. Let's start having our weekly lunches again."

They'd gone to lunch a total of three times, in the weeks Celeste was new at NWC. After that, he usually canceled.

"Dad, no. I need a break and some time to think about things."

Fred's demeanor turned on a dime again. "Fine. I'll have Marie start the paperwork."

As soon as the door shut behind him, Roz blew a breath out through pursed lips. "That went well."

Celeste opened a binder sitting on her desk—the portfolio of sketches and samples from the office remodel. She ran her hand over the swatches, concentrating on the rough texture of the upholstery she'd chosen for the lobby chairs under her fingertips. This was the last time she'd felt fulfilled by her work, and she was proud of what she'd done.

She didn't realize she hadn't replied until Roz wheeled her chair over to sit directly in front of her, taking both of her hands. Roz's hands felt hot, and it was then Celeste realized all the blood had run out of her fingers. She drew them back and rubbed them together to warm them up.

"Hey," Roz said. "I'm really sorry. I need you to know I didn't plan to do that. I don't know what came over me. I can't stand it when he acts like these issues don't touch him. I hate seeing how much it hurts you. And I hate that it holds you back."

She was right. It did hurt. It also hurt not to be trusted to make her own decisions about how she related to her father. She had to believe that he'd come around someday and fully accept her exactly as she was. It was too painful not to. Every time she pushed for it — mentioned a date's name or made a comment about current events that impacted the LGBTQ+ community, there was a chill she didn't want to confront, but she would have gotten there eventually, and the timing should have been her decision.

Rubbing her hands wasn't working. She reached for her tea and wrapped them around the paper cup, even though it didn't hold much warmth. She couldn't deal with being at odds with Roz right now, either, to say nothing of what it might do to Roz. In happier times, on the rare occasions when there was friction between Roz and Celeste, they'd turned to their respective mothers. Celeste's mom lived in California, and Celeste could call her later to vent, maybe even plan a road trip.

But the space where Kate had once been for Roz had been replaced with a gaping void of grief, and Celeste couldn't bear to leave her alone with that. Roz had behaved horribly today, but she hadn't been herself since losing Kate; didn't she deserve a little leeway? Celeste pushed down her own hurt, becoming a balm instead.

"I know, Roz, it's okay. You're right. I'd gone too long not saying anything. This is for the best."

"I'm sorry his reaction was so disappointing."

"Disappointing, yes, but not surprising. I guess as long as we didn't talk about it, I could still hope he'd react better."

"I'm sorry. I don't think he knows how to express it, but I know he loves you."

"I know."

There was a knock on their office door and it opened before either of them could answer. Barry, with a stack of cardboard boxes. "Oh my god, you two. Fred's trying to keep it quiet, but the whole office is losing their shit. Meanwhile, Mr. Bossypants is threatening a security escort if Roz isn't gone by noon."

Roz rolled her eyes. "No problem. I can't wait to get out of here."

"I've got a few more fires to put out, but we'll catch up later. I need details." He was gone as quickly as he'd come.

"Onwards and upwards, right?" Roz pushed off with her feet, sliding back to her own side of the office without leaving her chair. "I guess we'd better pack before your dad calls security."

"He's not going to call security." He wouldn't, would he?

"Oh, you never know," Roz turned, brandishing a box of paperclips. "I intend to steal as many office supplies as I can." She winked, then cast an exaggerated series of glances around the office before shoving the paperclips into her bra. Glancing down at the square protruding from her chest, she said, "Whoops, that's lopsided. Better give me yours."

Laughing in spite of herself, Celeste tossed her own box of paperclips to Roz, who stashed them in the other side of her dress.

An hour later, they were stepping back onto the elevator, cardboard boxes in their arms full of framed photos, Roz's instant oatmeal, Celeste's salt lamp. The doors were three inches apart when a hand shot through the gap and they shuddered open again. Breathless, Barry joined them. He was, inexplicably, holding the four-foot-tall potted ficus from the lobby. He looked like a kid who'd been cast as a tree in the school play.

"Guess what? I quit, too."

"Barry!" Roz exclaimed. "You can't quit your job. What about your health insurance and your 401(k) and your rent? At least Celeste and I have Mom's house so we don't have to worry about rent."

For a second, doubt flashed through Barry's eyes. Celeste knew he'd been unhappy with the ways his job had changed since Kate's death. She nudged him with her shoulder, leaning over to kiss him on the cheek. "We love you, Bear. We'll all be okay, right?"

Bolstered, he lifted his chin. "We'll be *splendid*."

Celeste saw Roz smile at this. Splendid had been one of Kate's favorite words.

As they toted their boxes through the lobby, Roz said, "Barry? Explain the plant."

"Well, of course I would have preferred a fish in a baggie, but Fred wouldn't let us have an aquarium in the NWC lobby."

"Um. What?"

"Jerry Maguire? Hello? Seriously, you haven't seen that movie? I am the Renee Zellweger to your Tom Cruises, and I am liberating this ficus as my grand gesture."

"Roz's mom wouldn't let us watch anything with Tom Cruise," Celeste explained. "She thought he was creepy."

They were on their way, a fresh start for all of them. Celeste assumed they'd catch a bus together, back to the house she shared with Roz, but when they exited the building, Roz turned in the opposite direction from the bus stop.

"Come on," she said, "We're going to YiaYia's."

Chapter Three

Andy

Most people think being on TV is a fun job. Especially a show like *Ardent Life Adventures*. What could be bad about traveling to interesting places to tell people about the local food and activities? Andy Arden wasn't having any fun, though, especially lately. He simply needed to get through this day. It wasn't going to be simple or easy, but once it was over, he'd be free to figure out the next chapter of his life. Step one was fortifying himself with coffee.

They never closed their locations to the general public before shooting, preferring to show real people enjoying the destinations they profiled. The only problem? It was sometimes difficult to get to the set adequately caffeinated. When "filming in the vicinity" signs were posted, people tended to start looking for celebrities, and stopping in a coffee shop increased Andy's chances of being recognized. The show kept things lean, often forgoing craft services on the days the shoot was surrounded by food, and Andy could never manage to leave himself time for breakfast in his hotel room. Man, he couldn't bear to do autographs and selfies today. He especially couldn't do intrusive questions. Of course, Pike Place Market was home to the world's very first Starbucks… and, of course, the line was already out the door. Andy hurried past, turning his face away from the crowd.

He was saved by Joe, his favorite camera operator. "There's a bakery around the corner," Joe told him, handing over a black coffee and a thick slice of banana bread.

"Thanks. Seen Liv yet?" Andy's co-host liked to get to set even earlier than he did.

"She's getting her hair and makeup touched up. She doesn't look any more excited about this than you do."

"Yeah, well. The network is determined to have us finish the season together. I understand why more people started watching when we announced the breakup, but I don't feel good about getting famous that way."

Ardent Life Adventures had been a modest success until a year ago, when Olivia's request for a divorce had caught the attention of industry gossip, a move that coincided with their network, The Geography Channel, making all of their content available for streaming. Then it became a *huge* success, and given their relatively low budget — rustic, DIY aesthetics were part of the show's charm — it was understandable that the network didn't want to let Andy and Olivia out of their contracts early. Olivia was more than happy to stay on. Andy, on the other hand, wanted a clean break as soon as possible. They had one episode left to shoot for their final season. As soon as they completed it, they could go their separate ways. Andy would be venturing out of town shortly to do his segment on the Olympic Peninsula's outdoor recreation opportunities. Today's shoot, purchasing and preparing ingredients from Seattle's Pike Place Market, was to be the last time they would appear on camera together.

Andy expected the market to be bustling already but, except for Starbucks, Pike Place was surprisingly slow to wake up in the morning. Groggy commuters cut through to get into downtown from the ferry docks, vendors were just setting up for the day. The cobblestones were freshly washed; shopkeepers arranged produce, pausing every so often to make an early sale. Seafood merchants swaddled shellfish and salmon in beds of ice. One by one, the newsstands and gift shops rolled up their gates. The flower stalls had mostly dahlias today: great anemones eight inches wide, in shades of crimson, gold, and magenta. Andy briefly thought about buying a bouquet for Olivia as a peace offering, before rejecting the idea. She would find it silly. Impractical. Patronizing.

Joe steered Andy to the tents that served as the production's base camp. Later, they'd shoot their cooking segment in a nearby restaurant's borrowed kitchen.

"So," Joe explained, "the meal is pretty simple this time: cedar plank salmon, root vegetable gratin, apple-blackberry galette. You'll shoot with the fish-throwing guys, the cheesemonger, and talk to one of the fruit vendors about apple varieties. For the blackberries, Charles has something slightly unconventional in mind." Joe pointed to the slope next to the parking garage. It was covered with a tangle of thorny, prickly vines clustered with plump purple berries.

"What? Why? Isn't there someone in the market who sells them?" Of course, there had to be a twist, but this was taking DIY a bit too far.

"Charles thinks it will be exciting. Apparently urban foraging is a hot new trend. Olivia was all for it, oddly enough." Charles, their producer, had always tried to get Olivia to shoot some of the more rugged segments with Andy, but she consistently demurred. Olivia liked to say she was a cute-après-ski-outfit kind of girl, not a hurtle-down-the-slopes kind of girl. Not today, apparently.

Andy peered down the hill. Well, why not? It wasn't like this was going to be a problem for him and being agreeable was the path of least resistance. "Fine. It's not like I haven't hiked more difficult terrain than that." He took a grounding breath and stepped into the hair and makeup tent.

Olivia was the very picture of upscale casual in jeans that Andy knew cost hundreds of dollars, high-heeled ankle boots, and a caramel-colored leather jacket. Her black hair was stylishly bobbed.

"Sticking to your uniform, I see?" She arched a manicured brow and gave Andy's Levi's, hiking boots, and canvas jacket an up-and-down appraisal. She had always wanted him to pay more attention to his clothes, but their contrasting senses of style were one of the things that made them popular with fans; Olivia leaned into sleek urban style even though her adoptive parents were from a small town in Nebraska. Andy almost always looked like he'd just stepped off a hiking trail despite being born and raised in Pasadena.

"Let's just get this over with, Liv."

"Fine, *Andrew.*"

After about thirty seconds of basic face powdering and yet another lecture from the makeup artist about the importance of daily sunscreen (Andy had a Mediterranean complexion that never burned in the sun, which had made sunscreen a difficult habit to acquire), he was ready to go. There was never much to be done with his wild, curly hair and he'd eventually persuaded them to just leave it alone. The segment they shot with the apple vendor went fine — Andy'd had no idea that there were so many types, and he was looking forward to tasting the tart they'd be making with two different kinds, which, according to Olivia, meant the perfect mix of flavor and texture.

Shooting with the fish throwers reminded Andy of a long-ago afternoon when they were seniors at Stanford. Olivia and Andy had driven his beat-up, third-hand Geo Metro all the way to Fisherman's Wharf to buy lingcod and sourdough bread, packing the fish carefully into an ice chest in the trunk. They spent the rest of the day making chowder to share with their friends, gathered on the futon and folding chairs in their tiny off-campus apartment. As broke college students, their kitchenware was fairly limited, and Olivia had laughed as they tried to jam all the ingredients into a too-small pot, continually skimming off the top as the mixture threatened to boil over. When they remembered they only owned two bowls, they served the soup in coffee mugs with hunks of buttered bread balanced on paper towels.

The seafood section of Pike Place smelled just the same as the San Francisco Wharf; it wasn't particularly fishy, but had a mineral, ocean smell. Olivia, trying gamely to catch the fish in her rubber-gloved hands, laughed the same way she had at the overflowing chowder pot when one flew past her outstretched arms and landed on the tile with a plop. Liv's laugh was good to hear. While she'd been more or less polite and professional, if brisk, since initiating the divorce proceedings, Andy hadn't seen Olivia let her polished guard down in a very long time — not since long before she'd presented him with divorce papers.

"Now," Charles was all business when it was time for berry picking, "the only way I could get market management to allow us in here was to promise we would make it *very clear* that this area is off limits to the general public. You've got some scripted copy I want you to read; it's on cue cards for you. Got it?"

"Got it." Olivia was already climbing through a gap in the cyclone fence.

Andy hesitated. It was mid-morning now and the market was filling with a flurry of tourists. Their production was attracting a lot of curious attention, and he had already noticed several people filming with their phones. And a tour bus was pulling up. "Maybe we could just stick with the apples?"

"Come on, Andy." Olivia snapped.

Fine. He'd better just get it over with. Andy squeezed through the fence, mustering his TV smile. It matched the one plastered on Olivia's face. They trampled through the thick brambles, which were already wreaking havoc on Olivia's tawny jacket, picking the ripe purple berries. Andy's cue card was first. "While blackberries are rare in other parts of the country, they are considered a noxious weed in Seattle. Luther Burbank introduced Himalayan Blackberry canes to the area long before anyone had ever heard the term 'invasive species.' Now they grow wild practically everywhere around western Washington. Preventing them from taking over your yard can be quite a struggle. Here at Pike Place Market, they use goats instead of herbicides to manage blackberry overgrowth."

Olivia picked up her cue to continue the spiel with perfect timing, though she seemed to be having a little difficulty negotiating the underbrush while reading from the cue card. "Blackberries can be used in many recipes that call for raspberries, though the seeds—" Her heel caught a root, and she lost her balance. Andy reached for her elbow, but she yanked it from his grasp. Unfortunately, a little too forcefully, and she tumbled backward.

She tumbled backward down a very steep slope.

Stopping only when she bounced off the fence at the bottom

of the hill, with a ladylike "oof" and a metallic twang.

Andy, Charles, Joe, the rest of the crew, and approximately forty mid-western tourists gasped in unison.

As if there might be a chance of pretending it never happened, Olivia scrambled back onto her feet. Andy was relieved. She probably had some scratches, but at least she appeared to have no major injuries. He was so relieved, in fact, that he chuckled. The laugh escaped before he had a chance to think better of it. Polished, perfect Olivia with twigs in her hair, berry stains on her expensive jacket, and leaves on her butt.

Laughing was a mistake.

With supernatural force, Olivia propelled herself back up the hill in what seemed like just a few enormous strides. It was actually kind of amazing.

"Are you fucking kidding me? You're *laughing* at me? *You're* laughing at *me*. You big. Stupid. MAN-CHILD." She gripped a handful of berries from his bucket, smashed them in his face, and stormed through the fence. Crushed berries tumbled down the front of his jacket. Even for Olivia, this was an extreme reaction. Andy stood, splattered with purple juice, baffled.

Baffled was how he'd been feeling for a year now. He'd known their marriage wasn't perfect. Whose was? He'd felt distant from Olivia for a while. Despite their success, working together could be rough. He'd known she harbored some frustrations with their relationship but had always thought they would figure it out together. Now, he'd had time to resign himself to the fact that his marriage was over, and Andy was ready to move on. He just wasn't sure quite how one might go about doing such a thing.

"Okay, team." Charles sounded put-upon but clearly already had a contingency plan. "Berries from a vendor it is. Andy," he took Andy's arm to guide him away from Olivia, who was yanking debris from her hair, "I think we'll give Olivia some time to cool off. We're on a tight schedule—we've got to get you onto the ferry tomorrow to catch the best weather because we want time to shoot both hiking and kayaking. I'll have Olivia do the cooking segment with Angela Lewis. They had a good rapport when Olivia shot her dining segment at Dandelion Bistro so I think the patter will be good, and since Angela is a chef, it might be an interesting twist. Take the rest of the day to relax, okay? You and Joe need to be on the boat by seven tomorrow morning."

Andy cleaned up as much as he could, then trudged uphill from the market, passing his hotel without stopping. He felt like his day had just been hit by Hurricane Olivia. Sometimes, he wondered if his whole *life* hadn't been hit by that particular storm. When they'd gotten together as college sophomores, Andy hadn't been able to believe his luck that she'd chosen him. Then, through their relationship, Olivia continued to make the big decisions for both of them right up until she decided it was time to end things. Maybe that was their problem; she'd gotten tired of that dynamic. He'd loved her; some part of him always would, but now that the true end was in sight for them it was time for Andy to get used to charting his own course again. Starting now; the rest of the day was unexpectedly at his disposal. He might as well enjoy the city a bit more, see some of the funkier, less touristy neighborhoods. Soon, he passed a divey-looking diner, definitely not a place Olivia would be caught dead, and went in for a burger and a beer.

Roz

Roz often went to lunch with Celeste and Barry in the restaurants near their office, but when they needed a pick-me-up, they made the trek to YiaYia's Bar & Grill. Barry insisted that the Greek diner's griddle, designed for pita, produced the best pancakes in town. The greasy spoon was about as far from chic as could be, with decor featuring plastic grapes, cheap prints of Greek landmarks, and a back room with a pool table and a perpetually sticky floor. In the ladies' room, a quarter could get you a spritz of "Odsession" from a hand-labeled, Cadillac-pink machine that would spray the perfume directly at you while you stood in front of it.

YiaYia's was five steep blocks uphill from the NWC offices, and Roz was propelled by righteous anger the whole way. Despite her high heels and the box of office mementos she carried, she walked fast, unable to stop herself from leaving Celeste and Barry half a block behind. She knew Fred had made her mother happy for a time, and their cordial post-divorce relationship baffled Roz. She merely tolerated Fred for her mom's sake. Recently, it had become clear that Kate had tempered his most insufferable qualities. In addition to being heavy-handed with content oversight, Fred's micromanagement of the office had gone to absurd extremes. Only last week, he'd ordered Barry to stay late and go from desk to desk to check the size of everyone's stapler — it turned out that the smaller-than-standard staples he was so upset about were the ones used by the photocopier's automatic stapling feature, not the result of a staff member's unauthorized mini-stapler.

Roz turned the idea of giving in to Fred over in her mind. She could return to the office, apologize, ask for her job back. He'd make her retract the *Unconvertible* column, but maybe it would be worth it to be able to keep helping people and maintain her ties to the community of fans who missed her mom as much as she did.

No, she couldn't stomach it. Letting Fred take away the column's ethical sensibility would be worse than not being able to write it at all.

Kate had always been adamant about an emergency fund, and even without her inheritance Roz had enough in savings to support herself for a while, but the idea of not working was intolerable. She didn't even like weekends; on idle days, she tended to fall into a pit of missing her mom that was too deep to dig out of. She usually spent Saturday and Sunday poring through the letters that came into "Kate Knows Best," occasionally answering some by email. Wheels were beginning to turn in Roz's mind as she grasped for ways to continue working. There was no way she was going to let Fred stop her from doing the work she loved. She'd figure something out. She had to.

An hour after their arrival at the diner, Roz, Barry, and Celeste lounged in a vinyl booth under an oil-on-velvet painting of the Acropolis, all three stuffed to bursting with pancakes, spinach omelets, and mimosas. Since it was eleven on a Monday morning, a few early lunch diners were starting to trickle in. With no place else to go for the day, Barry suggested ordering a pitcher of beer.

Roz was done wallowing. "What's our game plan here? I definitely need to start looking for a new job, but I think you two should go back to NWC tomorrow. I'm sure Fred would tear up your resignations. I can't let you be out of jobs on my account."

"I didn't quit because of you, Roz." Celeste sounded weary. "It's time for me to branch out into something different. I've been thinking about it for a while. Today was a wakeup call. I'm going to take a break to think things through. You might want to try that, too, Roz. You hardly took any bereavement time."

Before Roz could tell Celeste that spare time to be sad was the last thing she needed, Barry set his glass down with a clank. "Honestly, ladies, I was tired of working for that piece of shit. Sorry, Celeste, but we all know he's a low-key homophobe and kind of racist, too. I only stayed in that gig because I loved working for Kate, and you. I wouldn't be caught dead working there without any of you."

Barry was right as usual. "We all need something new, then."

Roz pulled out her phone and searched job listings. There wasn't much, but she did see one thing that looked promising. "Here's something: Reporter—features and human interest. Part time. Port Poulsen Gazette. It doesn't pay much, but at least that would be something to keep me sharp."

"Roz. Sweetie. Take a breath." Barry signaled their server for another round.

"What about my dad, Roz? I think he's serious about making trouble for you if you try to work for a competitor."

Roz blew a raspberry. "*Roz Connolly* isn't allowed to work for a competitor. I'll write under a pen name. Fred can't make trouble about something he doesn't know about."

Celeste said, "I think we should talk to a lawyer and—"

"Human interest sometimes includes an advice column." This might be too good to be true. "The Gazette doesn't have one right now. I could start it. And it's a pretty small paper. I doubt Fred would even notice."

"I'm sure he's got a Google alert set up on your name by now," Barry said. "Plus, with Kate's loyal readers, it won't take long for word to get around that you've got a new gig."

"I know. It'll have to be a secret." She'd need to rebuild her readership from the ground up, but that was an exciting prospect. She loved the legacy of her mom's column but had a touch of imposter syndrome. Was she good enough to build her own following from scratch?

Barry leaned forward. There was a glint of mischief in his eye. He was getting into this. "You know, there are so many female advice columnists, but not very many men. What if you gender-swapped your pen name? It would distinguish you and throw anyone who gets suspicious off the scent."

Roz waved the idea away. "Write as a guy? I'm not sure I have that in me."

"It doesn't have to be, like, bro advice." Barry said. "That's what makes it so good. The only men I can think of doing this are giving explicit sex advice, or incel bullshit. Your advice is sensible, mainstream, vanilla—"

"Hey!"

"Sorry, I call it as I see it."

Celeste slumped back in her seat and took a long drink. "Barry, please don't encourage her."

It was too late. Roz was thinking about it, and the more she did, the better it sounded. She was sure she could pull off the writing voice, but it wouldn't be easy, and that's what sealed the deal. The rush of a challenging project was making its way through her body, sending a tingle of adrenaline down her limbs. It might be exactly what she needed. "You might be right, Bear. What should my name be?"

"Here we go." Celeste rolled her eyes.

Barry rubbed his hands together gleefully. "Now we're talking. Okay, who's the first boy you ever kissed?"

"Gavin Turlington. Junior year formal."

"Okay, Ms. Late Bloomer. Let's call you…Gavin Garrett."

Roz wrinkled her nose but decided to let the late bloomer comment slide. "Why Garrett?"

"Alliteration for one. And because of Mrs. Garrett, you know, from the *Facts of Life*. She was always giving advice to Jo, Natalie, Blair, and Tootie?" He sighed deeply. "Okay, seriously, I'm not that much older than you two. You've never seen it?"

They shook their heads.

"Okay, well we are marathoning. Soon. Roz you are going to love Natalie."

They were well-accustomed to Barry's insistence on catching them up on what he called "seminal pop culture," which usually meant things he'd watched in after-school reruns as a kid.

He started explaining the basic premise of the eighties sitcom, but Roz was barely listening. Her attention was focused on the logistics of operating under an opposite-gender alias. It might work. She would need a credible resume. She pulled her laptop out and made some edits to her existing resume, drafting something mostly true but not connected to Rosalind Connolly in any way. She dug up a few writing samples from her unpublished pieces and attached it all to an email to the Port Poulsen Gazette. Her finger hovered over the send button, but she saved it to drafts instead.

"This is a very bad idea, Roz," Celeste said. "You don't have references, any sort of an online presence. What are they going to think when they search online you and don't come up with anything?"

That was a good point, but it wasn't enough to deter Roz. "Then I need to make some social media profiles, too. Can't do much about bylines, but at least that would make me look like a real person. Bear, can I borrow your face for a profile pic?"

"No way. I have over eight thousand followers. I'm not diluting my brand, even for you." He tilted his head and squinted at Roz's face. "Come with me. Bring your purse."

Barry bustled her into the ladies' room, where they pulled her hair back, removed her eye makeup and used artfully smudged eyeliner to give her a hint of a five o'clock shadow. He stripped off his plaid shirt and Roz put it on, buttoning it to the neck. She thought she looked pretty convincing, but Barry disagreed.

"Don't move. I'll be right back."

He returned with Celeste's glasses, classic black horn-rims that gave the right edge to her porcelain-doll face. On Roz they obscured her eyes and squared her features.

"And a hat!" Courtesy of Celeste, again. She ran cold and always had a knit beanie in her bag. Barry tucked Roz's hair in and regarded her critically. "Finishing touch, to bulk you up in the shoulders a bit." He handed Roz a gray canvas jacket. It smelled like the beach and had a faint spatter of deep purple stains across the collar.

"Where did you get this?"

"Borrowed it from a guy at the counter. A cute one, but probably straight. You should return it yourself."

"Are you serious?" How humiliating. She put it on anyway. It was still warm. She twirled for Barry in her full disguise.

"You look like a runty emo lumberjack, which is probably perfect for the demographic you're trying to appeal to."

He snapped a couple of close-ups. Backlighting from the bathroom window blurred Roz's features even more, but it still looked like a profile photo someone might pick because the lighting looked cool. The shots were perfect; Roz looked like her own twin brother. While Barry went back to their booth, she got to work setting up social media profiles, and within a few minutes she'd established a credible online presence for Gavin Garrett. This plan was bananas, but she didn't have any better ideas. She found her email to the Port Poulsen Gazette in the drafts folder and hit send before she could talk herself out of it. Her phone's swoopy sound confirmed that the deed was done.

She washed her face, peeled off the borrowed shirt and jacket, straightened her dress, and emerged from the ladies' room with an armful of extra clothes. Barry shrugged his shirt back on over his t-shirt and inclined his head toward the jacket's owner. The stranger's back was to them; all Roz saw was a head of dark, curly hair and a set of broad-but-not-intimidatingly-broad shoulders. Roz wiped her sweaty palms on her skirt as she approached him. This was so awkward.

"Excuse me?" She tapped him lightly on the shoulder. He turned and grinned, and Roz's heart thrummed in time to the nineties pop playing on YiaYia's sound system. "I think my friend borrowed this from you. Thanks." She held out the jacket.

"No worries." He twisted away to put it on the empty stool on his other side, then beamed in Roz's direction again. "I'm Andy." His grip, as she shook his hand, was warm and firm, setting off a zing in the backs of her knees. She steadied herself with a casual hand on the counter.

"You're probably wondering what that was all about." Roz wondered if she'd gotten all of the makeup off, and rubbed her chin.

He held up a hand to wave away her explanation. "Hey, none of my business. You three look like you're having a fun day."

"Well, we all quit our jobs today, so we're sort of celebrating. That's a weird thing to say, I know."

"Believe me, I get it."

"Anyway, we don't usually day drink on weekdays."

He smiled again. It was a hell of a smile. "I don't judge."

She smiled back, hoping she could come close to matching his wattage.

"Well. Thanks again. Enjoy your lunch."

"You're welcome again."

She turned to go, and Andy returned his attention to his burger. Roz thought she saw some of his energy sap away. Was he lonely? What the hell, she'd already done two rash things today, might as well make it three. "Hey, Andy, are you by yourself? Would you like to come sit with us? We've eaten but we're not in a hurry to leave." She shrugged in a way she hoped was charming. "We don't have anywhere else to go."

"Really?" His face brightened. "That would be great."

His eyes, warm hazel, met hers, and Roz felt that zing in her knees again. "I insist." She laughed and picked up his glass. "Come on. Join us."

"Okay. Thanks." He picked up his plate and brought it over to their table. Roz caught the tail end of a significant look between Celeste and Barry.

"Guys, this is Andy. We can't let him eat alone." Barry winked at Roz as he switched sides of the booth, moving to sit next to Celeste so Roz and Andy could sit with each other.

"I think you met Barry already, and this is Celeste."

"Nice to meet you both."

"Hi." Celeste gave him a limp smile. Roz could tell she still wasn't thrilled about the Gavin Garrett plan, but she'd come around. She always did.

"Andy, do you like pool?" Barry asked. "With four of us, we can play teams." He had a fierce competitive streak when it came to bar games, and could always get Celeste to play, but Roz, whose athleticism was limited to running in a straight line, usually opted to be a spectator.

"Sure. You two against me and Roz?"

The foursome spent the next few hours at the pool table, sipping their beer. Andy was an easy conversationalist, had a sweet smile that crinkled his eyes, and was a very good sport. Celeste and Barry played well together as usual, beating Roz and Andy easily in game after game.

The gameplay seemed to lift Celeste's spirits, too. Good. Of course she was upset, but everything was going to turn out for the best in the long run. Roz hoped she realized that.

"Dammit." Roz missed her umpteenth shot. "Andy, are you sure you don't want to switch partners?"

"Nah. Let me tell you a little secret about billiards."

He leaned close to her. She all but rolled her eyes, waiting for the thousandth well-meaning billiards lesson that would never take. Not that she would mind his hands on hers, she realized as she felt her face flush.

But instead of trying to help her to line up her shot, he stage-whispered, "If you like your partner, it doesn't matter whether you win." He winked and walked away from her.

Roz laughed, and caught a conspiratorial glance between Barry and Celeste.

"So, Andy," Celeste said, "you mentioned you're visiting Seattle?"

"Yep. I travel a lot for work."

Barry cut a glance at Roz. "Does your girlfriend mind you being gone so much?"

Subtle, Bear. If she'd been close enough, Roz would have kicked him in the shin.

"No girlfriend." Andy's eyes met Roz's. Above his beard, his cheeks were pink. "Dating is complicated, with my work." He leaned over to line up a tricky shot and Roz let herself appreciate the fit of his jeans.

Barry caught her looking and winked, then glanced performatively at his watchless wrist. "Oh gosh, Celeste. Look at the time. It's almost five. Don't you have to feed your dog?"

"No, he eats at sev — ow! Oh. Yes, we should go." She rubbed her ribcage. Barry's elbows were notoriously pointy. "Um, you two should stay. Bye!"

"Byee!" Barry scooped up their boxes and his plant and hustled Celeste out of the diner before Roz could react.

She found herself alone with a more appealing guy than she had managed to meet in six years on dating apps.

"Sorry about them. We did have a rough morning."

"I did too. I appreciated the distraction. This was fun."

"It was." She picked up her crumpled blazer from the booth and shook it out before slipping it on. Neither of them was eager to part ways. "Why don't I give you my number and you can call me next time you're in town?"

At the same time, Andy said, "Would you like to have dinner with me tonight?"

Tonight. Oh. While she was spontaneous in other areas of her life, Roz was a cautious dater. She stuck to the same sensible routine: text awhile to assess compatibility of personality and life goals, meet for coffee or drinks, a couple of dinner dates, test physical compatibility if that all went well. She liked it this way; it was easy to avoid mistakes. But if she were ever going to start being romantically impulsive, today was probably a good day for it; it wasn't like she had work in the morning. Andy was attractive, charming, and seemed unlikely to be an ax murderer. If an advice seeker wrote to ask if they should go out with the ruggedly attractive guy they met-cute right after losing their job, she'd tell them to go for it.

"Why not?" She smiled, hoping the deliberation hadn't been too plain on her face, or if it had, that he hadn't taken it personally.

"Know a place without plastic grapes?"

Chapter Four

Roz

The still-bright rays of the sun slanted golden through the city streets as the pair strolled down the sidewalk toward Andy's hotel. Roz's pale gray dress was fine for a nice restaurant, but Andy wanted to change out of his mud-dusted clothes. What a stroke of luck that she'd met him today; she needed to keep her mind occupied and with work temporarily off the table, getting-to-know-you conversation with a side of flirting was a perfect solution.

"So," he said as evening commuters hurried past, "did you grow up here?"

"I did, I'm a hometown girl. I left to go to college across the state, and then came back afterward. Celeste went to the same

school." Roz described how they'd shared a large friend group—
between the two of them they knew almost everyone on the small
campus—and an off-campus apartment. "I used to tease Celeste
for following me to college," she said, "but honestly, it was nice
to have her there. It's good to have somebody you know is always
going to be on your side."

"And you still live together? It's nice that you're so close to
your sister."

"Yes. Actually, we're stepsisters. Our parents got married
when we were kids. But they divorced when I was seventeen, so
I guess we're ex-stepsisters? It's not as complicated as it sounds.
We've only been roommates this time around for a few months.
Celeste moved in with me after my mom died. I don't know what
I'd do without her."

They'd paused at a crosswalk. Andy glanced at her, brows
drawn together. "I'm so sorry, Roz. It must be difficult to have
lost your mom so young."

"Well, I certainly don't recommend it." She stepped briskly
off the curb when the light changed, leaving him behind for a
second. She regretted mentioning Kate. Dead parents were not
an ideal topic for a first date. She pushed the sadness that rested
right behind her eyes to the back of her mind. After they cleared
the intersection, she asked, "Do you come to Seattle often?"

"No, I used to travel all over for work, but that job is
ending soon."

"What is it you do?"

He gave her a sidelong glance. "I'm basically a fancy
tour guide."

Must be some fancy tours indeed. They passed through the
revolving door of Andy's hotel into the swank lobby. Maybe
Andy's work involved the cruise business. She'd worked on a
story about the industry last year; it was seasonal here, ending in

the fall and starting up again in late spring. With Alaska weather turning cold, the ships that had been calling at the waterfront piers all summer to take retirees up the Inside Passage would soon be headed to Mexico. Staff accommodations on those ships were bare bones. If Roz were stuck in one of those tiny windowless staterooms below the waterline for five months, she might splurge on a fancy hotel before her next gig, too.

"Do you want to come up while I change?" Quickly, he added, "It's a suite, so you can wait in the sitting room."

She was on the verge of demurring when she saw Fred's friend Angela Lewis near reception. This was turning out to be a lovely evening that would surely be ruined by conversation with one of Fred's catty cronies. "Yes, thanks."

As soon as they stepped into the elevator, Roz pushed the door close button, hoping they would slide shut before Angela noticed her. Andy caught her eye and raised an eyebrow. She didn't want him to think she was overly eager to get to his hotel room, but if she said she'd seen someone she was trying to avoid he'd think that was the only reason she was coming up, and…it wasn't. The truth was somewhere in the middle. Now that they were alone together, she couldn't stop imagining what it would be like to take two steps across the elevator's polished marble floor, twine her fingers into his hair, and bring their lips together.

Before she could resolve the question, they arrived at their floor.

Andy held the door open for her as she stepped into the suite. "How about a glass of wine before we head out?"

A bottle stood on the credenza. It was a nice Columbia Valley merlot. "Sure," she said.

He pulled the cork and poured two glasses. When he handed one to Roz, his fingertips brushed the back of her hand lightly. A tingle rose on her arms, bringing up goosebumps, but it made perfect sense to feel a chill after coming into an air-conditioned hotel room from the sunny street. "Thanks."

"Make yourself comfortable. It won't take me long to change."

She'd dressed this morning knowing a confrontation with Fred was imminent, so she'd worn heels for extra confidence, but she hadn't expected to spend so much time on her feet today. Between the anger-fueled tromp to YiaYia's and the pleasant stroll she'd just taken with Andy, her feet were cramped and sore. She kicked the shoes off, flexed her toes on the plush carpet, and settled herself on the sofa with her glass. The wine tasted like blackberries and spice. As she drank, Roz felt some of the remaining tension ease out of her shoulders.

Fifteen minutes later, Andy emerged from the bedroom, hair and beard tidied, in an elegant navy suit and crisp white shirt, bringing the smell of sun and saltwater with him. "Tie? or…"

"Hardly anyone wears ties in this city."

"Cool." The corners of his eyes crinkled as he grinned. Andy joined her on the sofa, leaving a respectful distance between them. "Can I pour you some more?"

She held her glass out to him; he reached the bottle toward her. They both overcorrected and he missed her glass by half an inch. Magenta blossoms splashed across the skirt of her dove-gray dress.

"Shit! I am so sorry."

Her dress was done for, but maybe she could avoid transferring any of the spill to the upholstery if she held very still. "It's okay…could you grab a towel?"

Andy was back in a flash with a hand towel. He pressed it into the stain on her thigh; Roz took over, her fingers mingling with his.

"Believe it or not, I'm not usually this clumsy." Spots of color crept across Andy's cheekbones, and she felt his hand trembling a little. Adorable.

She laughed, intentionally catching his eyes with hers. "Really, it's fine. I know a great dry cleaner." Their hands were still touching. She glanced away, then back, expecting him to have shifted his attention to something else. He hadn't, and the eye contact was electric. Andy leaned in slowly. His lips when they finally met hers were gentle, slow, exploring.

"Is this okay?" he murmured when the kiss broke, sliding his hand up to cup her hip, bending his head to kiss the spot where her jaw and neck met, then her neck and shoulder. It was definitely okay, it felt amazing. Jolts of energy shot through her body every place he touched her. Maybe it was also reckless — she hadn't even known Andy twelve hours, after all — but didn't she deserve some fun after the day she'd had? Her stomach swooped as if she'd stepped off a diving board, and she answered Andy by wrapping her arms around him and pulling him closer.

Celeste

Celeste and Barry made it halfway down the block outside YiaYia's before giggles overtook them and they had to set their boxes down.

"Poor Roz," she said. "She didn't stand a chance."

Barry snorted. "I think she's doing just fine for herself. Besides, don't you think it was our turn to mess with her?"

"Maybe a little." Celeste bent to pick her things back up, then thought better of it. "Let's get a car," she said. "I don't want to carry all this stuff on the bus."

In the back of the rideshare, Celeste filled Barry in on the full details of Roz's argument with Fred. "I know she means well," she concluded, "but that almost makes it worse. It'd be easier if I could tell her off without feeling so guilty."

"Have you tried? Tell her you need to set your own boundaries with your dad, and you'll figure it out in your own time."

Celeste looked at him over the rim of her glasses. "How do you think that would go?"

"Okay, fair." Barry launched into a Roz impression. "But Celly I'm *only* trying to help. *I* know how to *handle* people like Fred."

They arrived at the house and carried their things up the walk. When they opened the door, there was a short break in their conversation while they greeted Bowie, Roz and Celeste's dog.

When Celeste agreed to move in with Roz, she asked about getting a cat. She'd always wanted one, but her apartment hadn't allowed pets. Roz agreed that a pet would be good for both of them and tagged along to the shelter.

In the lobby, there was a white pit bull with a single black spot on his nose, flippy ears, one eye soulful brown, the other ice blue. As soon as Roz and Celeste entered, he sprang up from where he'd been napping. Wagging his tail and grinning from ear to ear, he put his paws up on the railing to get closer.

"He's been here for almost nine months. He's deaf, and no one wants to adopt a special-needs pit bull. He's the sweetest boy," the adoption counselor told them as Roz leaned into his slobbery kisses.

Roz fell in love right away. "I can't leave him behind, Celly. How could you say no to that face?" It was pretty impossible, and Celeste couldn't say no to Roz, either.

So now instead of a nice, low-maintenance cat, they had Bowie. They'd both worked hard with him, learning sign language — Celeste's favorite was a thumbs-up to tell him he was a good boy — and getting him comfortable in his new home. Celeste loved Bowie, but he was definitely Roz's dog. She still wanted a cat, but Bowie was afraid of them.

"You give in to her too much," Barry said. "See Exhibit A." His tone was fond as he scratched Bowie behind the ears.

"She doesn't show it very often, but she's still grieving. We need to be gentle with her right now. Besides, I love Bowie." She made the sign for "sit," then gave Bowie a thumbs-up and a treat.

"Sure. But there's a difference between being gentle and letting someone walk all over you." Barry got glasses out of the cabinet and poured them each some water.

"She lost her mom. I could call my mine right now if I wanted to."

"Mm-hmm. And do you want to?"

She'd have to fill her mother in on quitting her job eventually, but honestly? "Not really. She'll be madder at my dad than I am and that's not helpful."

"But you would have talked through this stuff with Kate."

"Yeah." Months ago, she probably would have had a sit-down with Kate about feeling dissatisfied with her job and made a plan together. Kate had always been a balancing presence in Celeste's relationship with her dad.

She wasn't going to let Barry off the hook as the ringleader of Roz's harebrained scheme.

She kicked off her flats and laced up her tennis shoes. "I'll talk to her, soon. But Barry, why did you encourage Roz with this whole pen name thing? It's reckless and unhinged."

"It's only a bit of fun. We all needed to blow off a little steam. I doubt anyone will fall for it, but…she did look damn good."

Celeste clipped Bowie's leash on. "I hope it doesn't come back to bite her."

Later, after they'd walked Bowie and had fruit and cheese for dinner, Barry asked, "What do you think you're going to do, anyway? Roz is barreling ahead with journalism. I have no idea what the next move is for me, but I have a feeling you've already got something in the works."

"Can you keep a secret?"

"For you, always."

Celeste pulled out her laptop and showed him the interior design portfolio she'd been putting together. "I've been writing about style for a while and I have a little experience with the office remodel, but I want to do more hands-on work. I've even been playing around with a business plan so I can go out on my own."

Barry swatted her arm. "Hot damn, look at you go!"

"Don't tell Roz, okay?"

"Okay, but I'm surprised you haven't told her already. This is big stuff."

"I know, it's just, she would — "

"Try to tell you what to do," he finished her sentence for her.

"A year ago, I would have told her in a heartbeat. She's always been great with stuff like this. Opinionated, sure, but now it seems like she thinks her opinion is the only one that matters and I'm afraid she'll steamroll me."

"I get it. It's like she can't help herself; if someone has a major life decision to make, she thinks it's her duty to weigh in. I know it comes from a place of love and a lot of the time she's right. I have 'office manager' on my resume thanks to her." Roz had lobbied hard to get Fred to promote Barry from his administrative assistant role.

"I want it to be a done deal before I tell her. In the long run that will be easier for both of us. I don't want to give her something new to stress about. I think it's best, even though it might seem a little underhanded."

"You? Underhanded? Not possible," Barry said. A text came through to both of their phones. "Speak of the devil."

It was from Roz, and read, "Staying over. Don't wait up."

"That's not like her," Barry said.

"Yeah." Celeste typed back a reply. "The fake persona, then this all of a sudden after months of saying she's not in a spot to date. Should I call her?"

Barry's expression turned serious. "She's an adult, she can make her own choices."

"True." All the same, Celeste was worried Roz was close to the edge of something. It didn't take a mental health expert to see she was channeling her grief in frantic, disjointed directions instead of dealing with it. Celeste didn't know how to help, other than continue being there for Roz. It looked like Andy would be doing that tonight. "Speaking of adult choices, do you want to have a slumber party?"

"I thought you'd never ask."

They spent the rest of the evening doing at-home skincare treatments. Barry made Celeste watch *Jerry Maguire*. They stayed up late and Celeste kept expecting Roz to come through the door any minute, but she never appeared.

Andy

When the food arrived, Andy wasn't sure whether to wake Roz up. Their tumble on the sofa led to the bedroom, which led to skipping dinner entirely. One of them had mumbled something about room service at some point, but they hadn't gotten around to ordering before they dozed off. Andy woke up famished a few minutes after midnight and called down for sandwiches, figuring Roz would stir by the time they arrived. But she hadn't, and now he didn't know what to do. Olivia would definitely have wanted to keep sleeping. Olivia's attitude toward food was not what one would expect from a chef. She was happy to live on green juice and protein bars for days, preferring that to anything that wasn't—in her words—a thoughtful meal, skillfully prepared, with quality ingredients. Waking Olivia to eat a mediocre room service club sandwich would have been grounds for divorce.

Well.

Andy learned his marriage was over upon returning home from a rock-climbing weekend. They'd often vacationed separately; Olivia relished her alone time and preferred to spend her time off at spas or luxury resorts. Andy loved camping and hiking, anything that got him out under the open sky for long periods of time, and he could usually round up a buddy or two to join him.

It wasn't surprising to see her car missing from the garage when he got home; it wouldn't have been unusual for her to go out to dinner with a friend or to run a late errand. As soon as he walked into the kitchen it was clear something was off. Olivia's knives and cookware were gone, replaced by some new sets from a department store, still in boxes on the kitchen counter. Olivia had taped the gift receipts to the packages with a note: "In case you want to exchange these for something different." Andy blinked at it, bewildered, for several minutes, before continuing to search the house for clues. In the living room, Olivia's favorite painting, a Rothko-esque abstract seascape she had purchased while shooting the pilot episode of their series, was gone. An envelope bearing his name in her tidy script sat on their dresser:

Dear Andy,

I know this will be a shock and I am sorry, but this is the best way to do this. I am filing for divorce. I thought it would be less awkward to move out while you were away. My attorney's name is Grace Alejandro; her card is enclosed. We understand that it will take time for you to find your own attorney. When you've selected someone, have them call Grace. I have notified the network; Charles will call you tomorrow. I've also left chicken mole for you in the refrigerator and a few other things in the freezer. Heating instructions are on the foil.

This is for the best, Andy, truly. Love, Olivia

Leave it to Olivia to feed him even on her way out the door. Of course he called the next day, begging her to go to couples therapy with him. Andy believed the stagnation in their relationship was a phase they would pass through naturally, but that didn't mean he wasn't willing to work on it. Olivia insisted her mind was made up and there was no point in doing a post-mortem on their marriage. It took Andy the better part of a year to recover from the shock of thinking his marriage was maybe a bit boring, but solid, to learning it was over. His relationship with Olivia had been like catching an amazing wave; a great ride that carried him along until it spat him out on the rocks.

With Roz, he felt more like they were being carried away together, a ride they started the second she tapped him on the shoulder to return his jacket. He hoped she didn't think getting her in bed had been his endgame all along. This morning when he'd resolved to start moving on with his life, he never could have imagined he'd be halfway smitten with someone new by midnight.

Andy had never slept with a woman on the first date before. In fact, Andy hadn't even ever been on a true first date. In high school, he'd spent more time getting his Eagle Scout badge than with girls. His courtship with Olivia had involved friendly college hangouts that slowly developed into a companionable romance, then they were married. Since they separated, he'd spent more time puzzling through the end of his marriage than giving any thought to dating again.

Now he finally knew what it felt like to meet someone new and experience an immediate spark. She was beautiful, sure, but he also was charmed by the way she seemed to have fun playing pool even though she was terrible at it, how she'd taken the wine spill in stride, how she hadn't cared about the havoc they'd wrought on the meticulously made hotel bed.

"Roz," he whispered, shaking her shoulder gently. She slept on her stomach, one coltish leg straight, the other curled, arms wrapped around the pillow, auburn hair falling across her face in tangled strands.

"Mnmph." She buried her face deeper in the pillow.

"Hey. Roz," he continued to whisper, not wanting to startle her awake, "I ordered sandwiches."

"Hmm?" Her eyes blinked open. "Oh." A small smile. "Hi."

"Hi. Are you hungry? I got a turkey club and a grilled cheese. I wasn't sure if you have any dietary restrictions, though. We can order you something else."

She sat up, flicking the mass of hair over her shoulder. "I'm starving. Either one is perfect." She tossed on his t-shirt and helped him wheel the room service cart into the bedroom. They ate perched on the foot of the bed, watching a late-night rerun of *I Love Lucy*. Roz giggled as Lucy, increasingly intoxicated, tried to hawk Vitameatavegamin.

"This was my favorite after-school show as a kid," Roz said. "My mom loved it, too. We used to watch together on Saturdays sometimes."

"Lucy's great, but I was more of a *Star Trek* kid."

Roz punched him lightly on the shoulder. "That's Lucy's production company! Lucille Ball wasn't only a comedy genius, she was a brilliant businesswoman. Wait…listen to the theme song." The show was ending, and the familiar orchestral music played over the credits. "It sounds a lot like the *Star Trek* theme, right?"

"Wow. It does! How do you know that?"

She shrugged. "I might suck at pool, but you should see me dominate bar trivia."

"Smart chicks are hot." He waggled his eyebrows.

"Oh yeah?"

"Yeah."

As Roz shoved him backward onto the mattress, Andy reached for the remote and switched off the TV.

Chapter Five

Roz

Roz woke to the sound of the shower and daylight bleeding in around the edges of the curtains. Andy had mentioned needing to get to work early. She'd get dressed, then as soon as he was out of the shower, she'd kiss him goodbye and send him off with her number in his phone. She located her clothes and realized she was going to get some curious looks on the way home, with her crumpled, wine-stained dress. At least her blazer was okay. But where were her shoes?

Right, she'd kicked them off by the sofa. Roz scooted past the room-service cart and into the living room, where she encountered a middle-aged man in wind gear, toting a fancy-looking video camera.

"Um. Hi?" She was too surprised to say anything else.

He seemed surprised to see her, too, but didn't miss a beat before offering her a warm smile and a firm handshake. "Good morning. Sorry to barge in like this—I didn't think I'd be disturbing anyone besides Andy. I'm Joe. We work together on the show." He blushed, and Roz was glad for both their sakes she'd zipped her dress before leaving the bedroom. "I'm sorry. I had no idea he had company."

Roz gave her head a shake, as if that could clear the pre-coffee fog. She felt like she'd missed a few chapters of a book everyone else had read. "The show?"

"*Ardent Life Adventures?* Do you not..." He trailed off, and his blush deepened. "Oh geez. I'm really stepping in it here. Again, I'm so sorry. I'm sure Andy will explain everything."

There was no need. The pieces clicked into place. Andy had seemed familiar, but she'd written it off as a "just one of those faces" kind of thing. Roz didn't watch that type of program, but she had heard about *Ardent Life Adventures*, the show with the married costars embroiled in a high-profile divorce. Fred had even had their TV critic do a piece on it, which she hadn't read because she thought it was beneath NWC's standards to pile uninvited onto someone's personal drama.

So much for that. Roz had never even considered sleeping with a married man, even if he were separated. She didn't know the status of the paperwork for the Ardens, but either way this was too close for her comfort. Everything she thought was romantic and spontaneous last night now seemed cheap and reckless.

Her stomach lurched. A hangover? No. While Barry and Celeste had been hitting the pilsner pretty hard yesterday, Roz limited herself to three pints spaced out over the course of the day, alternating with water. More would give her a wicked headache. She'd only had half a glass of wine with Andy before becoming intoxicated by the chemistry brewing between them instead.

Oh, Andy. He'd seemed like such a great guy but obviously her judgment had been off yesterday. Of course he was too good to be true. Sure, she hadn't asked about his marital status, nor had she asked any follow-up questions about his work, but a decent person would disclose those things upfront. After what she'd seen her mom go through, Roz wanted no part of any public divorce drama, not even a small one, nor was she interested in being a rebound. She'd answered a letter from a woman in a similar position last month, writing, "There are plenty of unencumbered fish in the sea."

Well, chalk this one up to live and learn. At least it had been a fun night when she'd badly needed an escape.

Joe was still standing there, blushing apologetically, and the shower hadn't shut off yet. What was Andy doing in there, shaving his legs? Maybe he was stalling, waiting for her to get out. Good. Roz wasn't interested in an awkward conversation this morning, either.

"Excuse me," she said to Joe, "but I'm very late. Nice to meet you." She spotted one shoe under the coffee table and retrieved it. "I've got to get going." The other shoe was next to the couch.

"Don't you want to wait for Andy?"

She heard the shower shut off, which meant the clock on her escape was ticking faster. "No need!" She scooped up her purse, swept into the hallway, and was free. Even if Andy wanted to follow her, he'd at least need to put on pants first.

In a stroke of luck, the elevator doors opened as soon as she pushed the down button, and the car was empty. She leaned against the wall and checked her phone. Celeste had texted a goofy selfie with Barry, in sheet masks designed to look like panda faces. They'd had a sleepover after Roz texted to say she wouldn't be home.

In her email, she had a few administrative odds and ends from the NWC HR manager. And there was one message in the account she'd set up for Gavin Garrett.

> *Dear Gavin,*
>
> *Candidly, your resume doesn't have as much experience as I would like, but your degree is impressive, and your writing samples are engaging. I realize it's short notice and an in-person interview may be burdensome, but if you're available I'd like you to come in at 3:00 this afternoon. Please let me know if that does not work for you, otherwise I will plan to see you then: 2010 Front St., Port Poulsen.*
>
> *J. Jones*
> *Editor*
> *Port Poulsen Gazette*

Just as she should have expected Andy not to be as wonderful as he seemed, Roz should have figured that in a day and age where freelance journalism was usually arranged and performed remotely, the job *she* applied for would require an in-person interview. Her pen name plan depended on not dealing with employers in person. Ugh. Gavin should have applied for jobs in Duluth.

It was just as well that she wasn't going to have any sort of future with Andy. Getting this job was going to take all of her attention. There was plenty of time to catch the afternoon ferry, but could she pull off an in-the-flesh performance as Gavin Garrett? Roz cleared her throat experimentally. If she spoke in her lowest register…maybe? At least Barry was still at her house. He'd help with styling again. She hustled through the lobby and onto the first bus headed toward Queen Anne.

Andy

"I'm Andy Arden, and this is *Ardent Life Adventures*. Today, we're taking the ferry from the urban heart of downtown Seattle to Port Poulsen, where we'll show you this beautiful coastline in the best way: sea kayaking." Andy walked toward Joe's camera as he spoke. "I bet you don't think of rainforests when you think of Washington State, but that's exactly where we're headed for some hiking in the Hoh Rain Forest. Finally, we're going to find some trails for mountain biking."

They were on the outer deck of the ferry and even though he was wearing a mic, Andy was practically yelling so his voice could be picked up over the roar of wind and motors. He hoped they wouldn't have to dub it in post-production. He hated being stuck in that booth. "The Washington State Ferry system began more than a century ago as a mosquito fleet serving parts of Puget Sound. It's been operating since the fifties. With ten routes and twenty-one vessels, it is the largest ferry system in the United States and the fourth largest in the world. It's a great way to get around Western Washington, which is broken up by Puget Sound's intricate waterways. Some locals commute via ferry every day."

Andy reached the railing and leaned against it. "On this ride, we're being treated to beautiful views of Mount Rainier, the stadium district, and the Olympic Mountains. Look at that skyline view! Since you can drive your car right onto the ferry, it was easy to bring all of our gear with us. We're going to enjoy all the Olympic Peninsula has to offer."

"That was good," Joe said. "I think we've got it, but we can do another take if you want."

"Let's not. It's the last show, what are they gonna do, fire us?"

Joe chuckled along with Andy's laugh, but there was a regretful expression on his face, and Andy realized he was being a jerk.

"Sorry, man. I forgot not everyone is as happy to see the end of
Ardent Life Adventures as I am."

"I get it. Anyway, I'm not out of a job. The network offered to
put me on one of the luxury hotel shows." He grimaced.

Despite being twenty years older, Joe had matched Andy
paddle for paddle, hike for hike, skydive for skydive, while carrying a heavy camera. It was hard to imagine him being happy
filming glamour shots of swimming pools and opulent suites.

"Well, I am sorry."

"Don't be. Nobody blames you for not wanting to do
this anymore."

"Liv does."

"Yeah, but I heard she's been talking to the execs who run the
cooking channel. She'll land on her feet."

"If that makes her happy, I'll be glad. This isn't what I ever
expected to do. I miss writing." Before the show, Andy had been
a staff writer at an outdoor recreation magazine. "There's something about using language to describe places and experiences
that's so much richer than standing like a dumbass in front of a
camera. You know, they don't even let me write my own copy
most of the time."

Olivia set up their first meeting with network executives.
She'd been doing cooking segments on one of the network morning shows. When those went well, she'd signed with an agent
and started putting together concepts for her own thirty-minute
show. One of the ideas they pitched — the only one that got a
bite — was visiting a different destination each episode, profiling
restaurants and local dishes. The network had asked for a bigger
twist, and on the spot, Olivia suggested bringing Andy in, pro-
posing that he showcase recreational activities and then they'd
cook together.

That was that. She hadn't even asked him if he was interested, but she was so over the moon about the deal he couldn't say no. In fairness, he was happy to go along with it at the time. He thought it would be a good way to get someone else to foot the bill for travel. Half the time his magazine didn't have the budget to send him to the locations he wanted to write about. For their first season, it all seemed worth it, and he'd always been one to try things before ruling them out. Olivia was so happy, and the show was fun most of the time. Being recognized in airports or the grocery store was uncomfortable, but every once in a while, he had the gratifying experience of talking to a fan who'd gone someplace new after seeing a destination on their show.

The months after Olivia filed for divorce were hell. He wracked his brain wondering what he'd done wrong, but finally Andy realized that no matter what he agreed to do, he wasn't responsible for her happiness, and she wasn't responsible for his. It was better for them both to be free to find fulfillment on their own. He couldn't blame her for wanting to keep the show going, but it wasn't the right move for him. He knew Olivia respected that, deep down, and her recent hostility was a result of being uncertain about her future.

"Can I show you something?" Joe's question broke Andy's reverie. He'd pulled a tablet out of his bag and opened it to an album of landscape photographs. "I've been thinking about putting together a book. What do you think?"

"Joe. Wow, man. These are amazing." Joe's photos captured details Andy never would have noticed, a sapling in the foreground of a mountain vista scarred by fire, the gradation of colors in a slot canyon against a cerulean sky, golden monarchs gathered around a mud puddle.

"I'm glad you think so because I need someone to write accompanying text. It wouldn't hurt to have a recognizable name on the cover. Maybe even one of the 'Fifty Most Handsome Men?'"

There was a twinkle in Joe's eye.

Andy rolled his eyes at Joe's reference to his least favorite magazine feature. He'd refused to sit for the photo, so the network had submitted a publicity still.

A project like this could be good for him, too. He knew he was a good writer, and if the book sold well—which it probably would thanks to his notoriety, as much as he hated to admit that—it could be an effective way to position himself as more than a handsome face.

"I'd love to do it. Thanks for asking me."

"Oh, I wasn't thinking of *you,* you gargoyle. I was going to ask Chris Pine."

"Put the camera down. I'm going to throw you off this boat."

Joe clutched the camera to his chest and said, "You wouldn't dare."

Andy threw up his hands in defeat and sat on the bench next to Joe. It was cold out here in the wind, but they were both wearing the right gear for it and even though they weren't shooting any more footage, he wanted to watch the scenery.

"So, listen," Joe said. "I met a very nice, very pretty lady in your hotel room this morning. Do you want to talk about that?"

Andy considered jumping off the ferry, himself. A flush warmed his windblown face. Roz had been gone when he got out of the shower and he'd found Joe in the living room, but hadn't known for sure whether they'd crossed paths until now. He hadn't wanted to ask, in case they hadn't. "Um, yes. Roz. We met yesterday morning after the market shoot."

Joe's left eyebrow shot halfway up his forehead. "Yesterday, hmm? She didn't seem like she knew about the show. Left pretty quickly after I told her who you were. Why didn't you text me? I'd have waited in the lobby."

When they were married, Olivia had always been the one to

make sure Andy was up on time. After they separated, he slept through his alarm on Maui, causing them to miss the best light for a sunrise hike at Haleakala. Ever since, Joe had taken to stopping at Andy's room on early mornings to make sure he was up and on the move. Andy even gave him an extra key. It had never been awkward until this morning.

"I wasn't thinking. Sorry about that."

"You sure weren't. Don't take this the wrong way, kid, but lying to women doesn't seem like you." Most of the time Joe acted like a peer. He only pulled out 'kid' when he was disappointed in Andy. Joe had been married for almost thirty years to his high school sweetheart and was completely smitten. He called Carrie every night when they were on location.

"It's not. I didn't lie to her, exactly, I just…left some information out. I knew it was risky not to tell her, but it was so nice, you know? Hanging out with somebody who didn't know all the details of my baggage. We planned on going out to dinner, so I thought I'd get a chance to explain, but one thing led to another. Man, I royally screwed that up."

"You owe her an apology."

"I do, but I don't know how to get in touch with her. I don't even know her last name." Oh god, that sounded terrible. But she hadn't asked for his, either.

"I bet we can find her. Her name is Roz? That's probably short for Rosalind, Rosaline? Neither is very common. What else do you know about her?"

"She's a journalist."

"Well, there you go." Joe jabbed at his tablet for a few minutes, then handed it to Andy. "Boom. Send her a message."

The third result for "Rosalind, writer, Seattle" was Roz's bio page at NWC Magazine.

In her profile picture, Roz wore a turquoise top that set off

the red in the loose waves of chestnut hair Andy had adored
burying his hands in, and she was giving the camera a dazzling,
world-conquering smile. It was definitely his Roz, but she looked
different from yesterday. She put up a pretty good carefree front,
but there had been a sadness around her eyes, a guardedness that
was missing in this picture. Maybe it was because of the work
situation she'd alluded to, but he had a feeling it was more. She
hadn't wanted to talk about losing her mom, but he knew it was
recent. He hated the idea of her being in that much pain, and it
was even worse to think he'd hurt her more by withholding the
whole truth about himself. Joe was right, he needed to apologize
even if she didn't want anything else to do with him.

*"Attention passengers, we will be docking in Port Poulsen shortly.
Please gather your belongings and return to your vehicles."* The loudspeaker cut off with a crackle, and the deck attendant came out to
start getting the lines ready to secure the boat at the dock.

"Later, I guess." Andy wasn't sure what he was going to say.
He wanted to find a way to tell her about the spark he felt in his
chest when he thought about her, and the hope that came along
with it. Could he do that without scaring her off? Would she even
want to hear it? It was worth a try. He certainly couldn't mess
things up with Roz more than he already had.

Chapter Six

Roz

Bowie tumbled into Roz with a full body wriggle the second she came through the kitchen door.

"Hi sweet boy," she cooed, leaning down to scratch his ribs and accept a slobbery kiss. He tumbled over onto his back, and she knelt down, resigned to paying the belly rub tax. After a few minutes, he hopped up and cast a meaningful glance at his leash. Bowie was a fiend for snuggles, but his favorite thing in the world was going with Roz on her morning runs.

"Sorry pal. Not today." She needed to get into the shower, into Gavin Garrett mode and onto a ferry, fast.

"Good morning," Celeste wandered in, yawning. "Wow, you're a mess."

"Gee, thanks. I had a wine spill. And I left in kind of a hurry." Roz gave Bowie a final pat and stood up.

"Uh oh," Barry entered the kitchen wearing one of Roz's 5K t-shirts and a pair of Celeste's pajama bottoms. "You okay?"

"Of course. It's only that it was awkward this morning. Did you know Andy was Andy Arden from Geography TV?"

Barry stopped pouring his coffee to stare at her. "Did you *not*? I thought we were doing that thing where we pretend not to be impressed by famous people."

Celeste was equally blasé. "I thought we were being polite."

"We spent the whole evening joking about the two of you hang gliding in Peru."

"No, I didn't recognize him, you jerks. I just thought he was some hot outdoorsy guy."

"He is some hot outdoorsy guy. Seriously, Roz? Do you not pay attention to C-list celebrity gossip at *all*?"

"Not helpful, Barry." Celeste handed Roz a banana and a cup of coffee, before putting the kettle on for her tea.

"Good idea. She probably needs to replace some electrolytes."

"*Barry.*"

"No," Roz said. "You know I don't read the gossip accounts. I've never seen his show, and I had other things on my mind yesterday. Okay?"

He shrugged. "So, what happened? Are you going to become the new first lady of travel porn, or what?"

"I don't think so. No. I mean, he's attractive and fun. He seemed nice, but he didn't tell me who he was, and you know he's got that whole tabloid divorce thing going on. I don't want to get mixed up in that mess."

"But you like him?" Celeste fixed her with a penetrating look, as if she wanted to be sure Roz knew she was getting a taste of her own medicine. True, Roz had asked her the same question on the bus yesterday, but these circumstances were completely different.

"I did. But I hardly know him. Isn't it best to nip this in the bud before it gets any messier? Clearly, he isn't as great as I thought he was. Maybe he hooks up with a local at every location his show visits. I bet that's why his wife left him. Plenty of men have their nice guy act perfected because they know it'll get them what they want." Roz thought back to Fred, bringing her mother a rose before each date, giving her jewelry every anniversary, hitting on a series of assistants.

"Ain't that the truth," Barry said.

But Celeste didn't seem convinced. "You're leaping to conclusions. Andy didn't lie, did he?"

"No."

"And he isn't still with his wife?"

Barry had been looking Andy up on his phone and answered before Roz could. "Nope. They've been separated almost a year. I bet all the paperwork is complicated because of their show contracts and stuff."

"There you go," Celeste said. "I think you owe him a chance to explain."

"Maybe. But at best, he's on the rebound. I don't want to be a rebound fling."

"Sweetheart," said Barry, "we're in our thirties." (Roz was thirty, Barry was a few months shy of forty and loved few things more than pointing out they were in the same decade, if only temporarily.) "Everybody's on the rebound from something. Or they're an emotionally stunted wreck. Or they're workaholics. Or late wrapping up their quarter-life crises. Baggage-free relationships are for teenagers."

Roz wondered which of Barry's categories she fit into, as a thirty-year-old who hadn't had any relationship last longer than a few months. In her case, it genuinely was for lack of trying. She'd always assumed a suitable romantic partner would pop up when the time was right. The time had never felt right until…now?

But not today. "I have bigger problems. Gavin Garrett has a three o'clock interview in Port Poulsen. In person. Barry, do you think you can work your magic again?"

"Whoa. I can try, but do you think it's a good idea to do a face-to-face? That seems a bit bold, even for us."

"That's pushing the envelope, Roz," Celeste added. "Wouldn't it be better to see if there's a loophole for the shareholder agreement? If you get caught—"

"Celly, who would catch me? This editor is probably like ninety years old. Who else would ask for a face-to-face instead of a call? It's worth a try, at least. Let's all go. Pack a bag—we can go for a few days and make a mini vacation out of it." Yes, this was what they all needed right now. Roz found herself grateful to J. Jones for wanting to meet in person and providing a perfect excuse for a getaway.

"I mean, we can try to make the look work in person," Barry said. "Even if it doesn't, I could use a vacation."

Celeste still looked skeptical, so Roz deployed the puppy dog eyes she'd been using on her stepsister since they were tweens. "Celly, you always say you watch the ferries all day from the office but never get on one. We haven't been out to the peninsula since high school. Come on."

Celeste looked out the kitchen window. It was a beautiful day, perfect for a ferry ride. "That's true. Okay, I'm in."

Roz and Barry cheered, and by eleven they had Celeste's hatchback loaded with Bowie and their luggage for a week-long stay. Roz was wearing the best Gavin Garrett costume she and Barry could come up with, and they were on their way to the ferry terminal.

The ferry featured in some of Roz's fondest memories. Day trips and weekend jaunts with her mom, school trips on yellow buses packed into the belly of the boat, rowdy kids taking over all the vinyl booths along the windows. She never got tired of it; the hum of the motors, the novelty of driving your car onto a boat and being transported from the city to another world, even the crappy hot chocolate from the snack bar.

Even on cold days, Roz preferred to ride outside on the deck, letting the wind blast her hair and face, where she could watch the coastline, clouds, and whirling gulls.

Today, in spite of the autumn sun, the wind had a bite that blew through her denim jacket and flannel shirt.

After a quarrel with Barry about an impromptu pixie cut, they'd decided the best look for "Gavin" was to tuck her hair into a beanie again, letting her bangs peek out in front. Combined with Celeste's heavy-framed glasses, the look was classic hipster. Now, she let her hair fly free with the wind whipping through it. She was going to cram it back into the hat, so she didn't even care how tangled it got. Bowie sat by her feet, head lifted, black nose twitching in the air to take in all the new scents. On either side of the ferry, lush green coastline drifted past. An occasional late-season pleasure boater skipped by, and Roz waved at each one.

The Port Poulsen harbor hadn't changed much. Next to the ferry terminal there was a small marina with sailboat masts swaying in the light current. Behind a swath of grass of the waterfront park, Front Street ran parallel to the water, then wound uphill to a white-steepled church surrounded by century-old houses. Silhouetted against a backdrop of evergreens and early changing foliage, it all looked like something from a postcard.

As the ferry docked, Roz led Bowie away from the railing so the deckhands could connect the ramp for foot passengers to disembark. She met Barry and Celeste, who'd stayed inside with warm drinks and a Scrabble board, at the stairs that would lead them back to their car.

Barry looked at her with dismay, snatched the beanie from her hands, and began to rearrange her hair underneath it. "Honestly, Roz. Why did we even bother doing this at your house if you were just going to mess it all up?"

"I was going to fix it in the car!"

"Well, it's fixed now." He leaned back to take in the whole picture. "Looks okay, right, Celeste?"

She sighed before answering. "It looks fine, but I still think you should come clean. They liked your samples, which is the most important part."

"Nope." Roz buckled Bowie into his doggie seatbelt and climbed into the back seat next to him. "Gavin Garrett was invited for this interview, and that's who they're getting. Stop worrying, Celly. It will be fine."

Their car was at the back of the boat, which meant they had to wait for all the other drivers to crawl off before it was their turn.

"Which way?" Celeste asked.

"The offices are on Front Street." Barry was navigating. "I think you could park anywhere around here."

They found a spot at the curb next to a bookstore advertising new and used titles, with an attached coffee shop.

"Perfect." Roz said, hoping the chance to poke around a bookstore held enough appeal to get Celeste off her back. With any luck, in an hour or two, she'd have a job offer in hand and Celeste would understand what a good idea this all had been.

Celeste

Celeste browsed the bookshop shelves, taking a special interest in the section on Nordic culture. Port Poulsen had grown increasingly multicultural over the past few decades, moving away from its roots as a settling place for Scandinavian immigrants, but businesses like this one still had nods to the town's history. She pulled a few books on hygge off the shelf, but as soon as she opened one, she realized she wasn't going to be able to read them. Roz had once again appropriated her glasses as part of the Gavin Garrett costume. If this kept up, Roz was going to have to get her own, but hopefully this would be the last time. The whole thing was absurd, like something from a screwball movie.

How could Roz think this would actually work in real life? Celeste was surprised it hadn't occurred to Roz that she shouldn't appropriate a gender-nonconforming identity. Celeste was disappointed in Barry, too, for enabling it, but she wasn't letting herself explore that emotion. It would be too lonely to feel let down by all of the most important people in her life. As if he knew she needed comfort, Bowie pressed close to her legs.

She moved on to the cookbooks. She could at least look at pictures of food even if she couldn't properly read the recipes, but she only got a few pages into a book about Swedish bread baking when her phone rang.

The name on the screen read "Mom." Her finger hovered over the decline button, but they needed to talk and now was as good a time as any.

"Hi, Mom."

She heard wind chimes in the background, and the crow of her mother's rooster, Fred, who never seemed to know what time dawn was. Bianca George had been naming her most obnoxious pets after her ex-husband for decades now.

After her parents divorced, Celeste's mom moved to California and settled on the outskirts of Ojai, using her settlement from Fred to buy a property that had been, in turn, an alpaca ranch, a meditation retreat, and a sunflower farm. Currently, Bianca raised baby goats for the dairy down the road and conducted goat yoga classes.

Sometimes, Celeste struggled to imagine how her mother had ever been married to her father, but she'd been a different person then. Bianca, Fred, and Kate all met working for a local TV channel. Fred was an anchor, Kate a field reporter, and Bianca, a former pageant queen, did the entertainment reporting; mostly puff pieces that involved lobbing softball questions to actors on media junkets. She'd stayed on at the station after Fred and Kate left to launch NWC but quit when she was pregnant with Celeste.

Years later, Celeste asked her mother if Kate was the reason her parents split up. Bianca said, "No. They were good friends but there wasn't anything romantic between them until long after your father and I were over. I wouldn't have put it past Fred, but Kate wouldn't do that. I'd been chasing the spotlight all my life, and suddenly, all I wanted was to be with you, but that didn't feel right either. I didn't know myself, and I could sense your father slipping away. He was working so much on the magazine and I felt like we didn't have anything in common anymore. Part of it was that I didn't know who I was or what I wanted. I started searching."

This was part of the reason Fred had primary custody of Celeste. One of Bianca's quests to find herself led to a misdemeanor charge for marijuana possession, many years before it was legal, and she'd known she wouldn't win a court case against Fred's expensive attorney. So, she'd agreed to let Celeste stay with Fred during the school year, but Celeste spent summers and alternating school vacations in California. Privately, she thought her mother had been happy to be the fun parent, leaving the serious stuff to Fred, and after they were married, Kate.

"Hi, Button. Just checking in to see what's new with my girl."

Bianca had been calling more often since Kate's death. It had rattled all of them, losing her so suddenly. Celeste was grateful for the outreach. But conversations with her mother could be exhausting under normal circumstances, and this one was bound to be especially tense.

She took a deep breath and gave her mother a basic summary of the past twenty-four hours.

"That absolute jackass! I'm calling him right now." Divorce was good for Fred and Bianca's relationship, and they'd been on functionally friendly terms for decades now. Celeste tried hard not to upset that equilibrium.

"Mom, please don't."

"What about Roz? I could call her. Someone needs to tell her she has to let you fight your own battles."

Celeste stopped herself from laughing out loud. Her mom wouldn't understand what was so funny. She sighed instead. "No, Mom. I'll handle it." She wasn't sure quite what she meant by that—she hadn't decided yet.

"Do you have enough money? The yoga classes are doing well. I have a new corporate client and—"

"Thanks, but no. I'm doing okay." Money was the least of her worries, especially since—at least for now—she didn't have rent to pay.

"How about a visit? I'm fostering a litter of kittens right now and they're the cutest. I know you'd like that." She could hear the desperation to help in Bianca's voice.

"Maybe. Can I decide later?"

"Of course. I'll let you go, Button. Stay in touch. I love you."

"Love you, too. Bye, Mom."

Even though she hadn't wanted to pick up the call, Celeste felt

better. Lately, she felt like she'd traveled too far down the wrong
life path and been set adrift. Even though the circumstances
weren't the same, if anyone could understand that it was her
mother. Maybe she would go for a visit. For all her mother's idio-
syncrasies, she was the one person who always put Celeste first.

Roz

Climbing the stairs of the Port Poulsen Gazette offices felt like
stepping back forty years in time. The publication's headquarters
were in a small office suite above an antique store. The stairwell
had the dry, spicy paper smell particular to older buildings dedicated to the written word: libraries, newspapers, the best book-
stores. The butter-colored paint was peeling in places and the
stairs creaked, but the woodwork was original oak. At the top of
the stairs, a green-painted door read "Port Poulsen Gazette, est.
1932" in stenciled letters. Underneath, an index card declared "J.
Jones, Editor-in-Chief" in bold red handwriting.

Roz took a moment to make sure her hair was tucked away
under her cap. Under normal circumstances, she wouldn't have
shown up to an interview in such a casual outfit. Kate always
dressed impeccably and brought Roz up with the notion that it
was always best to err on the side of overdressing because like it
or not, first impressions make a difference. However, today was
certainly not a normal circumstance. Roz and Barry had decided
a laidback look was their best bet for maintaining a believable disguise. After all, it wasn't unusual for reporters to dress casually;
part of the job was blending in.

Roz figured J. Jones must be pretty eager to fill the role based
on the speedy reply to Gavin's resume. She was qualified and
experienced; this should be a piece of cake. She took a deep
breath, set her shoulders back, and pushed through the door.

The front room was lined with microfilm cabinets. Framed,

yellowed clippings graced the walls. There were bookshelves and a couple of old-fashioned desks made from honey-colored wood. A petite woman with chin-length locs and deep brown skin, in perhaps her early fifties, emerged from the door across the room.

"Hello. I'm looking for J. Jones." Roz remembered too late to use her deepest voice, and dropped an octave to say, "I'm Gavin Garrett. I have an interview."

The woman cocked her head and inspected Roz for a moment, her expression opaque. "I'm Jacqueline Jones. Come on back, Gavin."

Hoping she hadn't already blown it, Roz followed Jacqueline into her office. Unlike the rest of the building, this space had been updated and featured a modern, L-shaped desk. One portion faced windows overlooking Puget Sound, reminding Roz of her own former view from the other side of the same body of water. Two chairs upholstered in bottle-green microfiber faced the other half. Roz perched in one of them, ankles crossed. Then she remembered her role and scooted back, separating her knees in a way that she hoped appeared masculine.

Ms. Jones got right down to business. "So, Gavin, there isn't a lot on your resume, but I liked your writing samples quite a bit and since I can't pay much, I'm more interested in giving an emerging journalist a chance than being picky about experience. I'm a small operation right now and I'm looking for someone to help me fill human interest content. I just moved the Gazette from a printed biweekly paper to daily online updates with a Sunday print edition. I'm looking for someone who's social media savvy and creative, as well as a solid writer. Why don't you tell me a bit about what you're bringing to the table?"

"I've wanted to be a writer since I was a little kid. My mom was a writer who taught me there are interesting stories everywhere. She believed telling them was a public service. I want to tell those stories, too. I hope to do that in a way that helps people. I have to admit, I don't know a lot about the Gazette yet, but I know this community has many stories to tell. I could help you flesh out some regular features that might have broader appeal. Recipes, environmental stories…" She might as well go ahead and ask about the thing she wanted most. "Have you ever thought about adding an advice column?"

Jacqueline leaned forward, setting her chin on her fist. "Say more about that."

"It can be a very popular feature. Wild questions often go viral, which is good for social media exposure. Even when they don't, advice columns tend to have faithful weekly readers. I think people like reading about their neighbors' problems because it makes them feel better about their own lives."

"Have you done something like that before?"

Had she ever. But of course, she couldn't cite her real credentials. "I wrote the advice column for my college paper." That was true. She'd felt comfortable enough listing it on Gavin's resume because the byline was anonymous.

"Hm." Jacqueline finished the note she was writing, then looked up to make direct eye contact with Roz. "And Gavin, what are your pronouns? I use she/her."

Chapter Seven

Roz

Roz froze. She'd been expecting to be interviewed by someone who was out of touch and well past middle age — hopefully someone who wouldn't look too closely at her dubious masculine-coded presentation. Of all the questions she'd been prepared to answer, pronouns didn't make the list. How completely stupid of her.

This was her chance to back out, come clean. She supposed she had the option of claiming to be nonbinary or agender, but even in her panicked state, faking a marginalized identity seemed too wrong to consider. Acid nausea crept into the pit of her stomach, but changing gears once she'd committed to this plan was too daunting.

"He/him," she said, pushing the words out through her misgivings.

Jacqueline marked something in her notebook. "Great. We like to use pronouns on our correspondence here, but it's up to you if you want to or not."

Oh god. What a disaster. Roz nodded but the nausea was getting worse, until it rose to a peak and she squeaked out "Wait!"

Jackie's pen stopped moving and she looked up.

Roz took the hat off and let her hair fall down around her shoulders. It felt wonderful; her head had been getting so hot, and the wool was itchy. Roz also removed Celeste's glasses, which had been giving her a headache, and folded them into her shirt pocket.

"My real name is Rosalind — most people call me Roz — I use she/her pronouns, and I can explain."

Jacqueline leaned back in her chair and held up a finger. "Are you, by any chance, Kate Connolly's daughter?"

Gears clicked into place. Jacqueline Jones. San Francisco.

"Oh my god. You're *Jackie* Jones." Jackie Jones was a Hillman Prize-winning investigative journalist in San Francisco, and she'd been friends with Kate. They shared the kind of friendship busy professional women living in different cities could squeeze in, which meant they respected each other very much from a distance and often had lunch or drinks together at industry events or when work brought one of them to the other's city. A couple of years ago, Jackie quit her high-profile newspaper job and dropped out of sight. No one had known what happened to her.

Roz wasn't going to get this job, but it would be nice to catch up with her mom's friend. Maybe Jackie could give her some career advice or job leads. With a sheepish smile, she confirmed, "Yes, I'm Roz Connolly."

"Roz, you might not remember me, but I met you when you

must've been about twelve, at your mom's wedding."

"I do remember!" Fond nostalgia overtook Roz's disappointment at blowing the interview. "You gave me and Celeste those stuffed animals." It was a pair of sea otters with Velcro fasteners so they could hold paws. The girls had really been too old for stuffed animals, but it was a meaningful gift, a soft spot in a difficult day. Roz remembered now, Jackie had told them otters hold onto each other, because it didn't matter where they ended up as long as they didn't get separated. Roz still had them in a closet somewhere.

"My father remarried when I was about that age and his new wife had a son my age. We get along fine, but blending families was a big change and it was hard. I wanted to do something nice for you girls to help you deal with the big change."

"I adore Celeste — who is across the street in the bookstore, by the way — but getting used to Fred when it had always been just me and Mom was rough. I think that's one of the reasons I like to write advice. I could have used someone to write to, a time or two. Until recently, I worked with Fred and he's still no picnic. We had a difference of opinion about how frank I should be in an answer to a kid struggling with their parents not accepting their identity, and I resigned. Since I have my mom's NWC shares now, I'm technically not allowed to work for a competitor. That's why I applied for your position under a false name."

"What an absolute prick. I read that column. What happened to that child is unconscionable and I think you were right not to pull any punches." Jackie removed a file folder from her desk drawer and flipped through the contents.

"Listen, Roz," she said. "I didn't like Frederick George a whole lot when he married your mother. Kate was a smart cookie, but she had a real blind spot when it came to that man. I like him even less now. However, I'd still rather not be a knowing party to your violation of your shareholder agreement."

"That's completely understandable. Thank you for your time." Roz rose to leave.

"However," Jackie motioned her back into her seat, "since I don't know for certain that you're prohibited from working under a pen name, I can maintain plausible deniability. I wouldn't mind sticking it to Fred George a little bit by bringing you on board. And if you really want to try an advice column here, I'm up for that." Jackie slid the folder across the desk.

Roz couldn't believe her luck. Inside, she found hiring paper-work, website, email, and social media logins, and a list of story leads. "Oh wow. Really? Thank you so much, Jackie. I prom-ise I can give Gavin his own unique voice — no one will ever know it's me."

"As long as you keep your alter ego online only, I think it will be fine. You can work from home most of the time, but I'd like you to stay in town this week if you can. I want you to get a feel for the place. We have Nordic Fest coming up this weekend and I'm on the Chamber of Commerce, which means I'll be busy. I want good coverage of the festival."

Thank goodness they'd already planned to spend a few days away. "I'm free as a bird, but I need to find somewhere to stay. Celeste is traveling with me, along with our dog and a friend. I'll get online and look for a dog-friendly vacation rental."

"Go down to the marina," Jackie said. "There's a diner there, the Blue Plate. Talk to Erik Johansen — you're going to want to interview him eventually anyway, he's the Nordic Fest chairper-son this year. Erik knows folks in town and keeps a bulletin board where you'll find some ads for vacation lodgings. Tell him I sent you. The local hookup is going to be much better than what you can find online. In the meantime, I'll add an announcement about the column to our website to solicit some letters."

Right. She couldn't write an advice column until someone

asked her for advice. "That all sounds good, thanks." They shook hands, and Roz was on her way out the door when her curiosity got the better of her. "Jackie, I have to ask, what are you doing in a tiny town like this? You're an award-winning journalist. I'm surprised you aren't doing something bigger."

"I don't want something bigger, Roz." Jackie's friendly tone slipped away. Now she was cold and distant. "I had that life, now I have this one."

Message received. Roz was burning to know what would make someone give up a prominent position at a nationally recognized publication for a small-town paper one step above a free circular, but clearly it was a sensitive subject. "Thank you for this opportunity, Jackie. You won't be sorry."

Roz found Barry and Celeste right where she'd left them in the bookstore. Celeste leafed through a cookbook, Barry was curled in an overstuffed armchair with a novel and Bowie at his feet.

Barry gave Roz's appearance a once-over, taking in her dismantled disguise. "Aw, you didn't get it. Sorry, sweetie."

Roz grinned. "I did get it. I'll still be writing as Gavin Garrett. And get this. J. Jones, crusty elderly editor of the Port Poulsen Gazette is actually Jacqueline Jones, Mom's reporter friend from San Francisco."

Barry's mouth fell open. "No way. I totally remember Jackie. Formidable lady. We'd talk on the phone from time to time when she called for your mom. What on earth is she doing here?"

"She wouldn't tell me." The mystery gnawed at Roz. "But how great is it that I get to work for her? I need to stay here this week, there's a big Scandinavian heritage festival on Saturday that she needs help covering. Do you two want to stay in town with me? It'll be fun."

"That sounds nice, but we need a place that will take Bowie." It was as if Celeste didn't trust Roz to think through the practical considerations.

"Already on it. Jackie said we should go to the marina restaurant and ask the guy there. Let's go check it out. Anyway, I'm starving." She hadn't been very hungry all day, but now she was famished.

They had walked halfway to the marina when a small SUV painted a violent shade of fuchsia pulled up next to the curb a few feet in front of them. The side of the car was emblazoned with a heart-shaped logo and the words "Iris Indigo Fashions," and, smaller "Phoebe Sheppard-Shepherd, Wardrobe Consultant" underneath. A young woman bounced out of the driver's seat. Her outfit matched her car for flamboyance: Kelly green tights printed with small pink and blue daisies, a hot pink A-line dress with blue stripes, and a flowy yellow lace cardigan. Her curled blond hair was held back with a turquoise scrunchie.

"Hey, y'all." The woman didn't have an accent, but there was something about her manner, besides the folksy greeting, that reminded Roz of a vivacious southern belle. She popped the hatchback, revealing a rigged hanging rod. More garments, similar to the ones the blonde was wearing, dangled from the tailgate. The display bore a striking resemblance to the windsocks strung across the front of the souvenir shop down the street. Bright colors and cutesy patterns figured prominently in all of them. "I'm Phoebe Sheppard-Shepherd. Are y'all just in town for the day?"

Roz avoided looking in Barry's direction, knowing if they made eye contact, they would be rolling on the sidewalk in unrecoverable tears of laughter within seconds. They'd giggle about this one-woman clown car situation later.

Managing to keep most of the laughter out of his voice, Barry said, "Hello, Phoebe. That's a heck of a hyphenate."

"Oh, thank you!" Phoebe cooed. "Of course, my husband and I didn't plan it that way — I married my high school sweetheart, bee tee dubs — I just thought the names were so cute together I had to keep both of them!"

"Hi, Phoebe," Celeste returned the young woman's handshake. "I'm Celeste. We're just visiting for a few days."

"How nice!" This woman was an exclamation point, personified. "Would you be interested in doing a bit of shopping? I've got my mobile boutique all set up."

"Sure," said Celeste, who was a) always polite, and b) enjoyed looking at clothes, probably because c) she could do things like make a discarded pillow sham look like a stylish top. She handed Bowie's leash to Roz and stepped over to the car before flipping through the rack of clothes.

"Girrrrl," the extension of the single-syllable word, with Phoebe's aggressively friendly pronunciation, was way over the top. "How about you?" She gave Roz an up-and-down inspection. "Looks like you might be borrowing from your boyfriend here? I can help you pick out something real cute and comfy."

Before Roz could formulate a reply that was both sarcastic enough to satisfy herself and polite enough to avoid upsetting Celeste, Bowie whined. New people, especially those with energy as boisterous as Phoebe's, sometimes made him nervous. "Um, that's okay. Actually, Phoebe, it's been very nice to meet you, but I have some business to conduct down at the marina. Would you excuse me, please? Barry, Celeste, I'll see you down there."

Letting Bowie pull her down the sidewalk, Roz made her escape, finally allowing a giggle to sneak out when she turned a corner. She could hardly believe Phoebe was real.

It was a shame, though, if what Roz had heard about Iris Indigo was true. It was a multi-level marketing company only a hair on the side of legal from pyramid schemes, roping in women who wanted to work from home with promises of running their own business. The catch was, they had to buy their inventory outright, along with covering all of their other business costs, and many ended up losing money. Phoebe's aggressive sales tactics were probably due to a real desperation to keep on top of an untenable financial situation. No one deserves that, even if they are a bit much.

Roz knew of the Blue Plate because it had been featured in NWC. "10 Best Brunches a Day Trip Away from Seattle," one of the listicles Fred had become so fond of. It sat at the edge of the marina and catered to both locals and tourists. She walked Bowie through the waterfront park and along the marina buildings. Above the door hung a round blue sign with a stylized orange and white daisy in the center. A bell tinkled as she and Bowie stepped inside.

"Take a seat! Be right with ya." There was a hint of the slightly nasal vowels common in Scandinavian-American communities.

Since it was late afternoon, the place was deserted. At the front of the restaurant there was a counter with a pastry case featuring Danishes, cinnamon buns, and an assortment of cookies and pies. Yellow oak paneling lined the walls, and a shelf ran around the low ceiling bearing an assortment of ceramics. The walls were covered with art: modern paintings, oils of local landmarks and seascapes, cross-stitch samplers, and a few pieces of indigenous woodwork. It was pleasantly cluttered.

Roz found a table for four and opened the menu. The voice from his greeting had her expecting a Scandinavian grandpa, but from the kitchen emerged a man roughly her age; one of the most objectively beautiful humans she had ever seen. He looked like he belonged in Asgard, or at the very least on a poster for Swedish tourism. Tall, blond, tan, broad-shouldered, dressed in jeans and a flannel shirt. She checked to make sure her mouth hadn't dropped open. She really had to stop expecting old codgers around every corner.

When he saw them, a look of joy and adoration came over his face, but Roz didn't kid herself that it had anything to do with her. She'd seen this before. Her assumption was confirmed when he made a beeline for Bowie. Although some people were uneasy around a pit bull, there was a certain type of dog-lover who was always drawn to him, and Roz found herself liking these people very much. She wasn't sure if she automatically liked anyone who loved Bowie as much as she did, or if anyone who liked her dog possessed qualities that made them a wonderful person. "Look at you, you handsome boy! Are we gonna get you some food? Does he like new people?"

"He's deaf, so he can be skittish, but as long as you give him a minute to get used to you, he'll be fine. Sorry, I should have asked if he was allowed in here, but it was empty and I'm starving. I was hoping it would be okay."

"The health department would tell me to say no, if he's not a service animal, but I don't see the harm." He held a hand out for the dog to sniff. Bowie sidled right up and pressed his head against the man's knee.

"Looks like he's ready to be friends. I'm Roz, and this is Bowie."

"I can see why! Look at those gorgeous eyes. I'm Erik Johansen. What can I get you two? Can I scramble him an egg on the house?"

"His heart would be yours forever. I have a couple of friends joining me soon, but could I get a plate of fries for now?"

"Sure. Be right back with those." He gave Bowie one more pat and returned to the kitchen.

Bowie flopped onto his side under the table and promptly began to snore softly. Roz looped his leash around a chair leg and walked over to read the bulletin board. It covered an entire wall of the alcove where people could wait for a table when the restaurant was busy. In addition to rooms for rent, items for sale (including several candy-colored business cards for Phoebe Sheppard-Shepherd's fashion services), and lost pets, there was artwork and poetry. On a small table near the host stand there was a coffee urn, a stack of index cards, and a can full of colored pencils with a handmade paper label that said, "Create something while you wait."

Roz took a card, doodled a picture of a sailboat, and wrote, "Adrift? Gavin Garrett is the advice guru for you: G.Garrett@ PoulsenGaz.com." Couldn't hurt to start getting the word out locally with small-scale buzz marketing, she thought, thankful that Jackie had already set her up with an email address for Gavin. A shelf bore an eclectic assortment of mugs. Roz selected one with an orca on it and poured herself a cup of coffee.

With a burst of crisp air, Barry and Celeste bustled through the door. Celeste was wearing a new jewel-toned paisley cardigan knotted at the waist and carried a fuchsia shopping bag.

"You are such a sucker," Roz laughed.

"Some of her stuff is nice." Roz had to admit that with Celeste's styling (over her jeans and simple white tee, the busy pattern and bold colors had nothing to clash with, and the way she'd knotted it helped give shape to the boxy cut), it did look kind of cute.

"Most of the things are okay on their own," Barry added. "It's the head-to-toe look that's a bit much. Also, that woman was not going to let us leave until we bought something. She got me, too." He reached into the bag and took out a long-sleeved t-shirt with a black and white toile print on the raglan sleeves. Roz had to admit that it looked like exactly the kind of thing Barry would wear on a weekend.

"Hi there." Erik emerged from the kitchen with Roz's fries and a plate of eggs.

Erik's Nordic deity looks clearly had an even stronger effect on Barry than they'd had on Roz. His breath was coming, ever-so-faintly, in short, shallow bursts.

No one else would have noticed, except for Celeste, who was also eyeing Erik hungrily, but with an entirely different focus. "Fries! I'm starving." She skipped over to the table, giving Bowie a pat on the haunches as she sat.

"Guys, this is Erik. He's been super nice to Bowie. Erik, this is Celeste and Barry."

Celeste said, "Nice to meet you, Erik."

"Hi," Barry breathed.

"Hi Celeste, Barry." Erik held Barry's gaze an extra beat, a toothpaste commercial-worthy smile spreading across his face. "Nice to meet both of you. What can I get you all to eat?"

Roz ordered the house-made veggie burger, Celeste and Barry got fish and chips. When Erik brought their food out, he'd also brought a turkey sandwich for himself.

"Do you mind if I join you? I usually eat dinner alone before the happy hour rush, it'd be nice to have company."

"Of course," said Celeste.

"Please do," said Roz. Dining with handsome strangers was getting to be a habit with this group.

Barry simply beamed. Roz didn't think it was her imagination that Erik was beaming right back. She could practically see cartoon hearts beating in each of their pupils.

"So, what brings you all to town?" Erik asked between bites. "We don't get too many tourists this early in the week."

Barry, having recovered his faculties of speech, answered

before Roz did. "We all left our jobs yesterday. Roz has a new gig with the newspaper here. Celeste and I tagged along for the fun of it."

"Are you looking for work then? I could use some help here." In theory, Erik was addressing both Barry and Celeste, but he only had eyes for Barry. Roz caught Celeste's gaze across the table and hid a giggle behind her napkin.

"Sure." Barry was glowing. "I waited tables in college. I could put a few shifts in."

"Erik," Roz said, intruding on the smitten gaze between the two men, "we're looking for a place to stay this week. I checked for a vacation rental on the bulletin board but didn't see anything."

"There's probably not too much available through the weekend, with Nordic Fest coming up. But I tell you what—I've been meaning to rent out my house but never had a chance to post it. I sleep in the studio above the restaurant. It's easier since I have to get up so early to open for breakfast. My dad used to run this place and chair the festival, too, and I honestly don't know how he managed it all. I took the restaurant on a few months ago and I'm still figuring out the routine. The house is sitting empty. It's got three bedrooms and a nice view of the Sound. Would you be interested in renting it?"

Roz thought this seemed perfect. They agreed on a price and Erik got them his spare set of housekeys.

Erik finished his sandwich and was back a few minutes later with three slices of berry pie. "On the house. Tenants special." He set them down with a flourish. Barry's plate had a smiley face made of whipped cream.

Celeste dug into her slice. "This is incredible. What a nice man."

"Yeah," sighed Barry, "what a nice, nice man."

"Handsome, too, don't you think, Barry?" Roz added. Barry was staring moonily at the kitchen door and didn't seem to hear her. How refreshing. With Celeste quick to shut down any progress in her love life, and Roz's recent misadventure with Andy, maybe at least one of them could have some luck in the romance department.

A trio of windblown men dressed for working on the docks shuffled in, two well into middle age and one in his twenties. "Hi, fellas," called Erik, installing himself behind the bar. He began dispensing pints without taking orders. Clearly this was a regular crowd.

"I think I'll stick around and have a beer." Roz had a professional interest in absorbing some local color. "Do you want to take Bowie and go get settled in?" She handed Celeste the leash and the keys to Erik's house and moved to a bar stool.

The youngest member of the group was getting a hard time from the others. As Roz reached the bar, one of his friends gestured at her and said, "Hey, Steve, why don't you ask this lady what you should do? None of us sure as hell understands your wife, maybe another chick will."

"Uh, hey guys. Actually, we held the election for who would be qualified to speak for all womankind last week, and I lost by a hair." This got a laugh, which was a relief. This type of comment could go either way with groups of men in bro-mode.

She introduced herself. The men were Colin, Bill, and the youngest was Steve. Steve Shepherd, as a matter of fact, and Roz thought she might have an inkling about what his marriage troubles could be.

Steve took the seat next to Roz and laid out his problem for her. He seemed like a decent guy. Polite, obviously loved his wife, something which must require a saintly quantity of patience.

"Phoebe and I got married right after high school — we'd been dating since the eighth grade. I love her more than anything, but for the past two years she's been spending all of her time on her business."

Yahtzee. Roz made a go-on gesture.

"I'm not convinced it's bringing in very much money, and we don't need the income. Our living expenses are small, and I make enough for both of us. But she wants all this other stuff. A fancy car — her company calls it a reward, but we have to make the lease payment. Cruise vacations, stuff like that. I feel like I'm not enough for her, and she barely talks to me about anything but her business anymore. She's up late most nights updating her website and she's always on live-streaming sales on her phone. She always says she's too tired to — "

"I get the picture," Roz said, taking pity on him.

"Steve, buddy, listen," Bill was the oldest of the group. He thumped Steve on the shoulder, so hard Roz saw the younger man flinch. "She sounds like my third wife. Started breeding Persian cats and left me for a guy who breeds Siamese. Met him at a cat show. She's probably already planning to leave you for some metrosexual who sells tights."

"I'm sure that's not true. Have you talked to Phoebe about her priorities?"

"She talks about reaching the 'ultraviolet' level at her company, recruiting more people to work with her, going to the convention. It's like she doesn't want to talk about anything at all that she might…need me for."

Roz had a few ideas. It could help for Steve to see if he could find some other outlets for Phoebe's boundless entrepreneurial energy. As Roz, that was what she would have recommended. But as Gavin Garrett, she had an advice column to launch and needed to rustle up some material.

She walked over to the foyer and plucked the sailboat index card she had written earlier from the bulletin board. "I saw this on my way in. I'm crap at giving advice," she resisted the urge to cross her fingers behind her back, "but maybe you should give this guy a try?"

Steve pocketed the card. "I just might. No one around here," he gave Bill a pointed look, "has had any decent suggestions."

From: chefangela@Dandelionbistro.com
To: George.F@NWCmag.com
Subject: Your Stepdaughter

Dear Fred,

It's been ages. You should drop in to Dandelion for lunch some-time soon. We miss you! Of course, I've been so busy completing my cookbook that I haven't been there much lately, myself.

I heard that you and Rosalind have parted ways, professionally. I think that is for the best. Mixing family and business can be messy. As a matter of fact, I was recently asked to step in and shoot an episode of Ardent Life Adventures because Olivia Arden and her ex-husband have had some friction on set. Do you know Andy? I think Rosalind does – I saw them together at Andy's hotel when I was there meeting with some of the production crew. Small world, n'est-ce pas?

Best, Angela

From: George.F@NWCmag.com
To: Olivia.Arden@ardentlifeadventures.net
Subject: Guest Column

Ms. Arden,

It's come to my attention that you are currently in Seattle and may be looking for new opportunities as your television show wraps up. We have some recent vacancies on our writing staff and are seeking a guest writer for the "Kate Knows Best" advice column. I'm a great admirer. I think someone with your sophisticated viewpoint could lend some much-needed class to the column. Please call me to discuss details.

Best Regards,
Frederick George
Editor-in-Chief
NWC

Chapter Eight

Celeste

Erik's house was a lemon-yellow Victorian, two blocks uphill from Front Street. It had a wraparound porch with intricate woodwork, a swing, and a view of the harbor. They parked in the gravel drive and unpacked the car. Roz always teased Celeste for bringing too much, but if they were going to be here all week, it was a good thing she had. No doubt Roz would be dipping into her suitcase by Thursday.

Celeste put her bags down in a guest room on the first floor with a high cherrywood bed frame covered in a herringbone quilt and floor-to-ceiling bookshelves. She followed Barry upstairs, admiring the art hung on the walls along the way. Like the diner, the decor was a mix of antiques and contemporary art, most of which appeared to have been done by the same hand.

The largest bedroom had sky-blue walls, bleached wood furniture and stark white bedding. The final room was more modest, an office with a daybed covered in a soft-looking gray quilt.

"You should take the big room, Barry," she said.

"Shouldn't I leave it to Roz? She's paying the bill after all. She *is* paying the bill, right?"

Celeste laughed. "Of course she is. You know what she's like." Roz had always been generous with money. Since Kate's death she'd insisted on paying for everything. Sharing her inheritance was a way for Roz to find a silver lining in her loss, and Celeste tried to accept graciously without letting her go overboard.

She would try to chip in a bit for this trip, but Barry didn't need to. He was paying rent on a Seattle apartment, they weren't. "She'll want Bowie to sleep with her and that white bedding isn't compatible with dirty paws."

Celeste had seen how Barry admired the room—and for that matter, how he'd admired Erik back at the diner. This was certainly Erik's room when he was at home, and if Barry wanted to snoop through his closet a tiny bit, well, that was Barry's business.

Celeste made tea, pleased to find some of her favorite flavors in Erik's kitchen cabinet. Barry found a jigsaw puzzle and started sorting the pieces. She took a mystery novel from Erik's shelves and settled down with her tea, but she was only on chapter two when Roz burst through the door.

"I think I have Gavin Garrett's first customer," she exclaimed, and told them about the conversation she'd had at the bar. Every development seemed to pull Roz further into this scheme, but her luck wouldn't hold out forever. Something was bound to go sideways eventually. When it did, Celeste would be the one to pick up the pieces, but for now all she could do was go along for the ride.

Roz

Roz didn't mind taking the smallest room. It was cozy, and the only room with a desk. The twin bed was covered with a hand-made quilt that smelled of sage, lavender, and tea. The shelves were filled with painting supplies and art books, and a robot sticker on the inside of the closet door confirmed her hunch that this had once been Erik's bedroom.

She changed into boxers and an old t-shirt and went into the hall bathroom to brush her teeth and wash her face. When she returned, Bowie was a snoring white bagel in the dead center of the twin bed. Roz nudged him. She waved a treat in front of his face; he licked it half-heartedly before tucking his nose back under his tail. She gently tugged his collar, which earned her a half-raised eyelid. She shoved him, which resulted in an annoyed grunt, but no movement. He wasn't going to budge.

This was a problem. With the quilt pinned down by sixty pounds of stubborn canine, sleeping under the covers was out of the question. She could sleep downstairs on the couch, but if Bowie woke up alone in the middle of the night, he would panic and wake the whole house. His attacks of separation anxiety had waned since they brought him home from the shelter, but still happened occasionally and were hard on everyone.

There was an extra blanket folded at the foot of the bed. Roz wrapped herself in it and began the puzzle of fitting herself in comfortably. She felt him breathing against her, and his solid weight lulled her to sleep.

She woke the next morning when the room began to brighten. Followed by Bowie, who had evidently also had a restful night, Roz made her way downstairs. Bowie's ears and tail stood up the way they always did when he was excited to explore a new place, as if he needed to raise antennae in order to take it all in. There was a spring in his step as he padded along. The soft click of his nails on the floor was the only sound in the quiet house. Promising rays of morning sun angled through the windows of the kitchen, where Roz found half a pot of coffee and a note from Barry telling them he'd gone down to the Blue Plate.

On the way back upstairs to change into her workout clothes, Roz peeked in on Celeste. She was still sound asleep. Bowie lifted his head as high as he could and wagged his tail at the tall bed, but his attention snapped to Roz when she held out his harness. "You'll see her later. Come on, buddy. Let's go for a run."

Clearly, it was refreshing for Bowie to get a change from their normal neighborhood routes, because his nose was working overtime. Roz slowed to a walk and let him sniff the trees and fence posts they passed. In front of a large house with a sign out front that said, "Mrs. Muir's Bed and Breakfast," Bowie took a special interest in an azalea bush, turned around, and backed up to poop directly on it.

"Oh, thanks, pal."

He always did this, always had, for no reason any of the trainers could explain. He simply wouldn't go on the grass if a shrub was an option. At least Roz was used to it, had plenty of bags, and this morning he'd chosen a bush without thorns, although she hoped Mrs. Muir wasn't watching from a window. She pulled biodegradable plastic bags out of her pocket and cleaned the shrub up. "Okay, good boy…I guess. Wanna run now?"

She was straightening up when she heard a familiar voice. "Roz?" It couldn't be who she thought because that would be far too awkward.

Oh, but it was. Andy was coming down the front steps, squinting at her. Seriously? Of all the picturesque B&Bs in all the sleepy seaside towns, he had to walk out of the one where she was currently scooping dog poop.

Roz considered making a run for it—with her baseball cap and sunglasses, maybe he hadn't made a positive ID yet. Andy stopped right in front of her and set down the cooler he'd been carrying, blocking their path down the sidewalk. Nope, too late. "I thought that was you. What are you doing here?"

"Oh, you know, living my best life." Great. She had reconciled herself to not seeing Andy again. It was fine. In fact, it was preferable; he'd lied to her by omission, if not outright. He should be a ship passing in the night, perhaps a future cocktail party story. Definitely history. Which meant she ought to have guessed he'd pop up again. And he looked great, dammit, in a storm blue athletic shirt that showed the muscles in his shoulders and brought out the green flecks in his eyes. He grinned, and she felt a wobble in the backs of her knees.

She must have scowled, annoyed at herself for responding in spite of her resolve to be done with him, because Andy's smile drooped. *At least be civil,* she told herself, *it'll be easier to get out of this conversation if you don't make it a big deal.* She smoothed out her expression and forced a casual tone. "Actually, I'm here for work. New gig. You?"

"Well," Andy pushed his hair off his forehead, "I'm here working, too." He gestured to the SUV parked at the curb, emblazoned with the Geography Channel logo.

"Right. Mr. TV Star."

Andy deflated. "Roz, listen, I'm sorry I didn't say anything. When you didn't recognize me, it felt nice to be sure someone was genuinely enjoying my company instead of getting a thrill out of hanging around someone with a small amount of celebrity."

"Don't worry about it." She gestured dismissively with the hand holding the knotted bag, before she remembered what she was waving around and dropped her arm to her side. "No big deal. We're adults, you don't owe me an explanation."

"But I do, I—"

"Look, I've got to get going. Bowie gets antsy if we stay in one spot too long." (While this was generally true, at this moment Bowie sat patiently on the sidewalk, giving Andy his trademark pit bull grin: tongue out, eyes squinched, not a care in the world.) "Come on, good boy!" She scooped her hand forward to give him the 'Let's go!' sign, and thankfully he was happy enough to trot away with her.

Roz picked up speed as they ran toward the outskirts of town. Some nerve. How dare Andy show up, looking ruggedly sexy in his hiking clothes, being all…nice, after letting her think he was some normal, anonymous tour guide?

(A tiny voice in her head told her she had known all along that normal tour guides don't stay in suites in four-star hotels, and wasn't she perhaps looking for a reason not to add the complication of a genuine, decent guy, who she liked and who liked her back, to her life? Oh, and by the way if she wants to have a one-night stand, she can go ahead and have one without inventing reasons to be too mad at the guy to keep seeing him. She ran faster in an attempt to shut the bossy little voice up.)

Roz and Bowie followed the main road out of town. The houses got farther apart until they were passing rail-fenced cow pastures and long gravel driveways dotted with only the occasional house. As they picked up speed, she felt the stress of the past few days sliding from her shoulders, replaced by invigoration. It was a perfect fall day, cool and crisp without being cold, with just enough cloud cover to keep the sun from being too harsh. Bowie cantered along next to her left leg, stocky haunches rippling under his sleek white fur.

About half a mile down the country road, there was a trailhead that took them into the national park. Roz paused to check the bulletin board for bear sightings and other hazards. When she was out with Bowie, she had to hear for both of them. Seeing nothing of concern, she set out onto the trail. The evergreen canopy soared sixty feet above their heads. Prehistoric-looking ferns sprouted from fallen logs and it wasn't hard to picture a brachiosaur bending a long neck to munch on them. Twigs and fallen leaves crunched softly under their feet. The air was significantly cooler here, although the sun broke through the trees occasionally to dapple the ground and shrubs.

The trail skirted the edge of a shallow ravine filled with vegetation. Tall plants with dinner-plate-sized leaves reached so earnestly for all the filtered sunlight they could capture that they were almost completely flat, fallen pine needles puddled near the stems. A few downed trees crisscrossed the gap, dripping with moss.

The place seeped into her very being like a balm. If asked to describe the feeling with one word, she would have said, "Green." If she counted, she probably could have pointed to thirty different shades, but it was more than a color. The place was more alive than anywhere she'd ever been before. Roz had read about Japanese forest baths, the practice of renewing one's soul by spending time indulging the senses in nature, but she hadn't fully understood the concept until now. This place was cleansing some essential part of her, wiping the unwanted away, leaving only calm. She slowed to a walk, the better to take it all in, and began to notice more: a spider web still strung with morning dew; birds and insects flitting through the trees on either side of her; velvety moss coating fallen logs; the way the occasional deciduous tree's amber leaves contrasted with the backdrop of evergreens.

Her stomach growled, bringing her back to more mundane concerns. Having run off her nervous energy, washed into serenity by the forest, it was easier to put her problems into proportion. So what if Andy had happened to show up in the town where she was spending a week? She could probably avoid him until he left. (*Or not?* The tiny voice, which had returned with her slowing heart rate, prodded, *Why exactly, do you need to avoid him?*) He probably wouldn't be here for long. Didn't they shoot those shows pretty quickly? Roz turned, picked her pace back up to a jog, and made her way back to town.

The breakfast rush was ending when Roz arrived at the Blue Plate, toting her laptop bag but still sweaty from her run. She wanted to get a jump on work while eating breakfast.

Erik greeted her from the kitchen door. "Hey Roz. Barry went out to pick up the produce order. Get you some breakfast?"

"So he really is working here then?" she said, amused. Barry hated to be idle. "I'd love scrambled eggs and toast, thanks." She helped herself to coffee from the carafe near the front door. Bowie curled up in a corner behind the host stand and Roz secured his leash to a bar stool even though he was unlikely to move voluntarily anytime soon. As she sipped her coffee, Roz browsed the bulletin board. The index card she'd sketched for Gavin Garrett to replace the one she'd given to Steve the night before was missing. Good. She made a new one and a mental note to get some printed. Then, another card caught her eye. It was a sketch of an overturned glass of wine, shaded with red and purple pencils, and a verse:

> *My heart is aflutter because*
> *of a beautiful lady named Roz.*
> *I have traveled the world,*
> *but have not met a girl*
> *who will put up with all of my flaws.*

"Hey Erik?"

"Yeah?" He arrived with her plate of food and an egg for Bowie. If they stayed more than a week, she'd have to figure out how to get a dog's cholesterol checked.

"Do you know who made this card?"

He shook his head. "Not sure. It doesn't seem like something any of the regulars would do, but we did have a couple of guys in here this morning from TV. A travel show, I think. You know them?"

"Maybe." Andy, who else? Although she couldn't say she *knew* him. This wasn't what she would have expected from him at all. The poem was appallingly cheesy. So why did it give her a thrill to know she was on his mind? "I'm going to hang onto this, okay?"

Erik gave her a brilliant blue wink. "Fine with me. How'd you get on last night?"

"Very well, thanks. Your house is wonderful."

"Thank you." He wiped down the counter. "When Mom died last year, my father moved back to Norway—he was born in Bergen and came over with his folks when he was three—and he pretty much left everything as it was. I came home from Portland when she got sick and then when Dad wanted to leave me the house and the restaurant, I couldn't say no. It seemed so important to him to keep them in the family."

"I'm so sorry about your mom. I lost mine last winter. I live in her house, too, so we have that in common. It's funny, isn't it? Being surrounded by their things makes you feel better and worse at the same time."

"That's true. It took me a few months to move into the bigger bedroom. Redecorating helped."

Roz hadn't even moved Kate's clothes out of her closet yet. "What did you do in Portland?"

"I was an artist. Meaning, I was a server who did as much art as I could in my free time."

"Did you do these?" Roz gestured to the paintings.

"Most of them, yeah."

She didn't know art the way Celeste did, but she knew what she liked. "Erik, you should be doing this full time."

Erik replaced the tray he'd been working on and gave her a direct look. "You know, I like running this place. I enjoy talking to people, providing a gathering space. And when I get in a groove in the kitchen, it's meditative. I think once I get into a rhythm and hire more staff, I can delegate some things. Then I'll be able to find a few hours a day to paint, and that will be a perfect balance. It's nice to have Barry's help even if it's just for a few days, but I'm sure he's eager to get back to Seattle. It's hard to replace the kind of social life you find in the city." There was an unspoken question in Erik's tone, giving Roz the distinct feeling he was hoping she would contradict him.

"You'd have to ask Barry, but I think he's on a short-term lease and he's between jobs. And he's pretty amazing. Barry is one of my best friends and he was fantastic to work with. He's great at keeping things organized."

He smiled at her. "I might. Thanks."

Roz opened her laptop and connected to Erik's Wi-Fi. Morbid curiosity sent her straight to the NWC page. It was Wednesday, the day her columns normally went live, but she hadn't submitted one before she quit. She assumed Fred would rerun an old "Kate Knows Best," and wanted to know whether it would be one her mom had written, or one of hers.

NWC's website had profile pages for each contributor where readers could see all of each writer's content, a short bio, and if they liked, leave a comment. Roz's hadn't been archived yet, but she knew it was only a matter of time. The first thing she saw was a new comment here, timestamped the previous afternoon,

> *This is a personal message for Rosalind Connolly; I'm so sorry for the misunderstanding and hope to see you again soon. I think you're very special. You can leave a message for me at my hotel. Please do. Andy.*

Andy, popping up like a jack-in-the-box, again. Their website moderators usually took down comments like this; she had a feeling her friend Louise in IT let this one slip through thinking she was doing Roz a favor.

On the "Kate Knows Best" page, Roz saw that a column had indeed been posted today. She clicked through to the full text. As she read, her cheeks grew hot.

> *Note to readers: We have a guest columnist this week. Olivia Arden, star of Ardent Life Adventures, is filling in as our Kate. In addition to her training from the Culinary Institute of America, Olivia holds a psychology degree from Stanford University.*

> *Dear Kate,*

> *I (24, he/him) am working in my first job at a large tech company. Most of my coworkers are male and socialize together, bonding over craft beer and attending sporting events. I don't drink at all (both of my parents struggled with drinking, I just preferred not to start), and am not a big fan of spectator sports, although I am an avid cyclist and also enjoy paddle-boarding and skiing. My coworkers invite me along when they get tickets for a game or go to a sports bar after work. They do not invite any of our female or nonbinary coworkers, although there are a few women and one nonbinary person in our department. I go sometimes, but I don't have fun and I feel guilty about it. Should I stop going? Should I suggest inviting our whole team?*

Thanks,

No Bro

Dear No Bro,

Sometimes you have to play the game for a while before you can make your own rules. Fake it 'til you make it. You are new to a team that has been operating this way for many years; you can't change the system overnight. Suck it up and go out for a beer after work — you don't have to stay long. Your work buddies will notice you came along, and you can slip out after an hour or so. Maybe you can ride your bike to the bar. If you don't care for beer, try ordering a craft cider. Many non-beer drinkers enjoy those, and delicious flavors like pear and cranberry are increasingly available.

As for your female coworkers, it is not up to you to be their white knight. If they want to come along, they can invite themselves. No one helped me fight this battle in the culinary world, an environment that is just as sexist as technology companies, if not more so, and fighting it on my own has made me a stronger leader today.

Cordially, Olivia

Roz saw red. Until now, she had always thought that was a figure of speech, but crimson spots swirled in her tunneling vision. In one day, this is what had become of everything her mom built, everything she had tried so hard to keep going. She didn't know how Fred could possibly have known getting Olivia Arden to write the column would be salt in the wound, but she wouldn't put it past him to have done that on purpose. And if this was how Andy's ex-wife viewed the world, maybe Roz didn't need to feel guilty about connecting with him before the ink was dry on their divorce papers. She was banging on her laptop keyboard with furious fingers, in a mad cycle of type-delete-re-phrase, when Celeste entered carrying an armful of dahlias.

"Barry's pulling up around back, Erik." She found some vases under the counter and began arranging the flowers. "Roz, I saw the new 'Kate Knows Best.' You must be so upset. Do you want to talk about it?"

"Nope. Don't need to talk about it. Moving right on to getting even." Roz turned her laptop for Celeste to see what she was about to post as Gavin on social media.

"Oh Roz. I don't think it's a good idea to bait my dad like this. You could get in a lot of trouble."

"I'm *incognito.*"

"Okay, but—"

"Celly, listen." She kept typing. "I know Fred is your dad and you have to be loyal. I get that. But he's not mine, he was rotten to me growing up—he was rotten to you, for that matter—and I have to do something. I can't just sit here and let him turn my column, and Mom's magazine, into some bland, regressive, pile of…pabulum."

She hit the publish button on a post tagging Olivia's column, with a link back to her new alter-ego's website. "I lol'd @Arden-tLifeOlivia's parody advice column in @NWCmag. Surely this is a joke, because what kind of bozo would suggest the abstain-ing adult child of alcoholics 'suck it up and try a craft cider?!' I thought No Bro might like some real advice. Read my answer soon in my column, Mr. Garrett's Facts of Life: www.poulsengaz.com/advice."

"There, it's done," she said, but Celeste had disappeared into the kitchen leaving only the flowers behind. The adrenaline rush hadn't worn off yet. Roz did a quick search and found the profile she was looking for. She shouldn't do this. She should probably just email him like a sane and responsible grown up. As herself. But Roz already had a digital disguise — she might as well use it. Still logged in as Gavin Garrett, Roz found Andy's profile and typed. "'I think you're very special?' Weak. And is that maybe you leaving LIMERICKS on bulletin boards around my town? Niiiiiice. You need my help with your game, buddy. DM me."

Roz dug into her eggs, now cold and slimy, but she barely tasted them. By the time she was finished, her phone had blown up with notifications. Most were from "Kate Knows Best" fans; the column had a community of regular, dedicated readers, and several of them were now pinging Roz's personal social media accounts to ask what happened and where she had gone. Gavin was also getting messages and comments congratulating him on calling Olivia's letter out and asking when they could read the new column. And Gavin had gotten more than three hundred new followers in the past twenty minutes.

There was also an email in Gavin's inbox even more interesting than the one she'd expected from Steve, from "Pheebs99@webmail.com." Not exactly what she had been hoping for, but it would do nicely.

Before she could start drafting her column, she got a text from Jackie. "When we spoke yesterday, I didn't expect you'd lack the common sense to avoid engaging Fred or NWC directly. What were you thinking? Come see me, please. ASAP."

Celeste

Once the flowers were in water, Celeste had left them at the bar. She'd arrange them more carefully later, but she needed a break from Roz's spiral. Every time Celeste tried to steady Roz she got brushed off. She was sick of it.

In the kitchen, Barry and Erik were unpacking the produce. Barry caught the look on her face and understood it immediately. "Uh oh."

"Bear, she's impossible. Fred found a guest writer for 'Kate Knows Best' and she's replying to the column. She thinks it's fine because she's in disguise."

He laughed. "I've created a monster."

"It's not funny."

He put an arm around her shoulder and squeezed. "I know you're upset. But come on, it's a little bit funny. Let Roz and your dad fight it out between themselves. You have your own shit to worry about."

"I sure do."

"Speaking of which, did you finish your business plan yet?"

She pursed her lips. "No. Once it's done I'll have to have a conversation with Roz and I'm not ready."

The bell over the door dinged, indicating the arrival of a customer. "I'll get that," Barry said. On his way out, he added, "Finish your business plan. Worry about Roz later."

"Business plan for what?" Erik asked.

"A design company. I've been working as a style writer. I'd like to do something more hands on, although I'm not entirely sure what direction to take."

"Ah," Erik wagged a finger at her. "I thought you were an artist, too. You have the vibe."

"The paintings in the diner and your house are yours, right?"

"Most of them, yeah. The landscapes are from high school. My dad put them up and I haven't had the heart to take them down. The still lifes are what I'd been working on recently."

Celeste could see how he'd progressed as an artist. The recent paintings were photorealistic close-ups, rendered in crisp detail. A coffee cup from the diner, the cracked halves of an eggshell and a puddle of brilliant goldenrod yolk, a pair of polished wood knitting needles stuck through a crimson tangle of yarn, a scuffed rust-colored boat fender. All perfectly ordinary, mundane objects shown in sharp, balanced compositions.

"Beautiful work."

"Thank you. I was just telling your sister, I want to make more space in my life for art, but I like to mix in the practical stuff or else I spend too much time in my own head."

"That's why I prefer applied art to fine art," Celeste said. "I think there's value in creating attractive, practical spaces. Your house is beautiful, by the way."

"Thank you. I finally feel like I've made it my own."

"I wish Roz would do that. We live in her mom's house and she hasn't changed a single thing."

"Give her time. It sounds like she's been through a lot. You have, too."

Erik's words had more weight than he'd likely meant to give them. Was she giving Roz enough time and space to feel her feelings? It hadn't even been a year since Kate's death, and it had been such a shock. But how long would she have to put her own needs on hold?

"Listen, if you're interested, I could use some help with the Nordic Fest decorations. We need to do up the community hall and the park picnic shelter. My mom used to do it but to be honest I haven't even started. I know you're extremely over-qualified, but—"

"I'd love to." A distracting project to dive into was exactly what she needed.

Chapter Nine

Roz

For the second time in a week, Roz approached her workplace under a cloud of anxiety. Last time, she'd been sure she was in the right. Now, she had a nagging sense her temper had led her astray.

An hour ago, she'd still been in her grimy running clothes at the diner and as much as she didn't want to keep Jackie waiting, she didn't want to sit across from her smelly and disheveled. She stopped by the house to shower and change into jeans and a crisp white shirt. With her hair brushed and a bit of makeup, she felt more ready to march into a lion's den.

Roz let herself into the Gazette offices. Late morning light streaked through the wavy glass of the old building's windowpanes, casting hazy rectangles across the dusty front room. It was lovely. Had she already screwed up her chance to work here?

"Have a seat." Jackie beckoned Roz into her office. "I need you to understand that I agreed to our arrangement on a trial basis, at some personal risk." Roz opened her mouth to protest, but Jackie stopped her with a sharp look. "I know you're aware that this paper's reputation, and mine, could be on the line if Fred decides to go after you. I gave you a shot because of the respect I had for your mom—and the lack of respect I have for Fred. However," Jackie's tone wiped the relieved smile right off of Roz's face, "I assumed it went without saying that it would be foolish to call Fred's attention to ourselves—"

"Jackie, I know. I'm sorry." Roz couldn't contain herself any longer. "It made me so angry to see mom's column turned into trash, but I'll delete my posts."

Jackie held up her index finger. "Not so fast. Although I don't want to get into a pissing match with Fred, our website has had more traffic in the hours since your post than it usually sees in a week, and I'm getting emails asking when your response will be posted. Against my better judgment, I think we should go ahead and run your answer."

"Really? Oh my gosh, thank you." The legacy of "Kate Knows Best" was already tarnished, but it was still possible to build something better. Hopefully that was already starting. "Gavin will stick to answering the letters he receives from now on."

"Good. Does he have any?"

"One so far." Roz pulled the message up on her phone. "Do you know Phoebe Sheppard-Shepherd? I am pretty sure this is from her."

Jackie stuck a leg out from behind her desk, revealing the red leggings printed with ladybugs that she was wearing with her black jersey dress. "I'm familiar with her," she said. "I bought these just to get her to leave me alone. Although to be honest I do think they're kind of cute."

Roz laughed. "She cornered Celeste and Barry on the street yesterday. I barely escaped. What if we run the alternate response to the 'Kate Knows Best' column, then this letter and its answer as Gavin's first column?" Roz opened her laptop to the email and passed it over so Jackie could read it.

When she finished, she nodded her approval. "This sounds good. Grab a desk out front and draft something. We'll post it this afternoon, along with your reply to Olivia Arden's column."

Roz had never finished a column so quickly. It took her under an hour to refine her rebuttal to Olivia Arden's "Kate" column and draft an answer to Phoebe.

> *Dear Readers,*
>
> *As promised, here is my own response to this week's Kate Knows Best letter.*
>
> *Dear No Bro,*
>
> *You don't have to drink if you don't want to, and your after-work time is your own to do with as you please. You said you work at a large company; there must be other people interested in cycling, even if they aren't on your immediate team. Keep an eye out to see who bikes to work. Maybe you can get some people together to ride on the weekends. This could be a good way to network with people in other parts of your company.*
>
> *As for your coworkers who aren't cis straight men: While it is true that they can invite themselves along, culture change must come from within, and you have a great opportunity to be an ally here. When invited out, even if you decline you can say, "I don't drink but I hear Morgan is a home brewer. You should ask them."*

Or "Jessica is a huge Mariner's fan; you should offer this ticket to her." And why not suggest a whole-team activity that you will enjoy, too. (Trivia? Mini golf? A group hike? Community service project?) Remember that one of these people might be your boss someday, and they will remember your conduct and that of your colleagues.

Factually, Gavin Garrett

Dear Mr. Garrett,

Hi. Do you believe in signs? I found your card in my front yard and I thought it must mean that I should write to you for help. I've been trying to get pregnant for five years. I think we need to see a fertility specialist, but the treatments are so expensive. While my husband makes a decent living, I don't think we can afford them on his salary alone, much less the expenses of raising a child. For the past three years, I have been trying to build up a business so I can build my family. I'm an independent wardrobe consultant for a direct sales retailer. If (When! Gotta think positive!) I have a baby, this business will let me continue working without sending my child to daycare to be raised by strangers, because I work from home and my car and can set my own hours.

My husband doesn't seem to appreciate how much time I put into my business or understand that I am doing it for both of us. He asked me to give it up, but I've been putting the extra income away in a savings account for our future fertility expenses. It isn't much – growing my business means I have had to reinvest some of my profits there, but every little bit helps. Also, I don't think I can stand to be only a housewife, especially when I am not even a mom yet.

How do I make him understand?

Thanks,

Girlboss Wants a Baby

Dear Boss,

There are a few things going on here. First, you say you are work-ing hard and not banking much money. Have you thought about why that might be? It sounds to me like you are working with a multi-level marketing company. While these companies are not technically illegal, they operate very much like a pyramid scheme, with the people at the top profiting most from the labor of others. This makes it hard for people like you to get ahead or even make much of a profit. I encourage you to do a careful comparison of how much money you spend on your business vs. how much you bring in. Now calculate how many hours you spend "working" per week. Is the hourly rate worth the effort you are putting in?

I don't want to discourage you from working outside the home. You find it fulfilling to put your energy into a professional endeavor. However, I encourage you to think about different work. Ask yourself if there is something else you might be good at, and enjoy, that you could make some money doing? Pursue that. (On a side note, this columnist was "raised by strangers" in a daycare and turned out fine. Let's not pit mothers against each other, okay?)

Finally, I understand being concerned about fertility. This is not something you should have to worry about alone. Talk to your husband. Talk to your doctor, together, about what your options are, what they might cost, and what your insurance will cover.

Encouragingly, Gavin Garrett

Jackie approved the column as soon as she finished reading the draft. "Well done. This is a specific answer to your letter-writer, but you're also addressing a broader issue. Keep this up."

"Thanks Jackie." A positive response from her editor was a welcome change — even when she hadn't argued with Fred over the content of her columns, he had rarely been complimentary. Roz assumed he felt stuck with her because of Kate, and because she'd gained popularity with readers in her own right, but it was no secret that he didn't especially care for her work.

"I also have some ideas about features profiling local family businesses leading up to Nordic Fest." Roz checked the stats of Gavin's profiles. "Gavin's social media is getting a decent amount of attention, so hopefully that will get some more eyeballs on local interest stories — maybe even bring more people over from the city for the festival."

"Sounds good. Get to work! Let me know when you have something ready to submit." Jackie waved Roz out of her office.

"On my way. Hey, Jackie, how do you want me to handle interviewing locals?" She swept a hand over her lack of disguise. "I thought I could tell them I was Gavin's research assistant. Sound okay?"

Jackie snorted. "That will never fool anyone who knows any-thing about small newspaper budgets, but I'm sure most people won't give it much thought. Based on the amount I was asked to spend on a festival sponsorship, everyone around here seems to think I'm made of big city money."

Roz had been wondering about that, herself. Port Poulsen was charming, but she still didn't understand what the draw could be for Jackie over her high-profile career in San Francisco. Tra-ditional journalism was still a good old white boys club, as Roz knew only too well from her own experiences. The Gazette was a nice publication, but with Jackie's talent, she should be doing more than bake sale announcements and fishing reports. She'd get to the bottom of it eventually.

Olivia

Olivia was the only person in the theater watching the mid-morning screening of the latest rom-com. Sneaking away to see a matinee alone was her guilty pleasure when she was on location. She loved light comedies: the more absurd the premise, the better. She always got popcorn loaded with fake butter and soda loaded with high-fructose corn syrup, items she shunned at any other time. If anyone knew about this habit, they would reevaluate their opinion of Olivia Arden as a sophisticated woman with discriminating taste. She kept it to herself, and always wore a hat and sunglasses until the auditorium darkened. She'd never even told Andy where she was going, allowing him to think she was meeting with "ingredient vendors." He was always happy enough to have a free afternoon to go skydiving or whatever extra adrenaline rush he was after, and never asked too many questions.

Going to movies by herself had been Olivia's habit since high school. She'd never felt like she fit in with the other kids in her small Nebraskan hometown. They were fully entrenched in their Norman Rockwell, football, 4-H lives, and while they were nice enough, they didn't seem to know what to make of Olivia, who made profiteroles for the bake sale and wore basic, classic clothes instead of the latest from the noisy, cologne-soaked mall stores. So, after school sometimes, she'd escape into the darkened theater for a while, always telling her parents she'd been at a school activity or over at a friend's house.

Olivia's parents were great. They'd been in their late thirties when they adopted her from Korea as an infant and she was certain no child had ever been more wanted or nurtured. She hated the thought of disappointing them, which was why she'd believed it best to allow them to think it was Andy's choice to divorce. They were heartbroken; they adored Andy and had been eagerly anticipating grandchildren, but assured Olivia all they wanted was a happy, carefree life for her.

Marrying Andy had been the simplest decision Olivia had ever made. In addition to fitting in with her family, he was attractive, kind, and easygoing. They shared the same values and never argued. Their joint career success was more than she ever could have dreamed of. That was why it was so puzzling that every time she looked at him, she felt hot prickles of resentment. She couldn't pinpoint a single thing Andy had done to deserve it, but there they were all the same.

Always one to do her homework thoroughly, Olivia had found the best therapist in the area and approached the work with diligence, intending to learn how to be happy in her objectively amazing life. Instead, her therapist, Bert (she could not believe she had a therapist named Bert, but he was supposed to be the best), had helped her see that even though her life might seem perfect from the outside, wanting something different wasn't bad, and she was allowed to seek happiness even if it meant acting in a way that might disappoint others. Once Olivia's mind was made up, it was made for good, so she contacted an attorney, found a nice condo near the ocean, and told Andy she was leaving him. She hadn't intended to hurt him; she simply didn't see the point in dragging things out. So, she ripped the Band-Aid off.

She couldn't seem to stop herself from lashing out at him. Her behavior on set yesterday was shameful. Andy wasn't to blame for laughing at her tumble down the hill. After all, it was clear she hadn't been hurt and she probably did look pretty funny. It was the kind of thing they would have laughed at together two years ago. Now, Olivia intended to keep things businesslike and civil, but Andy insisted on being so damned nice to her and she couldn't stand it.

The evening Olivia spent shooting the cooking segment with Angela Lewis compounded her emotional turbulence. Angela was whip-smart, ambitious, and slightly bitchy in an exciting way. Being with a woman wasn't new. Olivia had realized in her first year of college that she was attracted to women as well as men. She'd even had a girlfriend for a while. Then she met Andy, who seemed like such a perfect match, and decided to chalk the girlfriend up to youthful experimentation because marriage to him seemed like the next logical step on the path to the life she envisioned for herself.

Bert encouraged her to try new things that made her feel uncomfortable, so when Angela asked her out for drinks after they wrapped their shoot, she'd gone, and allowed one thing to lead to another. And when Angela asked to see her again tonight, she agreed. It wasn't going anywhere serious, but what was the harm in having some fun?

Bert's advice was also why she'd accepted Frederick George's offer to write for "Kate Knows Best," but it was clear now that was a mistake. The turn-around time for the first assignment was so short she didn't have time to write a thoughtful answer. Olivia was afraid she was making a complete mess of her own life — who was she to tell other people what to do?

During the closing credits of the movie, she turned her phone back on and found an email from Frederick.

> From: George.F@NWCmag.com
> To: Olivia.Arden@ardentlifeadventures.net
> Subject: Feedback
>
> Dear Olivia,
>
> The reader response to your Kate Knows Best column was rather disappointing. However, all is not lost. It takes time to develop

one's voice as a columnist. Gavin Garrett's interference did not
help, but it's important to learn how to deal with pests like him.
Perhaps I can offer some feedback. Shall we discuss over drinks?
The Cedar Bar, 6:30?

Regards,

Frederick

It was a disappointment, but not a surprise. She replied,
agreeing to meet for drinks. Angela would be busy with dinner
service until at least nine-thirty. A face-to-face with Frederick to
discuss her reservations was the right way to approach this.

Andy

Although Andy was an experienced hiker himself, he liked to
present trails on the show for people of various abilities, so the
first stop he and Joe made that morning was the trail to Sol Duc
Falls. The round-trip hike was less than two miles but culmi-
nated in a stunning waterfall. Water cascaded down the rocks in
veils surrounded by lush evergreens, an ideal backdrop for a shot
where Andy spoke about Olympic National Park. The day was
sunny but the trail wasn't crowded. Their two-person approach
to these segments was a bit unorthodox but sending only a pho-
tographer and the talent (a term that had never stopped setting
Andy's teeth on edge) allowed them to be nimble, getting in and
out of natural areas quickly without trampling the environment
or attracting too much notice. Andy preferred to blend in, both
because it made the show better and because he didn't enjoy the
extra attention that came with a bigger crew.

The next trail they tried was more challenging, an eight mile
out-and-back with an elevation gain of more than two thousand
feet. Looking at the map, Joe groaned. "My knees aren't going to

miss this job."

"Are you up for it? You know I'll help carry the gear," Andy said.

"You always do. I'm game if you are." They used a lightweight camera, but it was still a lot to lug up a mountain.

The hike was worth it. Miles through mossy green cathedrals, opening to a spectacular vista of mountain peaks dusted with the season's first snow. Far off to the west, the Pacific Ocean glittered in the autumn sun. It wasn't the top of the world, but felt like it. At the cliff's edge, they sat on sun-warmed basalt, dangling their feet. Andy leaned back on his hands, taking in the view. Joe took his still camera out of his pack and, hoisting himself to his feet, walked a few steps and then snapped a photo of Andy. "That's your author photo for our book," he said.

"Let's take one of you, too, then." Andy reached for the camera. "Stand right there. You've got the ocean far off behind you, and if I take it from sitting down, you'll look epic."

Joe posed, hands on hips, head turned to the side to look off into the distance. "How's this?"

"Great," Andy said, "I think I got it, let me check…" Holding the camera in front of his lap, he leaned forward a bit to block the glare from the sun. "It looks g—ow!" He had moved to hand the camera back to Joe when a hot needle sank into his wrist. He dropped the camera over the cliff, as a yellowjacket buzzed away, bobbing along on the mountain breeze toward a patch of black-eyed Susans.

Joe didn't say a word, evidently struck speechless. In cautious increments, Andy leaned forward, afraid to look, but was pleasantly surprised when he did. "Joe, dude—it's okay. There's a ledge down there. Your camera is on a bush and I don't think it's broken. I can get it."

Joe shook his head. "It's okay, the only pictures not backed up are the ones from this week. It's not worth the risk."

"Come look." Andy beckoned him over. "We can totally get it."

Joe peered over the edge. The camera was about seven feet away, nestled in a scrubby looking bush. "Well, I guess it's worth a shot."

"Right. We need a hook…" Andy rummaged through their gear. With his Swiss Army knife, he removed the spring-loaded bar from a carabiner, leaving the c-shaped hook. "Give me your belt." He took his own off as well and attached them together. Now they had a rig to fish for the camera. Andy sent it over, but was still short of reaching the camera strap.

"New plan. Hold my legs." Carefully, Andy lay down along the edge of the cliff. With Joe holding his lower body, he was able to lean his head and shoulders over farther than he otherwise would have dared, and the length of his arm added to the belts was enough to reach the camera. Snagging it was another matter. One, two, three swings of the belts, and the carabiner merely grazed the strap, but on the fourth, it caught. Hand over hand, breath held, Andy hauled the camera up, reaching back to hand it to Joe before scooting back and dusting himself off. "Does it still work?"

"Lens is a little scratched, but I can swap it out. No big deal." Joe said. "How's your wrist?"

He had forgotten. The site of the sting was red and beginning to swell, but the pain was already fading. "It'll be fine. Ready to head back down?"

"Yeah, I'm dying to dig into that lunch Mrs. M. packed for us." Andy had already heard Joe's stomach growling. Although they'd eaten a substantial breakfast in Port Poulsen, it was after-noon now. Andy was hungry, too.

"Me too. At least down will be easy." Mrs. Muir was accus-tomed to providing afternoon tea, and he suspected the cooler might be full of cucumber sandwiches, but those would still taste good on this warm afternoon.

It took them well over an hour to get back to the truck, but they had plenty of water and some protein bars in their packs. When they arrived back at the gravel parking lot, Joe peered into the cargo area. "Hey Andy," he called. "Where's the cooler?"

"I don't know, man. You loaded it."

"No, you did. Remember, you said you'd put it in the truck while I was texting Carrie."

Well, shit. Andy remembered now. The cooler was still sitting on the sidewalk back at the bed and breakfast, exactly where he left it. He'd been about to load up the truck when he bumped into Roz, and the encounter had left him distracted and loopy. (*Twitterpated!* a voice popped into his head, from childhood viewings of *Bambi*, and yes, he did kind of feel like a Disney character in the throes of puppy love.) "Aw, crap. Sorry dude," he said. For a moment, the two men stared at each other, neither willing to believe the cold chicken or finger sandwiches or whatever had been in that cooler was lost, both famished.

Andy acted first, pulling out his phone to check for a nearby restaurant, but he didn't have a signal. "I don't remember passing anywhere to eat on the way out here, do you?"

Joe shook his head. "No. A couple of gas stations, but that's it. Listen, I think we're only about an hour and a half away from Port Poulsen. Should we head back? I'd hit that diner again."

Andy agreed. In addition to his hunger, he was exhausted and knew Joe was, too. And he had two more granola bars in his pack to tide them over. Better to go back to where they knew they could get a good meal than drive around looking for something closer. And, of course, he'd be kidding himself if he tried to pretend he wasn't itching to get back to Port Poulsen. With any luck, he'd run into Roz again.

His hopes were dashed when Joe drove them back into phone

range and he checked his notifications. A social media mention from someone named Gavin Garrett indicated that his attempts to reach out to Roz hadn't been well received. He couldn't give up, though. He'd be hard pressed to explain why he felt so certain about her, but when she'd touched him the other day to return his jacket, she was the answer to a question he had barely begun to think about asking.

He'd ruined it by not being straightforward. Maybe he didn't have what it took to be a good partner. Hadn't he spent his whole marriage disappointing Olivia? Roz was justifiably hurt and angry. What could he do that would be enough to make it up to her? He had to try. He sent Gavin a message.

If the way to win Roz's trust was to play Gavin Garrett's game, that was what he was going to do.

Roz

Roz was reading recent issues of the Gazette to get a feel for Jackie's editorial viewpoint and recent coverage of local news, but Gavin's notifications had been blowing up since the column posted and she could hardly read two sentences before her phone buzzed again.

> *RedLadyCyclist: Thanks for your column — being a woman in tech can be brutal and it's nice to see a guy who gets it.*

> *YesItsAshley: Olivia Arden's answer was better; women in male-dominated industries have to advocate for themselves.*

> *MicroChipsandDipsDude:* (Really? Roz read this handle with an incredulous shake of her head.) *Oh, good, another Social Justice Warrior criticizing the tech industry. Stick to advising lovelorn housewives.*

> *AstroBeatrice_87: Techbro culture starts in middle school.*

Robotics, math, and science clubs where girls are welcome are the best way to start encouraging women to advocate for themselves in these fields.

There were many more like this. Although the Gazette was a small publication, she'd tagged NWC in Gavin's social media post reacting to Olivia's column, effectively capturing the attention of avid "Kate Knows Best" followers. A bit of drama was effective bait for her fanbase. Gavin's email inbox was also filling up with comments and criticism, as well as a few questions from advice-seekers.

As the notifications continued to snowball, Roz considered turning them off for Gavin's accounts in order to focus more on her work. She couldn't; she was enjoying it too much.

The next buzz, however, did not indicate a comment from an advice column junkie, but a private message to Gavin. From Andy. "Hey, wondering how you identified me. Do you know Roz? I supposed you might as a fellow advice columnist."

She tapped out a direct reply, double-checking to be absolutely sure she was writing from Gavin's profile before she hit send. "Yeah, I do know Roz. Want help getting on her good side?"

He must have been online because he responded immediately. "You would do that? Why?"

Good question. Roz was acting on impulse and hadn't thought this through, other than wanting to mess with Andy as retribution for being evasive that first night together. But maybe through interactions with her "friend," Gavin, she could get to know him better in a way that protected her heart — and her ego. Of course, she couldn't say any of that, so she kept her answer simple. "I like Roz, you seem like a decent guy. Why not?"

"Okay."

"First of all, no more limericks, especially not embarrassing ones that use her name. Roz loves poetry, stop butchering it."

"Got it. What else? Flowers?"

Roz hated the way you had to cut the stems and change the water on flowers to keep them looking nice. She always forgot and wound up throwing out a limp, smelly bouquet of compost three days after they arrived. "No flowers. She likes plants, though. And baked goods are a safe bet."

"Thanks." The text bubble, with its telltale *someone-is-typing* dots, appeared and disappeared several times before the next message came through. "This is awkward, but I don't have her phone number or email. Can you please give me a way to contact Roz directly?"

If he only knew. However, she wasn't ready to speak to him as herself. She still felt stung and foolish about diving into their night together without having the full picture of who he was.

Was he the genuinely nice guy he seemed to be, or was it an act? Besides, it wasn't any more dishonest than Andy had been with her. Turnabout is fair play. Now, what would Gavin say, if he were real?

"Hmmm… nope. If she didn't give you her number, she might not want you to have it. If you can prove you're good enough for Roz, I'll put you in touch with her."

The dots appeared again, then disappeared, but no message came. There was her answer; Andy cared enough about her to send some half-hearted inquiries, but not enough to engage with Gavin. She gave up and went back to her research.

Ten minutes later, as Roz was getting ready to leave the office, Andy finally wrote back. "I'll give that some thought."

Chapter Ten

From: chefangela@dandelionbistro.com
To: George.F@NWCmag.com
Subject: Opportunities

Dear Fred,

It was delightful to see you today for lunch. You know I'm always happy to keep your table open. It was so thoughtful of you to ask if I have anyone special in my life these days – you always have had a nose for these things.

As a matter of fact, I've been seeing Olivia Arden. It's new, but she's quite a catch. We'll be spending time together at her hotel this evening. It's a shame she's been so determined to keep our relationship confidential – exposure could help both of our careers. Have I mentioned how much we enjoy a nightcap on the

*balcony of her suite? It's lovely to watch the boats on the bay.
How is your yacht these days? Still enjoy an evening cruise?*

*I was so pleased to hear that you will personally be reviewing my
new book! I hope I can count on you for a rave.*

Cheers, Angela

Olivia

Olivia chose a businesslike wrap dress and heels for her meeting with Frederick; putting on her polished, professional persona made her feel more prepared for this discussion. She was glad they were meeting at the bar in her hotel; she'd only have to step off the elevator and walk past the reception desk.

In order to avoid Andy, she was staying at a hotel on the waterfront and away from the rest of the crew. The lobby was decorated like a design magazine's idea of a mountain cabin, all knotty exposed beams and paneling, with a wall of windows to display the panorama of Elliott Bay. The hotel sat on a pier, creating the sensation of being on a ship, and Olivia's room looked right out onto the water. The harbor lights would come on soon, but for now the early evening sun still sparkled bright on the Puget Sound.

She hadn't met Fred in person yet, but when Olivia spotted an older man in a sharp suit with a frothy swoop of white hair, she knew it was him. He confirmed her hunch when he stood and stepped forward to kiss her on the cheek. Of course, he recognized her right away; that was something about being on television — she rarely had to introduce herself to anyone. It made her feel powerful.

"Olivia, I'm so glad you could join me. I took the liberty of ordering us a bottle of wine." With a hand on her lower back, he steered her to an expensively faux-rustic loveseat facing the window, where a bottle and two glasses were arranged on a low table.

She glanced at the label. Although she wasn't formally trained as a sommelier, working knowledge of wine was an important part of Olivia's work. She recognized the Chablis Frederick had chosen as overpriced and overrated. But this was business, and he was being hospitable. Her glass was already poured, fuller than she preferred.

"Thank you. Cheers." She turned her body so she could face him on the loveseat. This wasn't ideal seating for a work meeting. They'd both have to twist sideways in order to speak face-to-face. Then Frederick placed a hand on her knee, and everything became clear.

"Olivia," he said, his voice a murmur that made it more difficult to fight the urge to jerk her knee out of his grasp, "I know you're disappointed by the response to your first column, but I hope you won't let that deter you. Today's letter has a lively comments section and has already racked up twice as many page views as 'Kate Knows Best' usually gets. It doesn't matter to me that some of the reactions were negative; controversy can be good for business."

That's not what his email said. It was possible he'd had a change of heart, but more likely Frederick intentionally sent an admonishing message to ensure she'd meet with him.

She crossed her legs, effectively removing her knee from under his hand. "I wanted to discuss that with you. In retrospect, I don't think I'm the best person to be doing this work, and I also doubt it's the best thing for my own career at this time."

"Don't be silly, Olivia. You cranked today's column out in a few hours, on short notice. I'm sure you can do the same every week. You can write from anywhere, as long as we have an occasional face-to-face." He gave her an oily smile. "You can keep building your on-camera career, which will only benefit me in the long run." He leaned in, dropping his voice to a gleeful hush. "I understand that my former 'Kate Knows Best' columnist has become involved with your ex-husband. Won't this absolutely kill them? It's a perfect partnership, Olivia." He kept using her name. She wanted it out of his mouth.

He scooted even closer. She leaned away but didn't have room between him and the arm of the loveseat.

"Olivia, I have to tell you, I find you very alluring. I know you may not be interested in an older man like me." He emphasized the word man in a way that indicated he'd heard rumors about her sexuality, but she dismissed that as paranoia. Angela was the only person she'd been with since leaving Andy and they'd been very discreet.

Frederick continued, leaning in as he spoke. His arm slithered along the back of the loveseat, coming to rest behind her head. His breath smelled like cheese. "It would be nice to have a working relationship that allows us to see each other, socially. I'm not looking for a romantic commitment and I don't imagine you are either. I promise not to be jealous of any other attachments you might have. But it could be…fun." He traced a finger down her cheek and she almost gagged.

Before she could react, he executed the pounce she'd known was coming but didn't know how to stop without making a scene. He slid his hand down her shoulder and into the V-neck of her dress, as his face came toward hers, dry lips parted. So, Olivia did the first thing that occurred to her. She head-butted him. Hard.

"Ow! Goddammit!" He sprung up, pressing a napkin to his nose, which was bleeding. So much for not making a scene. Then, to her horror, he smiled. "The claws are out, hmm? That's fine. I don't mind temper from a passionate woman. Why don't you do some thinking about our arrangement and we'll speak in the morning after you have a chance to cool off?"

Olivia forced herself to stay calm as she stood, too. "Fat chance, you cretin. No wonder your stepdaughter quit. Oh yes, I know all about your personal connection to my predecessor." She'd overheard the NWC receptionist debriefing a friend when she went in to sign some paperwork; at the time she'd thought it was unprofessional, now she knew it was only the tip of the dysfunctional iceberg that was NWC Magazine. She managed to keep her voice from shaking. "I'm done. You can shove your shitty column straight up your disgusting ass."

His face was turning red, but Olivia didn't wait for him to respond. She turned on her heel and marched across the bar, head held high. By the time she got to the lobby, she was already starting to tremble and prayed the elevator would come before she fell apart.

When the doors slid closed behind her and she was alone, she leaned against the back wall of the elevator and forced herself to blow out a slow, steady breath. Earlier today, she'd felt terribly guilty about blowing up at Andy, but giving Frederick a piece of her mind felt magnificent, if terrifying. She didn't need to tame her sharp tongue; she simply needed to choose the targets who deserved it.

Frederick should know better than to follow her to her room, but the keycard shook in her hands as she let herself into her suite and bolted the door behind her. The lounge had been empty except for the bartender. Where were the paparazzi when you needed them? Even though she was totally justified in what she'd said, there was nothing to stop Frederick from spinning her resignation any way he liked, and with her reputation for a quick temper it wasn't out of the question that he would be believed if he claimed she attacked him unprovoked.

She needed to get ahead of that. Olivia opened her laptop and did some searching around the NWC website until she found the email address for the editorial board. She cc'd them on a resignation letter telling her side of the story.

It would probably be best to call her publicist and agent, too, but they could wait. She was flying to LA tomorrow for a publicity engagement and could speak to them then. In the meantime, she had a nice evening planned with Angela and wasn't going to let this ruin it.

Andy

The sketchy gas station beef jerky wasn't enough to keep Andy and Joe from being light-headed and irritable by the time they pulled into the parking lot behind the Blue Plate. Unfortunately, their arrival coincided with the dinner rush for the diner's popular meatball special, and there wasn't a single free table.

Andy was surprised to see Barry was at the host stand taking names. Andy gave him a one-armed bro-hug, introduced Joe, and asked what the hell he was doing there.

"Roz came for work and Celeste and I tagged along. The owner here needs some help and since I'm between jobs, I'm pitching in. Listen, I'd seat you if I could, but we're slammed."

"What about there?" Andy pointed to a table for four, where a woman was dining alone with an open laptop and a legal pad in front of her.

"That's Jackie, Roz's boss. She asked for a bigger table to spread out her work and she's a friend of the owner. I'm pretty sure she wants to be alone."

Andy wasn't going to give up easily. They were starving and exhausted, and there were three empty chairs at that table. Besides, it might be interesting to talk to someone who knew Roz. "We'll let her work. We just want some food. Please?"

Joe leaned into Andy's ear. "Dude, it's fine. Let's find some fast food or see if we can get something from the kitchen at the B&B."

"No way," Andy said, "it's my fault your camera's damaged, and my fault you didn't get lunch. We're getting dinner, we're getting it as soon as possible, and we're getting it here because you have been talking about fish and chips for an hour straight."

He turned his television smile on Barry, who clearly realized he was in a losing battle.

"I'll tell you what. If you want to ask her if it's okay to join her, I won't stop you."

Andy shot Barry a sidelong glance intended to say, "chicken," then sidled over to Jackie's table and turned up the wattage of his grin. He hoped he looked more charming than demented, but given the long day he'd had, it was probably a toss-up.

"Ma'am, I know this is a strange request, but my colleague and I have had a very long day, missed lunch because of a mistake I made, and these seats are the only free spots in the place. Could I trouble you to let us join you? I'm happy to buy your meal."

Her eyes moved slowly from her computer screen to his face and he was sure she was going to tell him to buzz off. "You're not going to go away until I say yes, are you?"

"No."

"All right then." She used her foot to scoot the chair closest to Andy out a few inches, which he accepted as the closest thing to a welcome he was going to get. He waved Joe over.

"Thank you."

While they waited for their food, Andy grabbed a stack of index cards and some colored pencils from the entryway. On one, he drew a gnome in a tall, pointy hat, with a speech bubble that said:

> *I've heard that you don't like my poems*
> *(Not even if they're about gnomes?!?!?)*
> *I have borrowed some verses*

None of which contain curses,
Now, please, can't you call on my phone?
(Your friend G.G. has my contact info. Really, please call. — A)

For the rest, he gave up on drawings in favor of words, pausing every so often to check a quotation on his phone. He tacked the one with the gnome drawing on the Blue Plate's bulletin board and tucked the rest into his jacket pocket.

Over their meals, Andy whispered to Joe, "I've been thinking about your book. I already have a few text ideas jotted down."

Joe sipped his beer and shot an apologetic glance at Jackie, whose typing had taken on an irritated staccato. "Awesome. I'd love your input about which photos to include, too. Maybe you can pick some of your favorites and get a rough idea of what you'd like to write about them, and we'll include that in the proposal."

"Sounds good, man. I'll sit down and go over all of them when I get home. Looking forward to it."

Joe chuckled. "The project? Or getting home?"

"Both, I guess. The show has been quite an experience, but I'm not sorry it's over." Hunger aside, today had been a good day. But he longed for quiet and downtime. He only hoped he would have the opportunity to see Roz again before he left.

After they finished eating, Joe went back to the B&B to call his wife. Andy stayed behind, nursing a piece of pie and writing out index cards. The pie was excellent, and he enjoyed being around the ambient noise of the weeknight crowd, but disappointingly, Roz never came in. He knew that she'd seen his first poem, which meant that she'd been here earlier today. Seeing her that morning had been an unexpected and pleasant surprise. Maybe if he bumped into her again, he'd get a chance to apologize before she ran off.

Their server refilled Andy's coffee. "Can I get you anything else?"

Jackie said, "Not now, but Erik, can you make me up a breakfast burrito and wrap it to go for tomorrow morning? I know it's not on your dinner menu, but I've been craving one all week, and this nice gentleman is picking up the check tonight."

Touché. But it was the least Andy could do. "Good choice. I had that for breakfast. Best one I've ever had outside a Mission district food truck."

Finally, Jackie cracked a smile. "Ah, I spent many years eating from those trucks. It's a good thing tacos are a relatively balanced meal, or I'd have been severely malnourished. I'm Jackie. We've already had dinner together; we might as well be properly acquainted."

He shook the hand she extended. "Hi Jackie, I'm Andy."

"Yeah, I recognized you. My son and I enjoy your show."

"Well, thanks. We're wrapping it up, though. I don't know if you've heard but Olivia—"

"I read about your divorce. I was sorry to hear."

"Thanks. Me too."

"Mm. Not your idea?"

"Hers." He looked down at his empty plate. "But I know now it's what we both needed. Olivia was brave enough to say so first." This was the first time Andy had admitted, out loud, that the split was for the best. He'd been slowly coming to this conclusion for several months—maybe even since he read Olivia's note—but until now it had seemed like a difficult truth to acknowledge.

Erik returned with the foil-wrapped burrito. "Hey Jackie, when you get a chance, I want to talk to you about getting some local arts and culture reviews into the Gazette again. I've been thinking about putting together a small gallery show, and I heard the theater over in Kingston is putting on *Twelfth Night* next month. It might be nice to showcase some of the creative efforts in the community."

"Sure," Jackie replied, poised to dig into her own slice of pie, "I've got some new writing staff on board and can generate more content now."

Andy began to have some qualms about being so candid. Not only did Jackie know Roz, but he didn't have any idea what other sorts of reporter connections she might have. "Listen, Jackie, that stuff I said about my divorce was strictly off the record." He tensed to leave.

"Relax, Andy. I don't do cheap gossip."

Andy settled back into his seat. "Yeah, well, I didn't used to *be* cheap gossip. Lately it's been hard to go anywhere without my picture ending up all over the internet." He remembered the surreptitiously taken phone photos that had surfaced a few times after he'd had lunch with female friends, thought about the images that might have surfaced online had he and Roz ever made it to a nice restaurant the other night, and better understood why she'd been upset he hadn't been forthcoming with her. "I never wanted to be in the spotlight."

Jackie lifted her right shoulder in a weary shrug. "Ah, but all the world's a stage. You can only control your own blocking and lines, not the audience or other players. It's all a cycle, Andy. I know it doesn't seem like it now, but everything blows over. You have to choose whether you want to write your own story or let other people write it for you. If your priorities are straight, and your actions are true to your intentions, the rest falls into place."

Andy finished his coffee and picked up his backpack. "Jackie, I hope you're right. See you, Barry."

While the bulletin board at the front of the Blue Plate was the largest he'd seen, and the only one that actively encouraged artistic expression, many of the other establishments in Port Poulsen also had corkboards for business cards, flyers, and lost pet posters. As Andy walked back to Mrs. Muir's B&B, he posted cards at the bookstore, the ice cream parlor, the pet supply shop, and the hardware store, where he bought a box of thumbtacks. Using these, he stuck the rest of the cards to fence posts, telephone poles, and mailboxes all along the street where he'd seen Roz and her dog on their morning run. When his task was finished, he returned to the inn. Before falling into a satisfied sleep, he messaged Gavin Garrett. "Borrowed a bit from other poets. Hope Roz likes them."

From: George.F@NWCmag.com
To: tips@UMAZ.com
BCC: chefangela@dandelionbistro.com

Subject: Olivia Arden pix

I thought you might be interested in the attached photos of Olivia Arden and Angela Lewis on the balcony of Arden's suite at the Soundview Hotel. I just happened to snap them from my boat. Hopefully they are not too racy for your site! Consider these a freebie from a concerned member of the public who wants the world to know who Olivia Arden really is.

Chapter Eleven

Roz

Roz took her coffee onto the porch, where she found Celeste and Bowie rocking gently on the pillow-covered swing. Bowie's eyes were half-closed; Celeste had a faraway look in hers and an open book in her lap.

"Morning," Roz said. Bowie's tail gave two thumps in return, and she wedged herself in next to him, stretching her toes out to join Celeste's rhythm moving the swing.

"How'd you sleep?"

"Great. I went to bed early for a change. I looked at the column's analytics before I turned the lights off and it had five thousand views. Gavin's social media is exploding, and I have twenty-two letters in my inbox to choose from for next week. This is all going so much better than I could have hoped."

"Congratulations," Celeste said.

"Thanks. You know the internet. Drama draws people in."

Roz didn't tell Celeste she'd woken up again later when her phone chimed with a nonsensical direct message from Andy to Gavin. Something about borrowed words. Still trying to get Gavin to hook them up—if only he knew the truth! But, he also wasn't trying very hard and wasn't serious about any of this; he was game-playing to pass the time. It had been fun to mess with Andy, but she wouldn't allow herself to imagine the possibility of anything real between them. Thank goodness work was giving her plenty to focus on. Every time she remembered what it had been like to spend the night in Andy's arms, she dutifully returned her attention to the advice letters in Gavin's inbox or the local interest stories Jackie wanted her to write.

Celeste closed her book. "What are you doing today?"

"Working on a few longer stories. Local business profiles, that kind of thing. You?"

"I volunteered to work on festival decorations for Erik. He needs help and with you and Barry busy, I need something to work on. Later I'll take Bowie for a walk."

"Oh! I found the best trail yesterday. Why don't we all go on a hike?"

Celeste stood from the swing, stretched, then released with a deep exhale. "That sounds nice. I'll go get my shoes."

Roz noticed the index card tacked to the side of the Little Free Library in front of a house down the block but didn't pay any attention to it. The one on the street sign at the corner piqued her interest further. When she saw another attached to a mailbox on the next block, she stopped to read. It was only a few lines of verse, superimposed over a sketched letter R. The handwriting on the card was familiar.

"Ooh, what's that?" Barry read over her shoulder. "A love poem?"

Celeste squinted at the card. "It's part of a Shakespeare sonnet. Remember Roz? We took that class together. There's an R — does it mean something to you?"

The meaning behind Andy's texts last night was becoming clear and it was time to fess up. "I think it might be from Andy. Did I…not mention he was in town?"

"You sure didn't," Barry said, "but I saw him last night at the Blue Plate. Where these are." He flicked the card.

"Andy's here?" Celeste said. "Isn't that a bit strange?"

Barry gasped, but it was theatrical and teasing. "He's stalking you!"

"He is not! He's here for work. I'm sure they schedule these shoots months ahead of time. It's a weird coincidence, that's all." Andy was turning out to be rather persistent, but nothing about his behavior made her feel unsafe. She didn't know him well (*yet*, interjected her subconscious) but she felt certain he wouldn't cross a firm boundary if she set one directly. Still, he obviously wasn't giving up as easily as she'd assumed he would, which was simultaneously annoying and flattering.

"Bowie and I bumped into him yesterday, and then after my run I found a card with a cheesy poem on it at the Blue Plate. So, I told him — well, actually, Gavin told him — how much I love poetry and that he should stop butchering it. And…I think I saw two more cards before this one."

"That's actually very sweet of Andy," Celeste said. "But what do you mean 'Gavin told him?'"

Roz could feel her shoulders creeping toward her ears. Celeste already disapproved of Gavin; she was going to hate this. "I kind of messaged him as Gavin? I wanted to see what he would say if another guy called him out, and what he would say about me to someone else. He doesn't make any sense. He basically lied to me about who he is, now he's doing all these grand gestures. I would tell one of my advice-seekers those are big red flags. But when I was with him, he seemed so genuine and kind. I don't get what's going on in his head, so —"

"So you lied about who *you* are." Celeste finished for her, crossing her arms.

"I guess? But I mean well."

"Maybe he did, too." Barry said. "He didn't really *lie* to you, right? He didn't tell you some things because they didn't come up."

These were valid points and Roz had no choice but to acknowledge them. "Okay. Fine. You're both right."

Barry untacked the card. "Don't you want to find the rest of these?"

Instead of continuing on to the trailhead, they spent the next hour wandering Port Poulsen neighborhoods collecting index cards. They had no idea Bowie had any tracking ability, but after a while Roz noticed that whenever they let him choose which direction to walk in, they found a card. He trotted along, nose twitching, tail waving happily. By mid-morning, they were back at the Blue Plate with a hefty stack of index cards.

Combining their memories from English classes with a little help from the internet, they placed the cards together to make up Shakespeare's twenty-third sonnet.

> *As an unperfect actor on the stage*
> *Who with his fear is put besides his part…*
> *O, learn to read what silent love hath writ:*
> *To hear with eyes belongs to love's fine wit.*

Andy must have seriously depleted Erik's stock of index cards.

Roz shook with laughter when she found Andy's gnome limerick on the bulletin board. She handed it silently to Barry, who held it so Celeste could read, too. Celeste giggled. Between chuckles, Barry said, "Oh, Roz. You've got to work things out with this guy. Imagine the valentines he'll write you."

She took the card back from him. "That's jumping the gun a bit, don't you think? But I am going to try to untangle the mess Gavin and I have gotten in."

"Hi friends," Erik called from behind the counter. "Barry, I didn't think I'd see you until later. You're closing with me tonight, yes?"

"Looking forward to it," Barry replied.

"And will you join me for dinner afterward?"

Barry beamed. "Absolutely."

Roz grinned at Celeste. They were both pleased to see Barry hitting it off with someone. It had been years since his last serious relationship, and although Barry was always upbeat, Roz sometimes got the feeling he was lonely. Deep down, she knew what a romantic he was, and he deserved someone who would appreciate his heart of gold. Roz thought Erik might be the winning candidate.

Romance was in the air today; Andy's poems were a pleasant surprise. She had completely expected him to forget all about her as soon as it became clear that it wasn't going to be easy to get her back into bed. Flipping through the stack of index cards in her hand, Roz smiled. Love poems. All over town. For her. Something in her chest did a tiny, excited hop. Roz had always pleaded practicality: "No flowers, please, they are expensive and they die; let's split this restaurant bill, it doesn't make sense for you to treat me when we make the same amount of money; what I'd actually like for my birthday is to have my car detailed," and so on.

The last romantic gesture that had truly thrilled her had been a playlist made by her college boyfriend, and that relationship had been a disaster even though he did have a great instinct for where exactly to put the Snow Patrol ballad. But this—she imagined Andy sitting down and choosing love poems with her in mind and flushed with flattered delight. Her favorite, Roz had to admit, was the ridiculous one with the gnome—an Andy Arden original. During their evening together, his playful streak had been one of the things that drew her to him, and here it was again.

The buoyant, hopeful feeling Roz got on that first night with Andy returned. Giddy, that was it. She felt giddy like a lovestruck schoolgirl. And in spite of herself, she liked it. She had to straighten this out, but it would be better to do it in person.

Andy's message from the night before made perfect sense now. Roz opened Gavin's direct messages and replied, "She loved them. Let's grab a beer tonight and I'll give you a few more pointers. How about the Blue Plate at seven?"

Andy replied immediately, "Sounds good. See you then."

Olivia

"Flight 452 to LAX will begin boarding shortly."

Olivia parked her suitcase near an empty seat and discreetly stretched her legs and shoulders. Although she was tempted to get a coffee—one last Seattle latte from the gourmet mocha kiosk near her gate—she refrained. She'd had a late evening and was hoping to take a nap on the plane. She didn't have to be anywhere until late afternoon but planned to run some errands before her appointment.

The family seated opposite was clearly bound for Disneyland. A small boy and a girl dressed as Peter Pan and Wendy chattered with barely contained excitement. They were small enough to share a seat and their feet dangled off the edge. Their father had returned with breakfast and was passing out hot chocolates to the kids and a coffee to his wife, who had one eye on her phone and the other on the children. "I'm going to need about six more of these today," she said, taking the first sip.

Olivia caught her eye and smiled. "They're so cute. I love the costumes."

"Thank you. I made them. I know you can buy them at the park, but I wanted them to have something different." The woman wrinkled her nose. "Most of that stuff is princesses."

"Well, they're adorable."

"Folks." The voice from the loudspeaker was jarring. "We have a slight delay due to a mechanical problem. Sit tight, we'll get you to California as soon as we can. We hope to know more in about an hour."

There was a collective groan from the crowd at the gate. The little boy looked up and asked, "Dad, why's everybody mad? Is Disneyland closed?"

"No, pal, we'll just be a little late."

Might as well settle in for a bit, then. Olivia sank back into her seat with resignation. Across from her, the children were now absorbed in a video on their father's tablet. He had his arm across the back of the seat, lightly brushing his wife's shoulder with his fingertips. Olivia felt a pang out of nowhere. She had no doubt that she'd made the right decision leaving Andy, but had she given up her chance at this kind of companionship for good? Even if she had, that seed of her discontent would always have been there between her and Andy, festering, poisoning their relationship. Unfair to Andy, unfair to her. She had to believe someday she would find the right partner.

Olivia had a novel with her but didn't want to start it until she got settled on the plane. She checked her phone; maybe she'd finally have a chance to catch up on some of the word games she played with her mother. While she was plotting the best use of a triple score space, a text notification threw itself across her screen. It was her agent, it said, "CALL ME" and included a link to a post from UMAZ, one of the trashier gossip accounts.

It was a video, opening with a publicity shot of Olivia followed by footage of her yelling at Andy at Pike Place, then a series of photos of her with Angela on the balcony of her hotel room. A robotic voiceover narrated, "Celebrity chef Olivia Arden is nothing if not fiery. Earlier this week, video surfaced of the culinary diva in an on-set temper tantrum at Seattle's Pike Place Market. UMAZ has obtained photos of Arden and Seattle-based chef Angela Lewis in what appears to be a passionate clinch on the balcony of Arden's waterfront suite at the Soundview Hotel. This raises new questions about her split last year from travel journalist and *Ardent Life Adventures* co-host Andy Arden. Was the bearded adventurer only a beard all along?"

As the robot voice said, "Lewis had this to say," a dm from Angela to UMAZ appeared on screen. "When Olivia and I cooked together, sparks flew. We couldn't contain our passion. I am a very sensual person—as you can learn if you buy my new cookbook, Dandelion Ginger, releasing next week."

The video concluded with the robot voice's announcement, "Olivia Arden could not be reached for comment."

They'd never even tried to reach her. As Olivia read, her face grew so warm, surely the people around her must see the flush. The contents of her stomach whirled. Who else had seen this? Probably everyone—the post already had several thousand likes and hundreds of comments Olivia couldn't bear to look at. She glanced around, paranoid. The mother across from her caught her gaze and something flashed on her face that didn't seem entirely friendly. Was there a hint of recognition in her eye? Olivia flushed more deeply; her cheeks felt like they were on fire now. She needed to be somewhere else. Anywhere else. She gathered her things with none of her usual regard for careful packing, and made her way down the row of seats, dragging her coat on the ground and stubbing her wheeled suitcase against the extended foot of a man at the end of the row. "Sorry," she muttered. But if he replied, she didn't hear. She hurried away from the gate and through the airport, past baggage claim, stopping only when she got outside. She boarded the first shuttle for an airport-area hotel she saw.

When the van pulled up in front of the high-rise hotel, she simply checked in. Why not? She wasn't going to Los Angeles today, that was for sure. Even if they still wanted her, there was no way she could do it. Not today. Olivia had a reputation for being tough, a reputation she had carefully cultivated in order to protect herself from ever being seen as the crumbling mess she felt like right now. The only way she could cope was to withdraw, lick her wounds for a while.

She wasn't all that upset about her romantic involvement with a woman becoming public. She'd thought this through while making the decision to leave Andy. After talking it through with her agent and therapist, she'd decided to avoid making any sort of announcement or statement, just to carry on her romantic life as she saw fit, allowing the public to draw their own conclusions. However, that had been before the media's attention to the divorce had made her a prime target for sleazy accounts like UMAZ. The licentious tone of the article was humiliating, but that embarrassment was eclipsed by her sense of betrayal. Angela had given a quote! When must she have done it…minutes after kissing Olivia goodbye as she got in her car for the airport? Although she hadn't been serious about a future with Angela, Olivia had trusted her. The most upsetting part of all of this was the degree to which she'd misjudged the other woman's sincerity.

She couldn't bear the thought of appearing onscreen with Angela after this, even though all of their footage was already shot.

As upset as she was, she still had obligations to fulfill. Olivia Arden was a woman who took care of her obligations. Before she gave herself over to a day wallowing in the velvety hotel robe watching sitcom reruns, Olivia made some phone calls. She called her agent to develop a response strategy, and Charles about making adjustments to the series finale.

She called her parents and asked them to stay away from any entertainment news for a few days. Thankfully, they didn't use social media and it was unlikely any of their friends or family would send them something like this. Olivia knew her folks wouldn't care about her having a girlfriend. They'd even met the girl she dated before she met Andy and liked her very much. They would be deeply hurt on her behalf, and she would hate that more than anything. "Of course, honey," her mother had said, "anything you need. We love you." Her father had simply asked if she was eating enough, and if her car was running okay. She must have had this exact exchange with them hundreds of times since she'd left home for college.

Olivia thought the last call would be the most difficult, but it turned out to be the easiest. "I'm so sorry to ask this of you, but it's necessary. Charles thinks the scheduling will be tight but workable, and they have everything ready to go if you say yes."

Listening to the measured, calm reply on the other end, Olivia nearly wept with relief. This, at least, was taken care of. "I don't deserve this. Thank you."

When she hung up, she did weep. And when she was done crying, she felt much better. Then, Olivia did what she did best; she made a plan.

Chapter Twelve

Roz

Roz's desktop at the Gazette was pen-scarred by generations of reporters, and while it no longer held a typewriter, she'd found a ribbon in one of the drawers. The chair was wood with vinyl upholstery, non-adjustable, and definitely would not hold up to the scrutiny of the expensive ergonomic consultant NWC used to make sure its employees weren't going to get carpal tunnel. The deep seat was wide enough for her to sit cross-legged, and if she pushed off from the desk the casters rolled across the linoleum with a satisfying rumble, like tiny bowling balls. Roz loved it. Although it was unlikely any major stories had ever broken in Port Poulsen, the old-fashioned vibe made her feel like a newshound in an old movie, like she should wear a fedora with a press pass stuck in the hatband. It was so different from NWC, but being here made her feel like she could find a new place to belong.

The next Gavin Garrett column wouldn't be out until the following week, so she was working on her profile of Erik and the Blue Plate. An easy interview to get, but what he was doing there really was interesting. He had plans to redecorate and had already updated the menu, adding vegan and gluten-free dishes and highlighting local ingredients. He hoped to someday add a small gift shop and gallery space to showcase his work and that of other local artists. He'd spoken about how his mom, an amateur folk artist of some local renown, would have approved.

That gave Roz an idea. There must be more multi-generational businesses in Port Poulsen; it was that sort of town. If other old businesses were also incorporating modern ideas from younger family members, it would be a fresh angle into her story. She could write about the way the town was evolving, moving from a sleepy blue-collar hamlet to a tourist destination with businesses that catered to weekenders from the cities. Even the venerable local paper was receiving a modern overhaul, and its leadership proved Port Poulsen was getting more diverse. Although, maybe Jackie wasn't as new in town as she thought; Roz didn't know where she'd grown up.

"Hey Jackie," she called into the office. "You're not from here originally, are you?"

Jackie laughed. "I'm from Sacramento. But my husband was born here."

Interesting. She should interview him. "Does he work in town?"

"No."

"Oh. What does he—" but the door to Jackie's office closed with a decisive click before she finished her question. Every time Roz got close to learning what had brought Jackie here, a door closed in her face. This time, literally.

Footsteps clomped up the steps and the door flew open. Today, Phoebe Sheppard-Shepherd was wearing red cowboy boots, black and white polka-dotted leggings, a short denim skirt, and an oversized sweater with a sheep on the front. Leaning hard into the shepherd theme, apparently. The outfit would have looked great on a first grader, or maybe an eccentric elementary school teacher. Phoebe deserved credit for being devoted enough to the brand to fully commit to outfits few twenty-something women would be caught dead in.

Roz had been so distracted by the clothes, it took a moment to see the sheaf of papers in Phoebe's hand and the manic glint in her eyes. "Where is Jackie Jones? I need to talk to someone about this."

Phoebe stopped waving the papers around long enough for Roz to see that it was a printout of Gavin's column. Terrific. She'd barely scraped out of trouble with Jackie yesterday, she didn't need another controversy. Maybe she could talk Phoebe down without involving Jackie. She glanced at the office door, which remained firmly closed. If Jackie was hearing this, she wasn't coming out.

"She's unavailable right now. Can I help you?"

Phoebe narrowed her eyes. "Who even are you?"

"I'm... the office assistant. We met briefly yesterday."

"Right, I helped your friends spruce up their wardrobes. You didn't buy anything." Phoebe gave Roz's jeans and plain black top a pointed glance. "My mobile boutique is parked outside, if you want to come down. I have a kimono top that would look great with your coloring."

"Maybe later. Let's take care of the reason you're here first." If this didn't go well, Roz could appease Phoebe by agreeing to buy the plainest thing in her collection. She used her most solicitous tone. "What can I do for you?"

"You published this letter yesterday that totally slandered my business. I've already had one home party cancellation and two more people turned me down for bookings. I asked for help, and instead I was insulted. That's unacceptable."

"I see. I'm sure insulting you was not Mr. Garrett's intention." Roz pretended to read the column, even though she knew every word. Insulting Phoebe really *hadn't* been her intent, but she did want to warn others away from businesses like Iris Indigo. She'd wanted to warn Phoebe away, too, but clearly that had fallen on unreceptive ears. "Can you point to which things here are untrue? I'll note them for Jackie and, um, pass the message along to Mr. Garrett."

"I've done better than that. I wrote a letter to the editor."

Oh great, Roz thought. "Oh, great!" Roz said. "You can leave it with me, and I'll make sure Jackie gets it."

"Gavin too, please." Phoebe held the papers out of reach. "I really think he owes me an apology and a retraction. Tell Jackie."

"I certainly will." Roz would wear that sheep sweater before she'd apologize. "To confirm, your advice letter was published anonymously. Do you want to remain anonymous for this piece as well? If we publish it, that is."

Phoebe's brows drew together. "I don't know why you wouldn't publish it. It's free content for you that I took the time to put together because I care about setting the record straight. But I do have that all worked out." She plonked the papers onto the desk and pointed at the signatures. "See, I wrote *this* letter as myself and you may publish my name at the end, but I *pretended* the other letter was written by someone else. Someone with a similar business." Her voice had dropped to a whisper by the end of her statement.

"I see," Roz whispered back. Then she returned her voice to a normal volume to say, "I will pass all of this along to Jackie, who has final say on selecting community letters."

"*And* Gavin. He needs to know how I feel about this."

Oh, he knows. "Of course. Gavin, too."

"And where, may I ask, is he? Doesn't he work in this office?"

"Uh, no. He works remotely most of the time. Computers!" Roz waved a hand at her laptop. "So convenient! But you have my word he will be completely aware of your message. I can guarantee that."

"Wonderful. Thanks so much, hon. Now what about that top? With your height, you'd look wonderful in one of my maxi skirts. Come on down and I'll pop the trunk!"

"Oh gee, I wish I could, but I'm swamped here." Roz's desk was empty except for Phoebe's papers. "With, um, errands I need to run for Jackie." She genuinely did have some research to conduct down at the boatyard. With a pout, Phoebe swept out as Roz exhaled with relief and gathered her bag. Knowing Phoebe, she'd stake out the office and know if Roz didn't really leave.

She'd gathered material for an article focusing on shops and restaurants like Erik's that were finding a balance between serving loyal locals and appealing to tourists, but Roz wanted to explore Port Poulsen's maritime roots, too. The waterfront had maintenance facilities for fishing and recreational boats. She'd include information about how the changes to the local economy were impacting the more industrial side of Port Poulsen.

The marina was neatly divided down the middle. The first half she was familiar with, where recreational boat docks served as a homeport for local boat owners and provided guest moorage to visitors. A long park stretched along that side of the waterfront, with a panoramic view of Puget Sound, picnic shelters, beach access, and a community center. The second half of the marina had moorage for fishing boats, a dry dock, dry storage for smaller boats, and a maintenance shop. The Blue Plate sat in the middle, serving both halves of the marina.

Roz waved to Erik as she passed the diner and made her way into the boatyard, sidestepping the spray from a hose and pausing to yield to workers moving a trailered sailboat across the yard. The shop at the back of the lot appeared to also serve as the boatyard office. A bell over the door tinkled as she entered.

"May I help you?" A teenage girl sat behind the counter.

"Hi," Roz said. "I work for the Gazette and am hoping to speak to the owner here. A…Colin Jorstad? Is he in today?"

"That's my dad. I'm Emily Jorstad. Dad's around but he's busy with a customer right now. You can wait if you want." Emily gestured to a row of chairs upholstered in shiny, cracked orange vinyl.

"Thanks," Roz said. She settled into one of the seats near the counter. From where she sat, she could see that the girl was working in a web design program. "What are you working on, Emily?"

"Oh," Emily flashed her a self-conscious grin, "this is a project for my business class, but I'm also hoping I can talk my dad into expanding into small boat rentals and tours. I'm setting up a website to show him how people can find us, book ahead, and leave reviews and comments."

"Emily," Roz said, "I came to talk to your dad, but it sounds like what you're working on is exactly right for my story. Can I interview you?"

Emily blushed. "Sure."

Roz spent the next twenty minutes talking to Emily about her proposal. She'd been helping out at the shipyard for a few years now and had a keen instinct for business, having seen the need to adapt to the increase in local tourism.

"So, do you think you'll take over here someday?" Roz asked.

"Maybe," Emily said. "I love it here, but I don't even really know what else is out there for me."

When Emily stepped away to help a customer fuel up their cabin cruiser, Roz returned to her seat and began organizing her notes. She was beginning to wonder whether she should try to catch Colin another day, when Steve Shepherd came in. Excellent luck: she had some questions for him.

"Hi," she said. "Steve, right?"

"Right," he gave her a small dorky wave, "you're...Roxanne?"

"Roz. But I get called Roxanne all the time. Hey, how are things going with your wife? Did you email that guy?" She knew he hadn't, but she wanted to know if he knew Phoebe had picked up the card and written in.

"Uh..." Distracted, he scanned the shelves of paint for the item he'd come in for. "With Phoebe, about the same, I guess. She was all fired up about something last night and was still at the computer when I fell asleep. No, I didn't send an email. I don't really want to broadcast my problems for other people to read on their phones while they're waiting in line at the grocery store."

"Ah. I see." The way people were so eager to anonymously send their biggest problems to a stranger had always fascinated Roz, but she had never gotten the perspective of someone who had consciously rejected the approach. Though she could see his point, she didn't agree; for every person who wrote her a letter there were dozens—if not hundreds—more who had a similar issue. If reading helped them, too, it was worth making some private matters public.

"Maybe I can help after all, if you have a few minutes." Steve stopped looking at the shelf and turned to her, his face an open book. He was desperate to solve things with his wife.

Having heard from both of them, Roz was in a unique position to help them sort out their differences. She could act as a kind of emotional translator. She genuinely wanted to help him, but solving their problem would also help her control the damage with Phoebe.

"You said she's been distant? Is she also not spending time with your kids?" This question was designed to get Steve's perspective on the fertility problem.

"We don't have kids yet. But we're both young. I'm twenty-eight, Phoebe's only twenty-six. We've been trying for a few years, but I'm not worried. We have plenty of time."

"I see. Have you and Phoebe discussed this?"

"I don't really see a need. It will happen when it happens."

And there it was. Both of them were so focused on a problem the other wasn't seeing. Maybe she could help this couple by getting Steve to be a little more tuned in. Roz leaned forward. "Steve, she might be more upset about this than you realize. I have friends who had a hard time conceiving and it really took a toll on their emotions. I think you should talk to Phoebe."

"Really?"

"Yes. If this has been festering a long time you are going to need to be straightforward."

"Okay. I'll give it a try." Steve's spirits seemed lifted, and after leaving a note on the counter for Emily, he left with his paint.

Seconds later, Colin—who she recognized from that first night at the Blue Plate when she'd met Steve—burst through the door with two other men, all three of them talking over each other in a way that was boisterous, but not at all friendly. "Listen, Harry," she heard him say, "I can do the job correctly and you can get all the way to Alaska, or I can do it fast and you'll need maintenance again in Victoria. Which one would you prefer?"

The older of the other two, a stocky fellow with salt and pepper hair in yellow all-weather pants and a plaid flannel shirt said, "Come on, Colin. I know you can get the *Skua* out of here by the weekend if you want to. You're bilking us on moorage. My crew doesn't start making full wages until we get up north."

"We're all losing money here, pal," said the younger man, who had pale, greasy skin, stringy dishwater hair and dirty coveralls.

"That's right, Will," said Harry. "We need to make sure this dockside pansy knows what the stakes are here."

"Guys," Colin put his hands out in a conciliatory gesture. "I'm doing what I can."

"I'll tell you what you can do," Harry snatched the clipboard out of Colin's hand and began slashing at the papers with his own pen. "We don't need paint, and can do without an engine tune-up, just change the oil. The belts should have some time left. Labor on the hull ought to be half what you've estimated here. If you're not done in that amount of time, leave it."

Colin took the clipboard back, his mouth a grim line. "Like I said, Harry, I'll do what I can. But I won't be held responsible for substandard work."

Harry leaned into Colin's face until his upturned nose was two inches away from the other man's chin, "Well, I won't be held responsible for my pissed-off crew."

Harry and Will slammed out the door, and Colin threw the clipboard down on the counter. "Arrogant mother-loving sonsabitches." Then he saw Roz. "Sorry, honey. These jack-asses think they know how to fix their own boat better than I do, even though I've been doing this for thirty-five years. I should shove 'em out to sea and let them fix it themselves. What can I do for you?"

"I'm assisting the new reporter for the Gazette, and I was hoping to talk to you about running a legacy family business. I can come back another time."

"Nah. Now's fine. Come on around back." He waved her

behind the counter, and ushered her into a dark, cluttered office.

Roz spent the rest of the afternoon with Colin, who, contrary to her initial impression of him as a cantankerous chauvinist, was affable, if a little too free with sexist terms of endearment, and seemed to know everything about boats. When she told him she'd like to use some quotes from his daughter in her article, he was so proud he hugged her.

Roz left with some great quotes in her notebook and bounded back up the hill to the Gazette offices. She could feel the article forming in her mind, and she liked where it was going. Tonight, she would see Andy again. They'd had a bumpy start, but nothing that couldn't be smoothed over by talking face-to-face and straightening everything out. Everything was turning her way.

When Roz returned to the newspaper office, Jackie was sitting on her desk in the front room, Phoebe's letter in her hands. She took a moment to read to the end, then asked, "Have you read this?"

Roz snorted. "No. You're not going to publish it, are you?"

"Actually, I am." Jackie hopped down. "The writing's not bad, and the letters-to-the-editor space is meant to give a voice to community members. I don't have to agree with them, I only need them to be an interesting viewpoint. I thought you of all people were in favor of dissenting voices."

Normally she was, but Roz had been hoping the Phoebe matter would die down. She'd said her piece already in Gavin's column, and her life was messy enough without a feud with a woman who was, if nothing else, extraordinarily persistent. Once in a while, her mother had gotten an angry reply from someone offended by the advice Kate gave them, but Roz had never expected to encounter a disgruntled advice seeker in person. Her saving grace was that Phoebe didn't know Gavin's true identity.

Still, Phoebe's letter was sure to be a whiny diatribe. It seemed unlike Jackie to think it had enough merit to publish. For crying out loud, Jackie had been an award-winning journalist at a major paper. Shouldn't she have higher standards?

All the wind that had filled her sails on the walk up from the marina whooshed out. She'd thought she was done with bosses who didn't back her up when she quit working for Fred.

"Wow. How can you not feel this is beneath you? Not exactly prize-winning journalism we're doing here, is it? What happened to you, Jackie?"

It took Jackie a long time to answer. She took a deep breath and exhaled slowly. When she spoke, there was ice in her voice. "Frankly, Rosalind, I don't care what's above or beneath me. I know you're used to writing as if you know the whole story when you've only seen a piece of it. You have to do that when you're answering advice letters sometimes, I get that. But you can't live your life that way. Your mom knew that, and I hope you figure it out soon." Jackie's coat and purse hung by the door. She put them on and yanked it open, saying, "I'm leaving for the day. Lock up when you go."

Alone, baffled, Roz picked up Phoebe's letter.

A Letter to the Editor Regarding Network Marketing,

by Phoebe Sheppard-Shepherd, Wardrobe Consultant, Tourmaline Level, Iris Indigo Fashions

Recently, this paper published a column that made negative statements about network marketing companies, and the people (usually women) who sell their products. I would like the opportunity to offer a counterargument in favor of these businesses.

I have been a fashion consultant with Iris Indigo Fashions for

*three years. During that time, I have made a profit (yes, a prof-
it — I do know how to calculate my balance sheets) of $17,263.45.
While that is a fraction of what my husband brought home during
that time, it's my money, free and clear, that I earned all by
myself. I made it doing work I enjoyed, representing and selling
a product I believe in, doing things I think are fun, like talking
to new people, facilitating parties, and hosting online sales. I
have made dozens of new friends through this venture, enjoyed
myself, built my skillset, and put a good chunk of money in the
bank. What's so wrong with that?*

*While it is true that many people who participate in network
marketing businesses don't make money, the statistics that are
often cited do not account for the fact that a lot of these people
aren't even trying to make a profit. They sign up because they
like the product and want a discount. Or they think they might
develop a sales business, but never follow through. How is that
the company's fault?*

*Have you been to the Peninsula Mall lately? Half of the stores are
closed. We have some great shops here in town, but few fashion
retailers. So, for our local women, shopping options are to drive
twenty miles to a big box store with low quality and a limited
selection, buy things online and hope they'll fit, or take the ferry
into Seattle. I offer an alternative. My clients tell me they are
grateful for the opportunity to buy cute, comfortable, high quality
clothes in their homes or from my mobile boutique. In turn, I buy
makeup from a friend, kitchenware from my mother-in-law, and
smoothie mixes from my neighbor. These companies offer women
in our community an opportunity to network with each other,
building sisterhood and friendships as we support one another.*

*I hope Gavin Garrett will consider that not all women who sell
for these companies are foolish victims. Many of us are smart*

*businesswomen who have recognized an opportunity. And the
next time one of your readers wants to buy some casual clothing,
I hope she will give me a call.*

Sincerely,

Phoebe Sheppard-Shepherd

Roz refolded the letter and slid it carefully back into the envelope. She still disagreed with Phoebe's position, but it had some fair points. Her desire to help Phoebe and Steve sort out their marriage troubles was sincere, but if she were being honest with herself, Roz had also taken pleasure in knocking Phoebe down a few pegs. That wasn't something she was proud of. Phoebe's childish outfits and boundless enthusiasm for her silly company made her an easy target. It was as if Gavin had been sitting on her shoulder, urging her to give in to her crueler impulses and offering the tempting ability to hide behind his persona.

Publishing the letter was for the best. It would make Phoebe feel better, and reading it might help Steve understand where his wife was coming from. She would try to make Gavin more empathetic in the future to avoid any further Phoebes cropping up, but she was relieved to consider this particular case neatly closed.

Chapter Thirteen

Roz

Although she generally believed any man worth her time should be happy with everyday clothes, Roz wanted to dress up for Andy tonight. Seeing her instead of Gavin was going to be a surprise, after all, and she wanted to make it an extra nice one.

She borrowed a floaty floral dress from Celeste. It was a bit short, and tight in the shoulders, but it would do. She undid her bun and her hair fell in bouncy waves down her back without any weird bumps or frizzy bits, a trick it performed only occasionally. She decided to take the fact that it worked today as a good omen for the date. She added her own soft, moss-colored cardigan, a pair of ballet flats, and a few swipes of lipstick and mascara. On the way out, she inspected herself in the crackly mirror at the top of Erik's stairs. She wasn't going to be on a magazine cover any time soon, but she liked the way she looked. Dressed up, feminine, but still breezy and casual. She wanted Andy to know she was making an effort without looking like she was trying too hard.

Roz wanted to be at the Blue Plate when Andy arrived. He'd be looking for Gavin and she pictured herself rising from her candlelit table — *note to self: ask Erik for a candle* — to reveal that she had been Andy's correspondent all along, and yes, she loved the poems, and yes, there's something special going on between them so let's explore it. Roz got to the Blue Plate at a quarter to seven and asked Erik for a spot in the back corner so she could watch the door, ordered a glass of wine and waited.

And waited.

Every time the door opened, Roz's expectation bubbled, but it was never Andy. She gave a small wave to Steve and Colin as they came in after work, looking beleaguered, but didn't see anyone else she knew. Whenever another local, boater, or tourist walked in, Roz's spirits sank further. Anticipation about seeing Andy filled her chest with butterflies. It wasn't unpleasant, but it was unusual; part of her wanted to slow down and savor every emotion. Another part — the nervous part — wanted to get the revelation over with as soon as possible. Would he understand she'd posed as Gavin out of a need to keep him at arm's length? Or would he say he wasn't interested in someone who plays games?

Barry stopped by her table to check in. "I'm sure he just got hung up," he said, refilling her now-empty wine glass. "Maybe his camera crew was trying to get a difficult shot or something. I bet he'll be here soon."

Roz gave Barry a wan smile, appreciative of the encouragement. But Andy knew how to get in touch with Gavin, and her phone, sitting on the table next to her fork, had not buzzed once. She left the second glass of wine untouched. She wanted a clear head when Andy arrived.

By eight-thirty, the restaurant was nearly empty. Port Poulsen was a town that rolled up its sidewalks early. Barry brought her a plate of chicken, pasta, and vegetables. Sitting down opposite her, he leaned over to squeeze her arm. "Better eat something."

She picked at the meal. Despite her disappointment about Andy, the food tasted good: the noodles had a buttery sauce and the faintest hint of nutmeg, the vegetables were steamed perfectly, the chicken was tender and seasoned with something smoky. Roz dug in with a bit more relish. It had been a busy day and she found herself rather hungry. "Thanks. He's not coming, is he?" She wanted Barry to tell her she was wrong, Andy wasn't that late, that he'd heard there was bad traffic.

"I'm sorry, Roz."

"It's fine," She popped the last carrot into her mouth and took a sip of wine. "I was expecting this, I guess. He must have just been bored when he put up all those notecards."

"If he were bored, he'd have played solitaire on his phone. I've seen you two together. He's into you. Trust me. Why don't you text him and see what happened?"

"Ew. No. I am not going to be one of those girls." The desperate girls, the groupies, the ones who couldn't take a hint. Her skin crawled at the idea, and she kicked herself for the dress and the lipstick and the elaborate plan to surprise Andy. "He's allowed to lose interest. No big deal. This will give me more time to concentrate on work."

Erik peeked out from the kitchen and gave Barry a small anxious smile Roz suspected she wasn't supposed to see.

"Oh, Barry! Your dinner with Erik." She stood, placing her napkin next to her plate, and gathered her purse and jacket.

"Look, Andy obviously isn't coming, I'm going back to the house to have a nice bath and go to bed." Roz pecked Barry on the cheek. "Have a great time."

Barry walked her out and flipped the 'closed' sign around before shutting the door behind her. "Don't wait up," he whispered with a wink. As she walked past the front window, he gave her a thumbs-up through the glass.

Roz grinned and returned the gesture. A second magical evening with Andy had been a long shot, but at least Barry and Erik could have a nice date.

Her mood dimmed again as she passed out of sight of the diner. She felt like a fool. But she'd had good reason to believe Andy would come tonight. The poems, the pursuit through Gavin…everything pointed to him having more than a passing interest in her. Maybe it had only been something for him to do to combat the boredom of being on location. Most heart-sinking of all, maybe he had somehow figured out that she and Gavin were the same person and decided he wanted nothing to do with her. Whatever it had been, it was over now for sure. Poems or no poems, Roz's self-esteem didn't accommodate third chances.

As she passed the industrial side of the marina, Roz heard rowdy laughter and a low wolf whistle, then the creak of the dock moving under the weight of people. She palmed her keys and quickened her pace, but the voices seemed to be traveling in the other direction, and after a couple of blocks she relaxed.

Celeste

Celeste savored having the house to herself. Bowie was sleeping in a corner of the kitchen, still worn out from their big morning walk, but he didn't count. She made herself a grilled cheese, opened a bottle of chardonnay, and settled in at the kitchen table with a library book about Scandinavian folk art. She was one bite into her sandwich when she heard the front door open. A few seconds later, Roz slumped against the kitchen doorframe and sighed heavily.

So much for an evening of solitude. Celeste closed her book and poured Roz a glass of wine. "You're back early."

Roz grimaced. "I got stood up. I'm not surprised. Andy has so much going on. I think I was merely a passing fancy. It's fine. I have a lot on my mind right now, too."

"I'm sorry to hear that. Maybe there's a good explanation." Roz ought not to take this personally when she hadn't even been honest with Andy about who he'd be having dinner with.

"Maybe. I'm going to brush it off and move on." Roz took a sip of the wine. "This is good. What are you up to?" She picked up Celeste's book and flipped through. "This looks cool."

"I'm looking for inspiration for the festival decorations. Erik hasn't done much except for buying a few flag garlands. This is fun, actually. I can do something whimsical since it's temporary and festive." She'd always focused on permanent design; home spaces, the NWC offices.

Celeste handed her sketchbook to Roz. She was going for a Scandinavian fairy tale feeling by creating oversized woodland decorations that would make the festival attendees feel as if they'd shrunk. It was a lot to do in a couple of days, but she was hoping to have some extra hands.

As if she was reading Celeste's mind, Roz said, "This is great, but do you have time to make it all?"

"I've already started framing out the papier-mâché and the centerpieces and tablecloths are ready. Can you help me put some things up tomorrow? Barry has been busy helping Erik with the food."

"I'm about done with the research for next week's long arti- cle. I can take a few hours around lunchtime." Roz paused, as if she wasn't sure about what she wanted to say. "I'm glad you're enjoying this. I want you to be happy."

That might be about as close to an apology for Roz's over-step with Fred as Celeste was going to get. She knew Roz meant these words now. Hopefully the sentiment would hold true when she said she wanted to move. "I want you to be happy, too. Work is good?"

Roz laughed. "You are not going to believe this." Roz laid out a whole saga about Phoebe and Steve: the infertility and the clothing business, the advice letter, Phoebe's editorial, and her disagreement with Jackie. "So now, I feel like this weird fly on the wall in their lives. They don't know what the other is thinking, but I know what they're both thinking, and I think that puts me in a position to help them. I'm not sure how to do that without making a bigger mess of it, but I'll figure it out."

Celeste got up to put her plate in the dishwasher. "It sounds like you put Steve on the right track. He needs to understand how much the fertility issue is worrying Phoebe, right?"

Roz nodded. "But Phoebe...I'm not sure how to get through to her. She seems smart, but she's deep into sunk cost fallacy with Iris Indigo. Logic isn't working."

"If she's determined to stay with that company, maybe she knows what's best for herself. I think you've done what you can and should let it be. They'll work it out on their own."

"I'm so close to being able to fix this for them."

This was typical of Roz: over-involved, over-invested, over-confident. She'd always had a penchant for helpful inter-ference, but now there was a relentless drive behind it that caused her to take things too far. Celeste pressed her lips together. "You can't always fix things for people, Roz."

"I know. But I have to try."

Celeste nodded and refrained from saying she didn't always

have to try, that sometimes the kindest thing to do was stay out of things.

Roz put her wine glass in the sink, stood and stretched. "Maybe something will come to me if I sleep on it. I'll feel better with a fresh start in the morning. 'Night."

"Goodnight."

It was getting late, but she still had a few things she wanted to research. Celeste put the kettle on.

Roz was halfway up the stairs when the front door opened and Barry entered, looking pale and rattled. He sank down to the bottom step with a thump and buried his head in his hands. Celeste put a hand on his back.

"Awful night," Barry said. "Awful."

"What happened?" Celeste and Roz made eye contact, alarmed. They weren't used to seeing Barry like this.

The kettle whistled. Celeste ushered them all to the kitchen table and got out three mugs. They sat in silence for a few minutes before Barry was ready to talk.

"Okay, so. We were ready to have a nice dinner. Erik made meatballs, which are actually Swedish, but he says Norwegians are great bakers but not so good at entrees that aren't seafood —"

"Bear." Roz made a move-it-along-gesture.

"Right. So, it was all very romantic. Low light, candles on the table. Then these boat crew assholes come in. I was their server at lunch, and they were a total nightmare, table of four and they went through five pitchers of beer, left a three dollar tip. Erik tells them we're closed but they won't leave — I put the closed sign up when you left, Roz, but I forgot to lock the door — and then I think they figured out we were having a date and were just being" — he paused, she could tell he was searching for the word he wanted to use, then spat — "Neanderthals about it."

Celeste's stomach dropped.

Roz said, "Oh no. What did they say?"

Barry shook his head. "I don't even want to repeat it. So, Erik picked up the phone to call the police, and they finally left, but punched a hole in one of Erik's paintings on the way out. Straight through the drywall behind it. I thought they might break the front windows." Barry took a deep, shaky breath and wrapped his hands around his mug.

"Poor Erik," Celeste put her arm around him and squeezed, "and poor you. Are you okay, Bear?"

"I'm okay, but I feel awful. I just stood there the whole time, I didn't say or do anything. It's been such a long time since I've had to deal with this sort of thing, and I just froze. When I was younger, I was great at taking guys like that down a few pegs."

"What was different tonight?" Roz asked.

"Erik." Barry answered without a hint of hesitation. "I like him so much, Roz. And it was his place and I guess I didn't feel like it was my prerogative to escalate the situation. You know, he's a pretty big guy and I'm sure he can hold his own in a fight, but he didn't even make a fist. He just looked so hurt, it broke my heart. While we were cleaning up, he told me he'd been scared about coming back here to live. It's still not easy to be out at home if you come from a small town, but he says everyone here has been pretty accepting. It really shook him up to have something like that happen in his own restaurant. I tried to get him to come back here with me tonight, but he said he'd better stay there to make sure they didn't return. He was patching the wall when I left — he didn't want the breakfast customers to ask what happened."

"I'm so sorry, Barry," Celeste said. "You shouldn't beat yourself up about this. You're not the one who was acting like a jerk. Did you call the police?"

"I wasn't sure if we should, but Erik said he trusts Sheriff Andersen. Still, all they said was to call if they make trouble again. There's not much they can do. Erik could press vandalism charges, but the sheriff said that it might be better to just drop it since they're leaving as soon as their boat is repaired. So, basically, the police are just as useless as me."

Roz stood up from the table and paced, already in fix-it mode. Celeste wished she would just let it be. "You're not useless," she said, "You just need a little more confidence. You should feel empowered to say something. Show Erik you're not a pushover, and that you insist he — and you — be respected."

"Yeah, Roz, you're right." Barry thrust his chin forward. "I hate letting jackholes like this get away with stuff. I'll resurrect my arsenal of snappy comebacks."

"That's the spirit," Roz declared, clapping him on the shoulder.

Celeste couldn't let it go without saying more. "Barry, you didn't do anything wrong. It's okay to be scared, or not know what to say. They were the jerks, not you."

Roz pushed her chair in, hard, bumping the table. Barry jumped. "But we can't just let them get away with that."

"He's not. Lay off."

"Fine. Maybe I'll just give them a piece of *my* mind next time I see them."

They drifted into separate corners of the living room, each lost in their own worlds. Celeste flopped on the sofa with a novel, but couldn't concentrate on the plot. Barry found a deck of cards and laid out a game of solitaire on the coffee table. Roz said she was going to try to get some work done.

Roz

On her laptop, Roz began outlining her multi-generational business article, but her mind wasn't really on it. The wheels turning in her brain were working on the Phoebe problem. She couldn't fix Barry's hurt feelings or Celeste's worry, but she could fix this. Publishing anything further on the matter was out of the question because it wasn't meant to be common knowledge that Phoebe was both the advice seeker and the author of the letter to the editor. But that didn't mean Gavin Garrett couldn't respond to Phoebe privately. Her mother had occasionally engaged in back-and-forth conversation with her letter-writers if she had more to say than was suitable to publish in the column; there was nothing to stop Roz from doing the same.

> *From: G.Garrett@PoulsenGaz.com*
> *To: Pheebs99@webmail.com*
> *Subject: Your letters*
> *Dear Ms. Sheppard-Shepherd,*
>
> *My colleagues have forwarded your letter to the editor to me. I understand it will be published in tomorrow's paper. I want to assure you that I had no intention of disparaging your chosen livelihood; I only wanted to suggest you do some critical thinking regarding the business model and costs vs. profits. I still hope you will reconsider the value of the money you are making with respect to the impact on your personal relationships.*
>
> *I'd like to encourage you again to discuss your concerns about conceiving with your husband. Often, one half of a couple is unaware of how much a matter like this is bothering their partner.*
>
> *Respectfully,*
>
> *Gavin Garrett*

After hitting send, Roz took Bowie out, then went upstairs to get ready for bed. She checked her phone as she brushed her teeth (How could anyone just stand there, doing nothing, for the two-minute electric toothbrush cycle?) and the reply was already in. It had been less than five minutes. Never a good sign.

From: Pheebs99@webmail.com
To: G.Garrett@PoulsenGaz.com
Subject: RE: Your letters

Gavin,

My husband asked me if I was worried about fertility tonight.
WOULD YOU KNOW ANYTHING ABOUT THAT? He said
he'd been told it might be something that was bothering me, and
he should ask me about it. I can't think of WHO would have told
him about this, IF NOT YOU. I wrote to you CONFIDEN-
TIALLY and I do not appreciate my PERSONAL BUSINESS
being interfered with in this way. WHO DO YOU THINK YOU
ARE??? Isn't the WHOLE POINT of an advice column that
you can ask someone questions without worrying that they'll go
TATTLING to your FAMILY???

No regards, PSS

Roz slammed her phone face down onto the bathroom
counter, as if that might stop the caps lock assault. She had been
too focused on telling Steve how to fix the problem and forgotten
to coach him on being subtle about it. As hard as it was to admit,
Phoebe had a right to be angry, but everything Roz had done
was an attempt to help. In her experience people who sent angry
emails this late at night usually came to their senses in the light
of day. She hoped she could ignore this and let it blow over. At
the very least it could wait until morning. She turned her phone
to silent, burrowed under the covers and let sleep overtake her.

Chapter Fourteen

Roz

R oz arrived at the Gazette bright and early the next morning, but Jackie's office was dark, the door standing open. She opened her laptop, hoping Phoebe hadn't sent Gavin any more messages overnight, and checked her email.

> *From: George.F@NWCmag.com*
> *To: G.Garrett@PoulsenGaz.com*
> *Subject: Collaboration*
> *Dear Mr. Garrett,*
>
> *I'd like to offer you congratulations on the success of your new column. Although I can't say the combative nature of your reaction to our most recent Kate Knows Best column was entirely*

professional, drawing the attention of our readers to your content was a shrewd business move. I'm impressed.

We should explore working together instead of in competition. I am still seeking a new columnist for NWC's advice feature, and you are obviously going to outgrow the rural market soon. I'm certain that a mutually beneficial agreement can be reached.

Please call the number below to make arrangements.
Frederick George,
Editor-in-Chief
NWC

This was so typical of Fred she ought to have seen it coming. It was possible he had recognized her as Gavin and was baiting her, but not likely. If Fred was onto her, he'd come at her much more aggressively. It was like him not to look past the surface of a profile photo — if he had looked at it at all.

Getting the better of Fred ought to be satisfying, but somehow, it never was. When she was sixteen, newly driving, and flexing her muscles of independence, Roz, Fred, and Kate had been sitting down to a rare dinner together without Celeste, who was at her mom's. The three of them tended to go their separate ways when she wasn't there, busy with school and work, content to microwave something or get takeout.

"I'm going to have to let Heather go," Fred remarked offhand to Kate while sawing through his steak, "she simply isn't working out. She's made several serious mistakes with my schedule, and her attitude is a bit surly for what I need from an assistant."

Kate set her fork down. She hated firing people. "She seems like a smart, capable young woman to me. She was very pleasant in her interview. I'll talk to HR tomorrow and see if we can assign her to something else."

"No. I want to make a clean break."

"We'll see." Kate returned her attention to her salad.

"It's my decision, Kate, she's my assistant."

Kate glared at Fred across the table.

"That's weird." Roz broke the uncomfortable silence, pleased to have some information that might help her mother. "When I saw you and Heather together, you seemed like you were getting along well."

"You haven't been in the office since winter break, Rosalind," Fred snapped. "Heather was new then and still on her best behavior."

"Yeah, but I was a few people behind you and Heather in line at the Greenlake Starbucks on Monday afternoon. I was supposed to be at school, so I didn't let you see me, but you seemed pretty friendly." In fact, the way Fred put his hand on Heather's back put Roz's hackles up, but she hadn't been sure how to bring it up without getting in trouble herself. If something was truly wrong here, speaking up was worth the risk of getting grounded for skipping class.

"Greenlake?" Kate asked, "Why would you need to go to Greenlake in the middle of a workday?"

Fred coughed and reached for his wine glass. "I was showing Heather how to follow up on a story lead. The interview at Lakeside Cycles?" Fred didn't conduct interviews; he handled the business end of the magazine and left content matters up to Kate and the reporting staff.

Kate sipped her own wine, "I see." Later, Roz had heard heated voices coming from their bedroom, and it was about a month later that Fred and Kate announced their divorce. Heather took a new job with one of Kate's contacts at a local TV station.

Roz always wondered how big her role had been in the end of the marriage. Kate assured her the end had been in sight anyway, but Roz didn't completely believe it. If she were honest with herself, her motivation had been getting the better of Fred, not doing the right thing.

The same impulse to lash out at Fred had been behind her revelation about Celeste; she couldn't deny it. He needed to hear it, and Celeste was never going to tell him. It motivated her response to Olivia's "Kate Knows Best" column, too. Gavin's advice was more helpful to *No Bro* than what Fred had published. Still, helping the letter-writer had come second to getting back at Fred for taking the column away. It wasn't a good feeling. But it was easier to hate Fred than it was to miss her mom.

> *From: G.Garrett@PoulsenGaz.com*
> *To: George.F@NWCmag.com*
> *Subject: Re: Collaboration*
>
> *Mr. George,*
>
> *I have an agreement in place with my current employer that I'm not interested in breaking.*
>
> *I was a big fan of your former Kate Knows Best columns. Believe me when I tell you that words cannot adequately express what Kate Connolly meant to me. I'm sad to say I am not impressed with the current direction of the column or your publication.*
>
> *Sincerely,*
>
> *Gavin Garrett*

The reply came so fast, Fred must have sent it before he even read her message all the way through.

> *From: George.F@NWCmag.com*
> *To: G.Garrett@PoulsenGaz.com*
> *Subject: Re: Collaboration*

Fine. If you want to write for a two-bit operation in a one-horse town, be my guest.

After she hit delete, Roz saw a new email from Jackie in her inbox. The subject line was "The questions you've been asking," and the body contained only a link to an essay published that morning on her former paper's op-ed page. Evidently Jackie still had contacts there.

Leaning Out, by Jacqueline Jones

If you recognize my name, you knew me as a reporter for this publication. I made my career and won some awards reporting on the emerging tech market and gentrification of this city. I've been on national television, and my book, Sales of the City, was a bestseller. You might now be thinking, "Yeah. Whatever happened to her?"

I've gotten awfully tired of being asked that question, so I've decided to answer it.

A little over a year ago, I moved two states north of San Francisco to a tiny coastal town, Port Poulsen, WA. The 80-year-old local newspaper was closing down. I bought it, changed the circulation model, and have been gradually re-envisioning how a local news outlet might best serve its community. It's not profitable or exciting: a day's big story might be a red tide that makes shellfish unsafe or a particularly noteworthy church bazaar, but it's where I need to be right now.

I've been asked many times why I would make this career change. Why would I move from a cosmopolitan city where my reporting won awards and national acclaim, to a small town where I don't have much in common with any of the locals? I didn't think I owed it to anyone to lay out my reasons.

I still don't.

I'm simply trying to live my life; it's not my responsibility to explain my choices so others can learn from them. But honestly, I'm exhausted. The path of least resistance is answering these questions once and for all.

When my husband of twenty years was diagnosed with pancreatic cancer, we didn't tell many people. Although my career brought me some notoriety, my family life was always a private matter and we saw no reason for that to change. I kept working through all of his treatments. I went back to work the day after his funeral. It was an election year and I had stories to cover. "Life goes on," etc. I continued keeping business as usual until the day I got busy working on a big story and realized I had forgotten to pick our ten-year-old son up at school. He was fine. He had, he proceeded to tell me, gone home with the same friend the other times I had forgotten to pick him up; times I hadn't even realized what I'd done.

I was horrified and ashamed. I'd been telling myself that continuing to work as before was my coping strategy. But I wasn't coping at all. And I certainly wasn't helping my child cope with the loss of his father. My husband's parents — his grandparents — live in this pretty town, with a dying newspaper. So, we moved here. I bought the paper and am trying to resuscitate it. I pick my kid up at school every day. We cook dinner together. I'm a room parent in the PTA, something — believe me — I never thought I'd do in my life.

Most of the people here know my kid and look out for him. I've had the talk with him about how he, as a future Black man, needs to be mindful about how he behaves in public, especially with the police. It's not right, I tell him, but it's more important to be safe than to be right. He'll need to know these things someday. But for now, the local sheriff lives down the street and is the assistant coach of his soccer team. My kid gets to be a kid. I know how lucky we are to have this, and I am grateful for it every day.

I understand that moving to a place like this is a privilege a lot of families don't have. It's not perfect here. But my son has already lost his dad. I won't feel guilty for making things easier on him.

My career as I knew it is gone. I couldn't care less. I've made a choice to be different, not less. This choice feels like more to me. Maybe someday, you'll find yourself choosing this, too.

As she read, Roz felt her cheeks flush with shame. She hadn't had the foggiest idea about Jackie's family situation. She'd thought maybe there had been a scandal at Jackie's old paper, a professional rivalry or something else that made her choose this safe local paper over her former high-flying life. Roz had been picturing herself as a spunky ingenue, giving Jackie pep talks that would gradually rebuild her confidence. What a fool. The choice Jackie made was the bravest one all along. Roz began typing a reply, starting and deleting several attempts before realizing nothing she could write would ever be good enough.

She sat until her coffee went cold, thinking about how she could possibly make things right with Jackie. Obviously, she owed her an apology, but that didn't seem adequate. After several minutes of staring at the blank email draft, her message alert pinged.

It was Andy. "Hi," he wrote.

"Oh, hello, stranger."

"Look, I'm sorry I missed our meet-up yesterday. Something urgent came up. I tried to cancel, and I just saw now that the message didn't go through."

A likely story. "It's fine." It wasn't fine, but what else could she say? "If you're not interested, say so. Roz doesn't deserve to be jerked around like this."

Bubbles appeared and disappeared several times before Andy's next message came through. "Aren't I kind of being jerked around, though? I wish you would just have her call me."

"After last night I'm glad I didn't. What if you had stood Roz up instead of me?" She chuckled bitterly at the irony as she typed.

"Then I would feel even worse. Look, I honestly do have a good reason, but it's complicated to explain. Can we talk in person?"

"I've got other things to do, dude. But if you're still in town tomorrow, I'll be around for Nordic Fest." She wasn't going to make special arrangements to see Andy again. But if she happened to bump into him…

"OK. I have a flight out of Sea-Tac on Monday, so I can stick around. Maybe I'll see you there. I hope I might see Roz there."

"I don't know what Roz's plans for the weekend are. I guess you'll have to wait and see."

Andy thought he'd been getting a friendly beer with Gavin. She'd been so focused on her hurt feelings at being stood up that she lost track of her own stupid deception. Still, if he were serious about her, wasn't that an appointment he wouldn't miss? She couldn't let him slide off the hook like that. Roz wasn't sure she was even willing to risk another let-down. Her head had been turned by Andy's grand romantic gestures, but when it came down to it, he had yet to prove himself trustworthy and her heart wasn't in any condition to weather a bad breakup. They'd missed too many chances and it was time to move on.

Celeste

Celeste spent the morning decorating the sheltered area of the park that would be the dance floor and beer garden. Frigga's Feast on Saturday night was the main event of Nordic Fest. All weekend, Port Poulsen's waterfront park would be filled with food tents, arts and crafts booths, cultural demonstrations, and fundraisers for local clubs. Erik said Frigga's Feast was the biggest party of the year, a banquet that turned into a rowdy evening of dancing.

She was turning the picnic shelters into a troll grotto, festooned with greenery and her papier-mâché trolls. These had horned helmets, bushy raffia beards and cute potbellies, and would stand on either side of the entrance. Celeste put Roz to work hanging bunting painted with traditional Norwegian rosemåling designs from the rafters, while she worked to arrange sprays of greenery and autumn leaves and made spaces for the trolls and mushrooms. The whole area, picturesque to begin with, was taking on a storybook quality.

Erik closed the Blue Plate after breakfast so that he could prepare for the festival, but was taking a break to have a do-over of his date with Barry. Since Erik did so much cooking for work, Barry said he wanted to feed him for once, and had spent the morning making a picnic. Celeste watched from across the park as he spread out a blanket and unpacked spiced chicken on skewers, a container of cut fruit, rice noodle salad, and iced tea in mason jars.

From the picnic shelter, Roz and Celeste had a pretty good view of the romantic lunch. Roz was spending more time watching the picnic than decorating. Even Celeste was having trouble keeping her mind on her tasks; they were so sweet together, and Barry looked so happy.

Roz called over from her ladder, "Erik brought flowers!" Erik was presenting Barry with a bundle of sunflowers.

"Aw, he's so great. I really like him for Barry," said Celeste.

"Me too. I would hate not to have Barry nearby but I wouldn't be surprised if he were thinking about spending a lot more time over here."

He was. That morning as he'd been making the chicken, Barry had told Celeste that Erik approached him about managing the restaurant. He was still mulling it over. They both knew not to tell Roz about things like that until they'd made up their minds. Once you said you wanted something, Roz would walk through fire to make sure you got it, but she couldn't temper her advisory impulses during the decision-making process. Right now, Barry was worried about things getting messy if he mixed a business and personal relationship with Erik. A valid concern — especially considering the family complications Barry had witnessed working at NWC. Celeste thought it would work out well; Barry didn't tend to take things personally and Erik seemed equally able to compartmentalize. She'd miss having Barry right there in Seattle, but Port Poulsen was only a ferry ride away.

Likewise, Celeste hadn't mentioned anything to Roz about her own upcoming changes yet, but she was looking for her own place — a spot where she could fill every room with projects without having to worry about anyone else, maybe even a home studio. It was time for them to separate their lives. She and Barry would both announce their plans when the time was right. Roz would be happy for them once she got over the inevitable irritation about not being asked for her opinion, but Celeste wanted to break the news gently so she didn't feel like she was being abandoned.

A group of three men were making their way up the dock. They rattled the door of the Blue Plate and, finding it closed, turned toward the park. The back of Celeste's neck prickled as she watched them make their way over to Barry and Erik. She couldn't make out any words, but heard sharp, confrontational tones and unkind laughter. Roz climbed down from her ladder.

"Oh no. Are those the guys from last night?"

"I think they must be. I saw them at the boatyard yesterday, too. Charming group." There was an edge of fear under Roz's sarcasm.

One of the men picked up Barry's mason jar, dumped it out, and tossed it into the nearby bushes, while another stepped onto the blanket, kicking at the containers of food. Erik stood and began talking to them in low, calming tones, hands outstretched, placating. At one point he gestured toward the Blue Plate.

Barry sprang to his feet and got right in the space of the guy in the front of the group, jabbing a finger in his face.

Celeste turned to say something to Roz, but she was already moving across the park.

The other man, unfazed, lifted his hand and casually struck the side of Barry's head with a blow that made him crumple. Celeste felt all of the air rush out of her lungs. Her own feet felt rooted in place. Erik pulled back his arm and punched the perpetrator squarely in the jaw.

The other two guys seemed more level-headed than the one who'd hit Barry. They picked their friend up, holding him upright with his arms over their shoulders. His head bobbed on his neck and his eyes were only half open.

Adrenaline hit. Celeste unglued her feet from the grass and rushed across the park to join her friends. Barry's eye was starting to swell. She pulled an ice pack out of the cooler and pressed it to his cheek.

"Thanks." He brought a shaky hand up to hold it in place.

After a moment of hesitation, she held a second ice pack out to the guy Erik had hit. He swatted it away and it landed on the ground. Erik picked it up and held it to his own knuckles.

The sheriff's truck pulled up and he hopped out of the cab. "What's the problem, folks?" Taking in the scene, he said, "Oh, come on now, boys. Didn't we already talk about behaving yourselves until you cast off?"

Sheriff Andersen took brief statements from everyone. Roz and Celeste both assured him that Erik had struck second, and in self-defense.

"Son," the sheriff said to Barry, "I can bring the one who hit you in for assault if you want me to. The judge isn't in until Monday, so he'd spend the weekend in jail. That means their boat won't leave tomorrow morning as planned. He's the captain's nephew, they're not going to pull out without him."

Barry cast a glance at Erik, "No," he said. "It's not worth it."

"All right," the sheriff said, clapping a hand on Barry's shoulder. "Fellas," he addressed the group, "I guess it's your lucky day. Colin tells me your boat will be ready to motor out of here tomorrow. I'd rather not have you stinking up my jail overnight. I strongly suggest you return to your vessel and stay there. I'll be sure to have the deputy on duty patrolling to make sure you keep up your end of the bargain. Do we have an understanding?"

"Yes, sir." They shuffled back down the dock.

"As for you two," he turned to Barry and Erik, "I don't like to see this kind of ugliness in my town; we pride ourselves on being a welcoming place. But for Pete's sake," he said to Barry, "watch your mouth in the future, son. It's not smart to go around provoking people like that."

"Yes, sir." Barry mumbled.

Roz and Celeste helped the guys pack up the remains of the picnic.

"Well, I tried, Roz," Barry said, "you told me I should stand up for myself, and I did."

"Barry, what did you say to him?" Roz asked.

Celeste wanted to yell at her that it didn't matter. All that mattered was that their friend was hurt and it could have been much worse.

"He said he could smell a couple of — well, I don't want to repeat the word he used — a mile away, so I told him he was such a mouth-breather, it was a wonder he used his nose for anything at all."

Roz laughed, "You're not wrong."

That was all she had to say? Yes, what they'd said was awful, but it was only words. Barry was lucky not to have been more seriously injured. "But was it worth it? Barry, your poor face." Barry's eye was swelling more by the minute and his cheekbone was starting to turn purple. Blood trickled from a nasty cut above his eyebrow. Seeing him injured like this caused a pang in her stomach that bottomed into nausea when she thought about how much worse it could have been.

Erik had a protective arm around Barry. His knuckles were bleeding and beginning to swell. "Come on, mister. Let's go get some fresh ice. Can you two take this stuff back to the house?"

"Of course," Celeste picked up the picnic basket and Roz folded the blanket, as Erik guided Barry toward the Blue Plate. As they walked, she felt her relief and fear curdle into anger — but not, as she might have expected, at the men. They weren't the only reason Barry was hurt.

Roz

They walked back to the house in silence. Roz was lost in her head, running through different scenarios. Her adrenaline was still coursing, and her thoughts raced. Barry could have been hurt badly if Erik hadn't been there. The entire situation could have escalated to something much worse if the sheriff hadn't happened along. But what if she'd been able to get there faster? Could she have helped more? Talked the aggressors down, distracted them?

"I should have said something sooner, or yelled," she said.

"Or we should have had Bowie with us — he might have scared them away." Her thoughts swung wildly. "But that's ridiculous, it's a public park and they had every right to be where they were, and you can't let bullies win because then what kind of a life would you have?"

"STOP. IT." Celeste slammed the gate behind them.

Her raised voice was such a surprise, Roz's mouth snapped shut immediately. Celeste had never shouted at her that way before, ever.

"I'm sorry, Roz, I can't listen to this anymore. It's so easy for you to tell Barry to stand up for himself when you're not the one people want to hit." She fumbled with her key and opened the front door.

"Wow." Roz dropped the picnic blanket in the front hall.

"Well." There was a tremor in her voice and her hands were shaking, but as Celeste unpacked the picnic basket, her gaze focused only on the cracked food containers and jumble of utensils, which she unloaded onto the counter with painstaking care, as if making an effort not to throw them. "Do you think any of this is salvageable?" She examined the fruit tray, which was dusted with grass and dirt.

"Toss it. I had no idea you felt that way. You didn't say so last night."

"I've given up on trying to talk you out of things, Roz. You don't listen to me. You never have."

"What? I listen to you all the time. I don't know how you can say that when I'm only trying to be a good ally. I'm standing up for your interests!"

"I never asked you to! I can stand up for myself, but you've never given me the chance."

"That's not —"

"Listen, I'm going to start looking for my own place when we get back to Seattle on Monday."

Roz was scraping the contents of Barry's containers into the compost pail. The implication of Celeste's announcement hit her with a painful shock. Celeste wanted to leave her alone again? "Oh, great idea, newly unemployed is the perfect time to sign a lease." She heard the venom in her reply; it wasn't what she wanted at all, but it was too late to dial it down. And what was she supposed to do, sit back and watch Celeste ruin her credit without saying anything?

"Why not?" Celeste had abandoned her clean-up efforts and finally turned to look at Roz. "It seems as good a time as any to make a new start."

"Celeste. You're going to need a security deposit, first and last months' rent, your landlord is probably going to want to see some proof of income. You don't have any of that right now." She grasped at practical reasons to change Celeste's mind. "Why don't you at least wait until you have a job lined up, then you can start looking for a new place in a few months?"

"I will figure out my housing situation, I will figure out my job situation — on my own. I'm not a child, I know what I need to rent an apartment."

"Fine." Roz began loading the dishwasher, glad she had something to keep her hands busy. She'd never had so much as a disagreement with Celeste before and didn't know what to do with herself.

"Fine." Celeste rinsed the silverware and handed it to her. Bowie whined and thumped his tail, hoping for a spoon to lick.

"Roz, please don't be upset," Celeste continued, lowering herself to the floor to pat the dog. "I didn't mean to bring it up this way, but I've been thinking about moving out for a few weeks. Getting you for a big sister when I was ten was one of the best things that ever happened to me but growing up in your shadow was…a lot. And lately I've been feeling subsumed by you."

"Celeste, if this is about last night, you had every opportunity to tell Barry to handle things differently."

"I did. You weren't listening. I told Barry he did the right thing keeping himself and Erik safe. You can't always argue with people like those guys without getting hurt. You're the one who told him to do something different. And to be honest, I'm tired of you ignoring everything I have to say."

"Oh, come on. When have I ignored what you have to say?"

Celeste threw her hands up, startling Bowie, who began to whine and tremble. "When I said this whole pen name thing was a bad idea, when I told you to be straightforward with Andy, when…" She hesitated, turning her focus from what she was saying to rubbing Bowie's chest, as if she could let what she'd started to say trail away.

Roz wasn't going to let her get away with that. Since Celeste had started laying everything out on the table, she might as well finish. "When what?"

"When I told you I wanted to deal with my dad myself."

Roz's stomach sank, but her anger bubbled up immediately. She thought they had settled this. "Celeste, you said you weren't angry! You said it was for the best! You are twenty-eight years old. It's time to stop worrying about whether your dad will disapprove of your girlfriends. It's almost like you're still living in the closet."

"I'm not 'living in the closet.' You know that. I simply don't feel the need to be confrontational about everything all the time. Roz, I said I wasn't mad because I couldn't handle being angry at you and angry with my father at the same time." Tears dripped down Celeste's face now. Bowie nosed at her chin. "I knew I was losing him. I thought maybe if I didn't get too upset with you, I could avoid losing you, too. I wanted to take the shortcut to a place where I had forgiven you and wasn't mad anymore. Instead, I keep getting angrier because you keep steamrolling me. I can't let go of the feeling that you took something away from me that I can never get back. I knew I'd need to have a tough conversation with my dad someday. Maybe soon, or maybe when I met a partner. I would have thought carefully about the words I wanted to use and the setting I wanted to do it in, and we would have had a nice, calm talk. If I'm prepared for these things, it's easier for me to pretend I can't tell how disappointed he is. Instead, you blew everything up because you were trying to win an argument. And I don't know how I'll ever get over that, to be honest."

"I had no idea you felt that way."

"I'm not direct like you are, but you also could listen more thoughtfully. I know you want to be a good ally, Roz, and I see you trying, but you need to listen to the people you're trying to be an ally to. Did you ever stop to think for a second about what your trans readers might think about Gavin?"

Roz felt Celeste's words like a physical blow to her stomach. "Wow. *Wow.* That's not how I was thinking of it."

"Yeah, I know. I'm not sure you were thinking about it at all."

"Okay, well…if I promise to try listening better and being more thoughtful, will you at least put off moving out until you find a new job?"

Celeste's fingers stopped moving behind Bowie's ears, and he looked up at her and whined. "No. This is exactly what I am talking about, Roz. I told you why I need to get out into my own space. I will be fine — not that it's any of your business, but I have about a year's worth of living expenses saved up, and a couple of freelance jobs lined up that start next week. Contrary to what you may think, I have resources."

"I guess you have it all figured out, then."

"I do."

A well of emotions built behind Roz's eyelids. She couldn't even tell if she was angry or sad, frustrated or guilty. Probably all of the above. It was unbearable—she was going to scream or fly apart or implode. She couldn't do that in front of Celeste, not now. Desperate to get out of the house, she snapped, "Fine. I'm going for a run."

Roz changed clothes as quickly as she could and was five blocks away before she realized she'd forgotten her phone and hadn't thought to bring Bowie. She felt another pang of guilt for inadvertently punishing the sweet dog, who was probably standing at the door wondering why he'd been left behind. Celeste was right. She was a horrible person who never thought about anyone but herself.

Chapter Fifteen

Roz

Her feet slapped against the pavement as she picked up speed, ignoring a car horn from a side street as she dashed across an intersection without looking. Yards and houses passed in a blur, and soon she was at the trailhead. She blew past the bulletin board and hurtled herself up the steepest trail. The trees offered her the privacy she craved, and the resistance offered by the incline felt good. Roz propelled herself by hammering at the ground with her legs as if she wanted to punish it.

How could Celeste have been harboring so much resentment toward her all this time without saying anything? (Oh, but she had, hadn't she? Only not loud enough for steamroller Roz to hear her.)

Why couldn't Jackie have simply explained why her career was taking a back seat to being a widow and mother? (*Because she didn't owe you an explanation.*)

What if Barry had been badly hurt? (*It would have been your fault. He was hurt and it is your fault.*)

Why hadn't Andy shown up? (*Because you're not good enough for him. And also, dumbass, he thought he was meeting Gavin to talk about how he could win you over. He didn't know you were going to be there. It's your own fault your hopes were up so high. You created this whole scenario by not being straightforward with him in the first place, and now your chance is gone. Nice work.*)

Your fault. Your fault. Your fault.

As she ran, the anger melted away until she was hollow. She'd blown it with Andy, may have ruined her job by being too pushy with Jackie, and Barry and Erik were hurt. Celeste was angrier than she'd ever seen her. All she wanted was to help, be a good ally like Celeste said, but she'd been so focused on what she thought they should do, she hadn't been listening to them at all.

It must have been nearly four o'clock; later in the day than the last time she'd been in these woods, and much warmer. The crisp morning air had given way to the pungent scents of decaying wood and overripe berries. As she climbed higher, strands of spiderweb clung to her sweaty face and neck. When Roz reached the top of the fifth hill she was panting, and her legs ached. Gasping, she doubled over, braced her hands on her knees and looked around.

Where was she? She hadn't come this far with Bowie, and the series of hairpin turns had messed up her sense of direction. She continued up. Maybe a vantage point would help her orient herself—if she could catch a glimpse of the water, she would know which way to go. Her hamstrings, so satisfied with the upward progress earlier, were cramped and protesting. After half an hour of trudging up the incline, she still had not broken out of the tree canopy, but she came to a bench at one of the twists in the trail and sat to rest.

Roz shivered. Her back was wet with sweat and it was cold now under the trees. She'd lost track of how many times the path had forked, or which turns she'd taken. She didn't have a jacket, food, or water. It was overcast, but the light had begun to wane, reminding her that it would be dark in a couple of hours. She'd put herself in a situation that was becoming dangerous. "What's the plan, Rosalind?" she muttered to herself, the words coming out in the inflection her mother had always used. Roz was used to being the one to take charge and come up with a solution. Maybe her advice wasn't perfect but at least she tried to help. Why wasn't a single one of those people here now, to tell her what to do for once?

Roz had been leaving her apartment when the call from Barry came. She was late for work, and she was missing the beginning of the morning writer's meeting. She assumed that's why he was calling, at Kate's behest. She accepted the call and said, "I know, I know. I'll be there in ten minutes, and they won't even be done with the news rundown yet. Tell Mom to hold her—"

"Roz." She knew right away from the way he said her name, the lack of affect in his voice, something was wrong. "Your mom is on her way to the hospital. She collapsed in the coffee room and was unconscious when they loaded her into the ambulance. They think it was a stroke. Celeste is coming to pick you up and take you there. Wait in front of your building, okay? She'll be there soon, Roz…okay? Wait there."

Roz wanted to answer but the words were stuck in her throat. She was too afraid any noise she made would be a sob or a scream.

Finally, she forced out, "Yeah," the word feeling inadequate. She needed to know what had happened, what was going to happen. She needed someone to tell her that the next few months would be difficult as Kate slowly recovered. Roz would probably have to help her with physical therapy, taking care of the house, but eventually she would be her vibrant self again. Anything else was unfathomable.

Celeste's car pulled up and stopped directly in front of the doors. Any other time Celeste had picked Roz up here, she'd scrupulously pulled into the alley to avoid blocking traffic, but today she ignored the annoyed honks of the car behind her. With mechanical stiffness, Roz lowered herself into the passenger seat and fastened her seat belt. Celeste squeezed her shoulder and pulled out into traffic.

Every red light was torture. Roz wanted to ask what exactly had happened. Did Kate say anything? Did the paramedics say anything? (Later, Barry would tell her that Kate arrived at work complaining of a headache, but she'd taken a painkiller and he hadn't thought much of it until he'd noticed, a few minutes later, how unsteady she was on her feet. He'd just gotten her to sit down when she collapsed in her chair.) Roz held her questions. She didn't think she'd be able to speak past the lump in her throat, and she was also afraid of the answers. Celeste drove in silence.

At the hospital. Rushing from the emergency room straight up to the ICU, then an interminable wait for Kate's doctor to come out and talk to them. Fred was there too, tie loose, hair messy, disheveled as she'd ever seen him. "I brought her advanced healthcare directive," he told Roz, his mouth a grim line. "She transferred medical power of attorney to you after our divorce, but I didn't think you'd know to bring a copy of the documents."

Roz stared speechless at him, her brain working slowly to process the words. Finally, she answered, "No. I didn't think of that.

Okay. Thanks."

Then, the doctor. Words like "oxygen deprivation," "inoperable," "brain death." Roz did her best to follow along, but the roar in her own head was so loud. At some point, she had taken Celeste's hand, or Celeste had taken hers. She squeezed until her knuckles ached. "You can go and sit with her now," the doctor was saying. "According to her living will, she doesn't want to be kept on artificial life support indefinitely if she has no hope of recovery, but we are required to wait twenty-four hours before removing support."

And then a day and a night at her mother's bedside in the ICU. Holding her still-warm hand, knowing it was only her shell Roz was sitting with. Her mother was already gone. Celeste in the chair next to her, Barry holding back tears as he asked what he could do for her. As if there were anything she could possibly ask for that would make things okay, or even tolerable. The nurses, too. The nurses were so nice. Unbearably nice. Urging her to eat something, at least drink some water. "Please, honey, maybe just a little juice?" But she couldn't, she'd lost all sense of her body as something capable of eating and drinking. She heard Fred, on the phone with the magazine staff and the board, then he left, saying he'd start to write an obituary, call a florist, the funeral home, Kate's friends.

The organ donation people arrived a few hours in. Yes, Kate was registered as a donor. Yes, of course Roz wanted to help others. They needed to ask some questions, it's standard, there's a conference room they can sit in to talk. Celeste will stay with Kate. Although she knows it's irrational, Roz doesn't want her to be alone.

Roz answered the basic questions about Kate's health to the best of her ability. "Has she used intravenous drugs?" Of course not. "Has she ever been associated with a gang?"

"I beg your pardon?" Roz choked.

"These questions are standard, ma'am."

She couldn't help but laugh at the absurdity. "I think she almost got in a fight once at the Nordstrom Anniversary Sale. That's about as close as it gets." Of course they didn't laugh. Surely they wondered what the hell was wrong with her, cracking a joke at a time like this. (What exactly is the proper response to being asked if your Eileen Fisher-wearing mom is in a gang?)

All right. So, this is what happens when your loved one is an organ donor and it's time to stop life support. She'd seen this dramatized countless times on prime-time TV so she thought she knew how it worked: the family says their tearful goodbyes and they turn the machines off, the monitor flatlines. A long beep. A handsome doctor looks at the clock and calls the time of death. So clear, so final. But in real life, it doesn't make any sense to turn off machines that are keeping perfectly good organs viable. Roz was a practical person. The tidy Hollywood closure was not more important than the people whose lives could be saved. *You wouldn't want it another way. Neither would she.*

The doctors came in and did some tests. They said she could stay with her if she liked, but it may be difficult to watch. Roz didn't want to leave her mother alone with them. She stayed. The doctor said it was a good learning opportunity for a medical student, to whom it was explained how to tell beyond the shadow of a doubt that a brain is beyond repair. They determined it was time, and let Roz know she could leave when she was ready ("Take your time, but the transplant team is waiting..."). They would take her mother to an operating room so that two people could have new kidneys, someone could have a new heart. Her skin would help a burn victim, someone would see again through her corneas. Medical miracles. So many people, so lucky.

They promised to make all the necessary arrangements with

the funeral home; everything would be made easy for her. In a few months, she would get a thank-you note from a woman able to travel to see her grandchildren for the first time since she started dialysis. It wouldn't make the loss worth it, but it would make it feel slightly less senseless.

This is how you say goodbye: squeezing a hand that still feels alive, kissing the warm cheek, whispering into the ear you know can't hear to say you love her and you wish you'd told her more often, that you're not ready, but you promise you'll be okay. And then Roz simply...left. She got into a car as if she was a whole, normal person and drove away from the hospital.

Since then, she'd been alone with this. Sure, Celeste understood some, Kate had been a second mother to her. But Celeste's mom was alive and well. And she'd had Barry and a handful of other friends, the brief, brilliant hope of Andy. Bitterly, Roz congratulated herself for managing to screw up all of her remaining important relationships over the course of a few days. The one person who would have loved her no matter what, was gone.

It landed like a stone dropped onto her chest. Kate would never be there. Not if Roz got married someday, had children. Not when she needed to figure out how to cook a Thanksgiving turkey. Not to help her figure out what to do with the mess she had made of her life. Never. It wasn't fair. She wasn't ready.

She brought her feet up onto the bench and curled her arms around her knees. The floodgates had opened, and Roz couldn't seem to stop the tears now that they'd started. On an intellectual level, of course she had understood that her mother was gone for good, but she'd been so busy missing Kate moment to moment, the idea that she'd have to get used to missing her forever hadn't been real until now. Roz choked on a sob, tear tracks tracing through the dried sweat on her face. She shivered harder with a chill that came from the inside out.

"Okay," she said aloud, "you're okay. You're fine. Stop crying, stupid, because you can't afford to get dehydrated right now."

Kate would be so disappointed in the way she'd behaved recently, all for the sake of her column. Who was she to be giving advice to anyone? On top of the mess she'd made of everything, she couldn't even find her way out of these woods.

Retrace your steps. She heard it in Kate's voice. It was what her mother would have told her to do, had she been here, and it was the sensible approach. She'd been so sure she could fix things if she kept going up, find a shortcut by continuing to push forward, that she'd gotten herself even more lost.

Roz stood and turned down the hill, pulling her arms into her t-shirt to help retain body heat. When she came to a fork in the trail, she did her best to remember which direction she'd come from. The topography was beginning to look familiar. Rounding a corner, she looked up to see a doe in a clearing, no more than eight feet away, frozen. Roz froze, too, not wanting to panic her. The deer held her gaze for another moment, then calmly turned and returned to the tree cover with delicate steps.

The first thing she would do when she got back was going to be an apology to Celeste. She couldn't take back what she had done, but she could promise to listen more attentively to her sister's needs in the future. That included, she supposed, supporting Celeste in finding a place of her own. If Celeste let her, Roz would help her pack and apartment hunt. Or she'd stand by quietly if that's what Celeste wanted. Roz also owed apologies to Barry and Jackie. She owed it to herself, as well as her friends, to spend less time talking at them and more time learning from them.

Andy…well, he was a lost cause. He'd gotten tired of being jerked around by "Gavin," and she couldn't blame him. That must have been why he didn't show up last night. She wouldn't allow him to string her along anymore with his backpedaling messages. Although she was preparing to swallow several helpings of her pride, Roz had her limits.

As she approached the fallen tree where she'd first realized she was lost, she caught a glimpse of hot pink through the underbrush. "Hello?" she called, her voice breaking with relief.

"Hello!" A voice called back. The pink turned out to be a stylish nylon hiking jacket, worn by a woman around Roz's age, who also sported designer leggings and a small day pack. As she came closer, her immaculately groomed brows knit in concern. "Are you all right?"

"Yes. No. Well, kind of." Now that she actually had to explain herself to someone, she realized she must look like a mess, with her sweaty face and running mascara. "I feel so stupid. I came out here without my phone or any water or a jacket, and I…well, was kind of upset and not paying attention to where I was going, and I have no idea where the trailhead is."

"Here, I think you should sit down." With a light hand on her arm, the woman guided Roz to the fallen tree, removed her pack, and rummaged in it. "Put this on." She proffered a long-sleeved tech fabric shirt. Roz accepted it gratefully. Next out of the pack were a bottle of water and an energy bar.

"I can't take all your stuff. I'm sure I'll be fine if you can point me in the right direction for the road."

"Don't be ridiculous. I've been hiking for half an hour. It will take you at least that long to get back to the trailhead. You need to take care of yourself before you can keep going."

To her great embarrassment, Roz burst into tears again. Between sobs she choked out, "I'm sorry. I'm a total mess. You're being so nice to me."

The other woman laughed.

"What's so funny?"

"It's just that I'm rarely accused of being nice."

Roz squinted through her tears. "Oh." She recognized the concerned face in front of her from a shameful midnight internet search, performed after she'd found out who Andy was. *Oh.* "Um. Are you Olivia Arden?"

Olivia sighed and shrugged. "Guilty."

Roz grimaced. She couldn't imagine a clearer sign than this chance encounter to tell her it was time to start being more straightforward. "Olivia, this is strange and awkward, but I have to tell you, I've sort of been seeing your ex-husband."

"Oh!" Olivia exclaimed, peering at Roz's puffy face with more scrutiny. "Oh my god. Are you Rosalind?"

"Yes. Well, Roz." A torrent of words issued forth from Roz's flustered mouth. "Andy told you about me, I suppose. I'm very sorry, I know your divorce is quite recent; it must be strange to think of him dating, especially while you're still working together. Don't worry, I'm pretty sure he's no longer interested in me — he stood me up last night with some bullshit excuse about his message not sending." In for a penny, in for a pound, she kept going. "Also, I'm sorry about your column, I was so angry with my stepfather and it's not your fault." Olivia stared at her. Roz swept her hand through the air as if to wave her own words away. "You probably don't even know what I'm talking about and that's going to be an even longer story and I should definitely be on my way if you're sure I'm going the right direction."

"Roz. Relax. For heaven's sake, breathe." Olivia said, putting a hand on her arm. "First of all, your stepfather is a piece of trash. I don't know what I was thinking when I agreed to write for him, so you don't need to worry about that. Second, beyond wanting him to find someone who makes him happy, I'm not concerned about Andy's love life. Third, he really is terrible at making sure texts go through before he puts his phone on airplane mode. He didn't stand you up, he was probably on a plane, or live on air. You see — well, actually, you should see for yourself if I've got a signal." Olivia removed her phone from her pack and opened a video clip. It was from the previous night's Lionel Lenord talk show. Sitting on Lionel's couch, looking ruggedly handsome in an olive V-neck sweater and dark jeans, was Andy.

"We're back, with Andy Arden, star of *Ardent Life Adventures*. Andy, you're half of one of reality television's most talked-about divorces. This morning, news emerged that Olivia, your, er, temperamental ex-wife, is having a fling with Seattle celebrity chef Angela Lewis. We were actually scheduled to have Olivia on tonight to talk about your series finale, but she wasn't able to make it. What do you have to say about all this?"

Andy smiled tightly. "Well, first of all, Lionel, I wouldn't exactly call what we do reality television. Yes, our marriage was a big part of the show, and it's become obvious to me since we announced our divorce that a lot of people tune in hoping to see personal drama, but all we wanted was to have a good time showing people the fun things to do and eat in the cities we visit."

"That's fair," Lionel broke in, "But — "

Andy continued smoothly, with a charming smile. "And I'll let you in on a secret. I don't get upset very easily, but I've had at least as many bad days on set as Olivia. I've never once been described as temperamental. Isn't that strange?" Lionel tried to interject, but Andy kept talking. "You know, Olivia and I were lucky to have had the chance to do *Ardent Life Adventures*, but it can be a lot of pressure. We're often jet-lagged and under time and budget crunches. It's not easy to be in a good mood all of the time, but whenever Olivia is a little cranky, a video ends up on social media."

"I bet she's a doll," Lionel conceded with a heavy dollop of sarcasm. "But tell me, Andy, when you married her, did you know she was a lesbian?"

"No." Andy answered, eliciting an audible "ooh" from the studio audience. Andy continued, "I knew she was bisexual. Liv had a girlfriend before we met. If she has a girlfriend again now, good for her. Really. We're not married anymore, and a person dating whoever they like shouldn't be considered scandalous or even newsworthy. I hope I have a new relationship soon, too. It's none of my business. It's none of your business, either." He turned to the camera. "Or yours." The microphones picked up another collective gasp from the audience.

"Well," Lionel minced. "She certainly is lucky she has you to come here and defend her, isn't she?"

Andy turned a charming, edged smile in Lionel's direction. "I'd say you're lucky I was available to come on your show tonight and deal with this crap, instead of canceling the appearance altogether, Lionel. Olivia doesn't need me to defend her. She's brilliant and assertive and can do fine on her own. She's also smart enough to know she doesn't have to put herself out here to answer intrusive questions if she doesn't want to. This kind of bull—"

BEEP. The censor cut him off.

"That's about all the time we have, folks. We'll be back after the break with another song from our musical guest!" Lionel's smile looked like it was going to shatter his face. As the theme music played, Roz could see Andy removing his microphone and exchanging a few heated words with Lionel before striding off stage.

So, this was what Andy was doing last night. The fact that he was willing to put himself out to do the right thing for someone he cared about only made her like him more. How irritatingly complicated.

Celeste

Celeste finished cleaning Erik's kitchen, then walked back to the park to finish the outdoor decorations. She didn't regret anything she'd said, but she wished she hadn't blown up. She'd let her resentment fester too long and spoiled all her careful plans to talk to Roz gently and rationally when they were both in the proper headspace. Still, she wasn't worried. Roz often dealt with her feelings by running them out. Celeste knew her well enough to expect her back in an hour or so with an apology followed by a few days of bruised ego.

When she returned to Erik's house and didn't find Roz there, she didn't think much of it. Roz needed time to cool off and deserved to take it. But when it had been four hours since Roz ran out the door, Celeste knew something was wrong. Roz would never stay away that long on purpose; her temper flared easily but cooled down just as quickly. Celeste called Barry's cell to ask if he'd seen her.

"No. What happened?"

Celeste recapped their argument. "This is not how I planned to do things. Barry, I feel awful."

"I'm sorry Roz took off, but you know what? I'm super proud of you. That was a long time coming. How did it feel?"

"It felt good at the time but now I'm really worried."

"Erik and I can take his truck and start looking, okay? We'll start at the waterfront and downtown, you check the neighborhoods around the house."

"Okay."

She grabbed her car keys and patrolled the streets around Erik's house. Bowie rode shotgun and his nose twitched at the open window. "You probably know exactly where she went, huh boy?"

Celeste was about to park and let Bowie's nose lead her to Roz when her phone rang.

Chapter Sixteen

Roz

Olivia closed the app after Roz finished watching the video. "I begged him to do the appearance instead of me," she explained. "He said he had somewhere he needed to be, but after he saw this…" She pulled up the UMAZ site on her phone and passed it to Roz.

Roz's blood boiled as she watched the grainy video of Olivia and Angela on their hotel balcony. "That's disgusting. I'm so sorry."

"Andy thought so too, which is why he agreed to rush down to LA to do Lionel Lenord, and then took a late flight back here to finish up his filming. He's a pretty good guy."

Every person Roz had misjudged ought to all get together and start a club. She sighed. "I will add him to the list of people to whom I owe apologies. Speaking of which, do you mind if I use your phone to make a quick call?"

"Go ahead."

Roz didn't know very many phone numbers by heart, but she knew this one. "Celeste?"

"Roz! We've been looking all over!"

"I got lost, of all the stupid things."

"Where are you? I'll come get you."

"I'm on the trail a couple of miles outside of town. I'm borrowing someone's phone—you won't believe whose. I'll explain it later."

"I'll be right there."

"Celly, don't hang up!" She knew she'd see Celeste very soon, but she couldn't wait another second to apologize. Roz turned away from Olivia and lowered her voice. "I have to tell you I'm so, so sorry for what I said to your dad, and I'm so sorry I haven't been a good listener. I'm going to be better from now on, I promise. When we get back to Seattle, I'll help you pack up and look for a new place if you want to, but I'll give you whatever space you need to figure out what's next for you."

There was a long moment of silence on the other end of the line. Then, finally, "That means a lot, Roz. Thank you. Now, where exactly are you?"

That's right, Roz had intended to take Celeste and Barry to this trail, but they'd been distracted by Andy's poems. "If you follow the main road out of town, there's a gravel parking lot on the left side of the road and…"

Olivia took the phone from Roz's hand. "We're about a thir-ty-minute walk from the parking lot at mile marker six on Route 108. I'll walk out with her to make sure she gets to you okay, she's shaken up."

Standing and brushing the pine needles off her leggings, Olivia extended her hand to help Roz up. "Shall we?"

"Thanks. I'm sorry I ruined your hike."

"You didn't. I wasn't going to go much further anyway. The outdoors was always more Andy's thing, but I thought while I was here with some time to kill, I would give it a try."

"I hope you don't mind me asking, but why *are* you here?"

"Change of plans in the shooting schedule. We were going to use a cooking segment I shot with Angela, but I don't want to use that footage anymore. I talked our producer into sending me to reshoot with Andy, here."

"I see. You make a good team." Roz tried to put a bright note into her voice, not wanting to sound jealous of Andy's ex.

"Professionally, yes, but this will be the last thing we do together for our show. I'm hoping to line up a new series. That's why I agreed to guest-write the "Kate Knows Best" column. I thought it would be good to get some extra exposure. I suppose I succeeded," Olivia said with a bitter laugh.

"I think I owe you an apology." She stopped and turned toward Olivia. "I was trying to tell you earlier—I'm the one behind that Gavin Garrett post about your column. As a matter of fact," Roz did a little bow, "I am Gavin Garrett." She felt so silly admitting it out loud. "I set up an alias to write under because Fred said I'd lose my NWC shares if I wrote for a competitor. And I was so angry with him for turning my column over to a new, inexperienced person, I wasn't thinking at all about how hard the assignment must have been for you. I still would have disagreed with your advice, but I could have been kinder about it."

"You don't owe me anything. Clearly Frederick orchestrated the whole situation. I could kick myself for being so naive."

"He can be very charming when he wants to be."

"You weren't wrong about the column, either. I think I have

a lot more work to do on myself before I'm in a position to tell anyone else what to do."

Roz almost said, *Me too*. The idea had barely started to form and she wasn't ready to say it out loud yet, but today had made her realize it was time to grapple with her own demons. It had been very convenient to hide behind other people's problems, but maybe it was time to come out and face her own.

Olivia continued, "Listen, Roz. It's completely over between me and Andy. I'd be happy to see him move on."

Roz shook her head in an effort to pretend she wasn't invested in Andy. "That was really just a fling for both of us. I'm sure he doesn't want anything more to do with me."

"Believe me, Andy isn't a 'fling' kind of guy. You should call him."

Meeting Olivia painted Andy in a new light for Roz, but she was left feeling more apprehensive than she had been before. It was much easier when she could brush him off as the guy who'd been dishonest with her and stood her up.

"Do me a favor? Don't tell him I'm Gavin, okay? I need to do that myself."

"I understand. Until then, your secret is safe with me."

Celeste

She didn't see Roz at the trailhead when she parked, but Bowie seemed to recognize the spot, tugging her forward onto the path. They'd just turned a bend when he whined and pulled the leash out of her hand.

She heard Bowie's excited yip and Roz coo, "Hi Buddy!" from around the next corner.

Celeste had never been so relieved to hear Roz's voice. When she made the turn, she saw Roz crouched down to greet Bowie as he pushed his head into her chest.

The woman with Roz was hanging back, and Celeste called out to reassure her. "He's friendly, just overexcited. We're working on his training."

"Oh, it's not that," the woman said. "I'm sure he's a very nice dog. I'm allergic." As proof, she sneezed.

Roz stood and led Bowie away, crushing Celeste in a hug. "Celly, I'm sorry. I'm so sorry."

Celeste patted her back. "It's okay. I'm just glad you're safe."

The other woman sneezed again, and Celeste looked over at her. She was stunning, but she also looked somehow…familiar.

Roz broke the hug. "Celeste, this is Olivia Arden."

That explained it. "Oh my, that *is* quite a coincidence. Hello."

Olivia's smile was radiant enough to cut through the chill of the woods. "Hello. It's lovely to meet you…"

"Celeste. Thank you so much for helping Roz."

"It's my pleasure." Their hands lingered, clasped, a few seconds longer than normal, and Olivia squeezed before she let go. Her hand was warm, but calloused. A chef's hand.

Olivia looked like she'd stepped out of a catalog, while Roz was shivering and bedraggled. She should get her home.

"Well," Celeste said, hoping Olivia could tell she was reluctant to leave, "we should get going."

Olivia sneezed again and Roz laughed. "Yeah, Bowie is giving this poor woman an allergy attack."

"Oh dear," Celeste said, then added, "you know he's really Roz's dog. I'm more of a cat person, myself." As soon as she said it, she wanted to slap herself on the forehead. Why did she feel the need to say that?

Olivia smiled again and said, "I'm not allergic to cats."

"Good," Celeste said. Good? What was she doing? She felt a pull toward Olivia, but even if Olivia felt it, too, anything between them would be wildly messy. Olivia was in business with her father. Roz was involved with Olivia's ex. "Well. Bye." What in the world was happening? She wished the forest floor would open up and swallow her, but at the same time she felt an impulse to link arms with Olivia and walk down the path together.

"Thanks again," Roz called, as they made their way down the trail. As soon as they were around the bend, out of sight, she nudged Celeste with an elbow.

"What?" Celeste said, but Roz just cackled.

"Nothing."

Roz

"Hang on," Celeste said, as soon as they got into the car. "Let me just text Barry and Erik to let them know I've picked you up."

"You called them?"

"Of course I did, Roz. You left your phone and wallet at the house and we had no idea where you were. They've been out looking for you, too."

Somehow, Roz had pictured everyone going about their usual business until she'd called. She ought to feel warm and supported, but she felt worse for ruining everyone's afternoon, especially when they were all working on the festival.

"I'm so sorry. I screwed everything up."

Celeste blew a deep breath out through pursed lips as she put the key in the ignition. "I meant every word I said, but I shouldn't have dropped it on you all at once like that. I never wanted to upset you so much."

"Celly, don't apologize. I should have been a better listener this whole time. And I shouldn't have gone off like that without my phone. I'm upset about a lot of things. I'm realizing, I'm not sure what to do with my life right now, either. I've made a huge mess of things with Andy." That thick, choked sensation returned to the back of her throat. She hated crying in front of other people, even Celeste, but the floodgates were opening again. "I miss Mom, so much. I can't stand that she isn't here anymore to talk about all of this stuff."

"Oh Roz," Celeste pulled the car onto the gravel shoulder and twisted over to hug her. "I miss her, too. Since the funeral you haven't said much about her and I knew you didn't want to talk about it, but I've been so worried about you. You just didn't seem to want any help."

It must have looked that way from the outside. "I feel like I should be able to cope with it on my own. I'm a grown woman — one whose job it is to tell other people what to do — sitting here crying about my mommy."

"That's not realistic, Roz. I don't think anyone is equipped to deal with a loss like that on their own. That's not what you'd tell someone who wrote in to the column, is it? You'd tell them to be patient with themselves, that grief is a long process. You'd encourage them to see a therapist or find a support group, or at least lean on family and friends. Why do you think you have to hold yourself to a higher standard?"

"I'm supposed to be the one with all the answers. I've always felt better if I took care of things myself."

"How is that working out for you?" Celeste gave her a sidelong glance.

"Awesome. Maybe you should be the new 'Kate Knows Best' columnist. You should call your dad and tell him."

Celeste's face hardened into resolve. "I definitely still need a break from Dad. I will always love him, but I don't respect his values, and I don't think he respects me." She pulled back onto the road and drove through town, to the Blue Plate. "Come on. We need comfort food."

"But they're closed today."

"It's okay." Celeste winked. "I'm tight with management."

She led Roz through the back door of the kitchen.

Erik, who was sliding a meatloaf and a tray of roasted vegetables out of the oven, directed his dazzling smile their way. "Roz, I'm so glad you're okay. That trail system is more complicated than it seems—I always check the map before I start a hike."

Roz gazed around at the preparations Erik and Celeste had underway for the next day's feast: the work surfaces of the kitchen were crowded with tidy rows of bread and cookies. The shelves lining the walls were filled with Celeste's beautiful centerpieces; wildflower arrangements in mason jars, around which were tied wide ribbon bands painted with simple rosemåling flowers and whirls. Celeste had also used fabric paint to stencil designs on solid-colored tablecloths; these were draped over a few extra chairs in an unused corner of the kitchen. Roz hadn't realized how much work Celeste had been putting into this project. The banquet was going to be beautiful. And, if the peek she'd had into the refrigerator was any indication, delicious.

"Erik, the food looks wonderful. Your parents would be so proud."

"I hope so." Erik wiped his hands on a dish towel. "I'm nervous. Everyone has such high expectations, it's a lot to live up to. Celeste has done a gorgeous job with the decorations. That reminds me." He touched a tablecloth. "I am pretty sure my mother had some platters with a very similar design. They're probably in the attic. We should use them."

"That would be lovely," said Celeste. "We can help you look for them later."

"Roz!" Barry thundered down the stairs and engulfed her in a hug. "Didn't we already have enough drama today?"

She shrugged, feeling sheepish. "I didn't mean to worry everyone."

"Rule number one of dramatic tantrums. Take your phone."

Barry tapped his own phone for emphasis.

"I know, I know. Believe me, I'm never setting it down again. But you'll never guess whose phone I borrowed."

As Celeste opened a bottle of wine, Roz filled Erik and Barry in on meeting Olivia. After they watched Andy's talk show appearance on Barry's phone, he pulled up the tabloid article about Olivia and Angela. "Hm," Barry clucked and shook his head, "Angela Lewis is a good friend of Fred's, right? Does anyone else think this seems awfully tidy?"

"I hadn't thought about it." Until meeting her today, Roz had a picture of Olivia as conniving and ruthless, in league with Fred to steal her column away. She realized now that wasn't at all the case, and a seed of unease was growing. "Do you think Fred and Angela are behind those photos?" Roz shot a glance at Celeste. She might have been on the outs with her dad, but this was a pretty serious allegation.

Celeste surprised her by nodding, "I don't want to think that of him...but he does like to take his boat out at night. Poor Olivia."

When Barry excused himself to get some painkillers from the upstairs apartment, Roz turned to Erik. "How's he doing?" she asked, "And, how are you? What happened to you guys this afternoon is a lot scarier than me getting lost on a trail like a dumbass."

"I'm all right," Erik said. "I think Barry is, too. This isn't the first time something like this has happened to either of us, but it's the first in a pretty long time. My hand kind of hurts, though." He grinned and shook it out.

"I'm glad the *Skua* will be gone tomorrow." Roz was tempted to head down the dock to give the men a piece of her mind.

"Me too," said Barry, bounding back down the stairs, "although I wouldn't mind another chance to get a solid punch in."

Erik kissed him on the cheek. "Punching is not your forte, my dear. But you may carry this salad to the table."

Olivia

Her phone buzzed while she was getting ready for the shoot. "This is Celeste. Thank you again for helping Roz."

Olivia wrote back, "Anyone would have done the same. I'm glad I was there. And it was nice meeting you both."

"It was nice to meet you, too! Roz says she forgot to give you your shirt back. Do you want us to drop it off somewhere?"

"I don't want to put you to any trouble…" Olivia didn't need the shirt back—it was just a freebie from a company that wanted to feature their products on the show—but she was glad it might give her a reason to see Celeste again. Their conversation had been so rushed and focused on Roz, but Olivia had felt an undeniable charge of attraction between them. She needed to know if it was real.

"It's no trouble at all." Celeste added the biggest smiling emoji.

"Are you staying near downtown Port P? I can swing by after shooting my segment."

"Yes. I'll send you the address. It's a yellow house with a big porch."

"I'll be there around eight."

"See you then. If you're not too tired, maybe you can join me for a cup of tea."

Reading that gave Olivia a burst of energy. She definitely wasn't going to be too tired. "I'd love to."

Olivia put her phone away and returned to the makeup chair. The network crew had set up a small trailer in front of Mrs. Muir's. Even though they didn't need much wardrobe or space for hair and makeup, there was hardly room to turn around. Maybe she ought to feel foolish flirting with Celeste so soon after her disastrous dalliance with Angela Lewis, but she didn't. Meeting Celeste today felt like coming home, and she was tired of being safe and careful. There was a time when she would have laughed at someone for following a feeling like this, but Olivia wasn't the same person she used to be. She was ready to trust her emotions.

Andy appeared in the doorway of the trailer. "Hi," he said, hovering on the threshold.

Olivia stood and hugged him, holding on for a long time. He froze for a moment before returning the hug. "You okay, Liv?" He pulled back and looked her in the eye.

Careful not to smear her eyeliner, she looked up and blotted at the moisture seeping through her lower lashes. "Fine," she smiled. On tiptoe, she kissed him on the cheek. "Thank you."

Andy gave her a bemused smile. "You're welcome. So, you ready for the last supper?"

"Ready. Let's make this a great one."

Side by side, they stepped into the blazing lights of a television-ready kitchen for the last time.

The shoot with Andy was a breeze. Maybe because it was the last one, maybe because, compared to the public humiliation she'd experienced recently, a broken pie crust didn't seem like a big deal. Olivia found herself less worried about perfection and more interested in having fun in the kitchen. Leaving Andy had been the right thing for both of them, but maybe there was friendship in their future.

Assisted by television magic — courtesy of Mrs. Muir, who'd cooked extra portions from Olivia's recipes — Olivia produced a big enough meal to feed everyone, so that they could all sit down to eat together before most of the crew caught a late ferry back to Seattle, then scattered to their respective homes. Joe suggested shooting footage of the crew meal to run over the end credits of the final episode; it would be a warm coda for the series as well as a way to thank all the behind-the-scenes staff, most of whom had traveled from location to location with Andy and Olivia for three years.

The bed and breakfast had plenty of room in the backyard. Someone had found paper lanterns and strung them along the roof and around the pergola, casting the garden in a dreamy glow. It was warm enough to be comfortable outside in jackets and sweaters. The slight chill in the air made Olivia's hot meal taste even better.

The whole gathering had the air of a family reunion; bursts of laughter, snippets of chatter about what everyone would do next, platters passed from table to table. Andy traded good-na-tured barbs with the hair stylist and admired Joe's family photos. Everyone was polite to Olivia, but she could tell they didn't quite know what to make of her presence among their familiar chatter. She'd wasted three seasons being so worried about appearing unprofessional that she'd remained aloof from everyone.

After the last bite of dessert had been eaten, Olivia took off her apron and walked to the address Celeste had given her. Dusk was turning into night, and in one of the yards she passed a woman and her daughter packing away a table with a sign that read "Dahlias, $5." There were three bouquets left; a mix of anemone and puff-ball flowers in sunset shades, arranged in old spaghetti sauce jars. On a whim, Olivia bought all three, told the girl to keep the change from her twenty-dollar bill and walked the rest of the way balancing the three jars in her arms.

The house Celeste had directed her to was a buttery-yellow Victorian with a wrap-around porch and a view of the lights dot-ting the harbor. She rang the bell, and a few moments later it was opened by a man in his late thirties, one of his eyes rimmed by a plum-colored bruise. "Hi Olivia," he said. "I'm Barry. Come on in."

Celeste and Roz were in the living room with an intimidat-ingly attractive young blond man, poring over a photo album. Roz's dog was curled next to their feet. "Hello," Olivia said.

"These are for you, Roz. I hope you're feeling better," she handed Roz the jar in her right hand, which was full of yellow and orange flowers. "And these are for you," she told Celeste, indicating the other two bouquets, which were in shades of pink, purple, and deep red. "Just because, well, I thought they were pretty." Olivia felt a flush spread across her cheeks.

"How beautiful," Celeste said, leaning in close to take them from her. "These are some of my favorite colors."

"Yes, thank you," Roz said. "These are lovely. And thanks again for your help today. Let me introduce Erik Johansen. Erik is a chef, too."

"Pah." Erik made a dismissive gesture, "I'm a cook."

"Don't sell yourself short," exclaimed Barry. "Olivia, Erik spent the whole week in the kitchen making food for the Nordic Fest banquet tomorrow, on top of running his restaurant."

"And Celeste created all the decor," Roz added.

Olivia had been feeling a bit awkward, unsure of how to approach Celeste as someone she was interested in romantically. Shop talk would get her into her comfort zone. "Tell me all about what you're planning," she said, finding a seat in an overstuffed chair.

Erik told her about the meal: salmon filets, Swedish meatballs with noodles, roasted potatoes, salads, rye bread, and enough pastry to send a football team into a carb coma. "Also, lutefisk and pickled herring to satisfy the traditionalists."

"I've been having so much fun with the tablescapes," Celeste said. "I love the dichotomy of Scandinavian design; some of it is so streamlined and modern, but then there is also a lot of whimsy. It's been nice to be hands-on instead of writing about it."

"I didn't realize you were a writer, too." Olivia had wanted to look Celeste up online but didn't know her last name. All she knew about Celeste so far was that she was a good friend to Roz.

"Well," Celeste began, "I was. I used to write the design column for NWC. It was a bit of a mishmash: interior decorating, DIY trends, party planning. I fell into the writing thing because of my dad. I'm sort of looking for my next act."

"Your dad?"

"Oh sorry—I thought you knew since you're working with him. My dad runs NWC."

The pieces fell together with a nauseating clunk. Of course. How could she not have realized that Celeste was Frederick George's daughter? Olivia's dinner somersaulted in her stomach. The idea that such a kind, lovely person had been raised by that odious man was mind-boggling.

Celeste continued, "When Roz resigned, I realized I couldn't work with him anymore, either. So," she shrugged, "here I am."

"I should have mentioned," Olivia said, "I'm also finished working for NWC. I hope it's not too awkward to say, but I found working with your father…" she searched for the right word, not wanting to hurt Celeste's feelings, "…challenging." Now was not the time to say more about what had happened with Frederick, although Celeste might find out someday if Olivia's outreach to the NWC board of directors found any purchase.

"I understand. He is not an easy person. I'm taking a bit of a break from him, myself."

"Fred is the opposite of an acquired taste," said Barry. "The more exposure you have to him, the less you like him."

Olivia opened her mouth to comment, but instead she sneezed four times in a row.

"Oops, your dog allergy!" Roz said. "Celeste, why don't you take Olivia out to sit on the porch, and I'll bring you both some tea?"

Olivia allowed herself to be ushered onto the covered porch. Lamplight filtered through the living room curtains and illuminated the wide, rough floorboards. Olivia sat on one corner of the porch swing. Celeste settled at the other end, unfolding the blanket that had been tossed over the back of the swing to cover both of their laps. Over tea, they began the process of telling each other the stories, big and small, that made them the women they were.

There were silences, too, where they simply sat and rocked comfortably, bathed in the glow from the house, warmed by the tea and blanket. It felt strange to be so at home with someone she'd met so recently and had good reason to shy away from; Olivia didn't know if matters were settled with Frederick George, but whatever happened, being involved with his daughter wasn't going to help. And she wasn't sure exactly what had happened between Andy and Roz, but she knew Andy well enough to know his interest was sincere.

It would make sense to walk away, but she couldn't. This felt different from what she'd had with Angela, which might have been exciting but was never warm. It felt more like those first days with Andy, when she sensed the person she was sitting next to would be significant in her life.

Chapter Seventeen

Roz

Roz went to her room, intending to work. Barry and Erik had fallen asleep on the couch in front of a movie, Barry's head resting on Erik's shoulder. Celeste and Olivia were on the front porch with their tea. The sounds of their murmured conversation drifted up through Roz's open window. Maybe if she had done things differently, she could be having a lovely, quiet evening with Andy. But there wasn't anything she could do about that now.

She could at least do something useful. Roz pulled down the hallway trapdoor that led to Erik's attic and climbed the ladder, flashlight in hand. She reached up to switch on the bare bulb installed in the ceiling. When light flooded the space, she laughed. It was so orderly. Storage boxes — the kind you specifically buy for boxing up household goods, not odd sizes begged, borrowed, or stolen from the liquor store — were stacked in perfect rows around the perimeter of the attic. Each one was labeled meticulously in a tidy, feminine script that must have belonged to Erik's mother. Finding the platters Erik wanted to use tomorrow would be a breeze. How very different from her own mom, whose haphazard approach to packing led to items that fit in the same box being placed together with total disregard for function or easy unpacking.

The last time Roz helped Kate with boxes, she was seventeen and a few months away from leaving for college. They sat at the kitchen table, unwrapping glassware.

"Mom. This box has books in the bottom."

"I know. Books are too heavy to pack on their own, so I put a few in the bottom of each box. Pile them in the living room, will you?"

With a heavy teenaged sigh, Roz carried the stack of books to the other room and set them down in front of the fireplace. "I can't remember how we had these shelved," she said, wishing she could blink and have everything in their house back where it had been before Kate's marriage to Fred.

"We'll find new places. How boring it would be to put everything back the same way." Kate entered the room with her own stack of books. "Look, if we start now, we can arrange them by color." She placed a red book at the far left of the shelf, and a blue one towards the right, then began looking around for yellows and greens to put in the middle.

Roz sat back on her heels, "But don't you wish everything could be back the way it was? You wouldn't fix your mistake if you had the chance?"

Kate turned her attention away from the books and back to her daughter. "What mistake do you mean? Marrying Fred?"

Rolling her eyes, Roz gestured at the room around them, filled with boxes and other moving-related rubble as if to say, "Obviously."

"That wasn't a mistake." Kate sat back on the rug, crossing her legs in front of her. "Listen. Honey, just because relationships end, it doesn't mean they shouldn't have begun. I know it doesn't make sense to you, but we had a lot of good times before things went wrong."

"I guess."

Kate leaned forward to put her hand on Roz's knee. "Rosalind, my heart, I don't ever want you to run away from things because they might not be perfect or last forever. That's no way to live. Fred hurt me, but laying blame doesn't help anything. It doesn't mean the happiness wasn't real."

In a corner of Erik's attic, Roz opened a box labeled "serving ware" and found several platters painted in bright, swirling patterns. She set them near the ladder to carry down for Erik, then glanced around at the remaining boxes, stacked around the edge of the room as if they were reinforcing the walls of Erik's tidy house.

Roz had boxes like this, too, but they were full of her own stuff. When she inherited Kate's house and moved back in, she'd tossed the contents of her apartment into boxes and stored them in the basement with the intention of going through them sometime to get rid of what she didn't need.

Roz had stacked a lot of things around herself so that they stood between her and the reality of her grief, and not just physical stuff. She'd have to deal with it all eventually, decide what she should gently let go of to be replaced with something that suited her better.

At least for now, the advice column needed to go in the discard pile. She had wanted it to keep her feeling close to Kate. Instead, it had been a pipeline of distractions. Was she even any good at it? She'd behaved reprehensibly this week, merely for the sake of the stupid column. "Unacceptable," Kate would have said; Roz could practically hear it.

Her behavior towards Andy had also been over the line. She should probably cut her losses, chalk this up to a lesson learned for the next guy who came along.

She thought about Andy's wide, sly grin spreading across his face; the crinkles at the corners of his eyes; his stupid, sweet poems; his easy laugh. She'd learned a lot this week, but Roz didn't want insight to tuck away for her next romance. She wanted Andy.

Celeste

It was getting chilly on the swing, but Celeste didn't want the evening to end, and sensed Olivia didn't, either.

"Are you cold?" she asked.

"A little. Maybe I should get going."

"Or you could borrow a sweater."

A slow smile spread across Olivia's face like warm honey. "Or I could borrow a sweater."

Celeste returned the smile. "Be right back."

She brought back two cardigans and another blanket. When she handed Olivia a sweater, their fingers brushed. Gently, Olivia tugged Celeste down to sit next to her instead of at the opposite end of the porch swing. Then her fingers brushed along Celeste's jaw, and their lips came together. When their tongues met, Celeste tasted jasmine tea in the kiss. Olivia's lips were soft but still dusted with sugar from the cookies they'd been eating. Sweet, sweet, sweet. The kiss was gentle, slow, warm and comfortable. Like easing aching muscles into a warm bath.

When they finally broke it, they both giggled as if they'd encountered something unexpected. Like the time Celeste tried a chocolate truffle that turned out to be filled with popping candy that fizzed on her tongue. All of those times she said she was waiting for someone worth making a fuss over, it had been a purely theoretical concept to her. Now she understood on an irrational, chemical level and the realization broke over her like a discovery. The solution to a puzzle she hadn't been aware she was trying to solve.

Considering Olivia's history with her father, it was going to be an even bigger fuss than she'd ever anticipated. "This could get...complicated," she said.

"I don't care." Olivia replied, and kissed her again, this time less gently.

After the second kiss, they curled up together on the swing, Celeste's head nestled in the crook of Olivia's shoulder. It was getting late, but for now, they were content to stay there together gazing out into the evening, until they both dozed off to sleep.

Roz

Roz was desperate to talk to Andy. She wished she could apologize, explain, thank him for being patient with her. But it was too late to disturb him. She'd come off badly enough already, no need to add late-night phone calls to the mix.

Roz had never gotten invested enough in a relationship to feel heartbreak, not in the romantic sense, at least. Was thirty too old to experience that for the first time? Maybe she had simply never learned how to do it. Besides, was "heartbreak" even the right word to describe the way she felt about what was happening with Andy? She had known him less than a week. Surely she couldn't call it lost love. A missed opportunity, maybe. Whatever it was, she had mishandled it. While Roz couldn't do anything about whatever feelings Andy had for her or didn't, she could certainly apologize to him for her behavior.

Roz's eye fell on a stack of index cards on the desk in her room. She'd grabbed a few from Erik, intending to put more handwritten "Ask Mr. Garrett" ads on bulletin boards around town before heading back to Seattle. Maybe a taste of his own medicine was the way to Andy's heart. Bent over Erik's childhood desk, by the light of the gooseneck study lamp, Roz composed her own poem. She went through three drafts before she realized no amount of effort would turn her into Elizabeth Barrett Browning. The slapdash, silly nature of Andy's poems were what endeared them to her. Hopefully he would feel the same way about hers.

Throwing a hoodie on over her pajamas, Roz snapped Bowie's leash onto his collar and walked down the block in the direction of Andy's bed and breakfast. Bowie's nose was to the ground and his tail bobbed, enjoying his bonus late-night outing. The Geography Channel SUV was still parked at the curb, and she lifted a wiper to secure the poem against the windshield. An ear-splitting clamor broke the evening quiet as the vehicle's alarm went off. Bowie glanced at the truck with mild interest, and gave Roz a look that said, "What's all this fuss about?" as she clamped her hands over her own ears. Roz was thankful to have a deaf dog. Unbothered, Bowie squatted over his favorite azalea bush.

As lights began to come on in neighboring windows, Roz tugged the leash. "Come on, Buddy! Let's go." But he adjusted his stance and stared at her, immovable. Roz clapped a hand to her forehead. One of the front windows on the second floor of the B&B went up with a scrape, and Andy's curly head leaned out. "Roz?"

She gave a little wave. "Oh…hi."

Chirp. Andy shut the alarm off. "Don't move. I'm coming down."

She could probably run — she'd be halfway down the block before he got out to the sidewalk. Should she leave the poem behind and make a break for it?

Before she could make up her mind, Andy emerged from the front door and jogged down the walk. "Are you out for an evening walk or is this some sort of elaborate scheme to steal our equipment?"

"Oh, yeah. I was dying to get my hands on some… camera thingies."

"Very convincing."

"I'm not sure your alarm is quite loud enough."

"Yeah, sorry about that. Is your dog okay? It must hurt his ears."

"Bowie is deaf, he's fine. My ears on the other hand…"

"We keep a lot of equipment in the truck, so it has a sensitive alarm." Andy raked his hair off of his forehead. He must know how good he looked when he did that. "So, um, what brings you out this evening?"

Roz's cheeks went hot. Well, hotter. She reached toward the wiper, then hesitated. "Is this thing going to go off again?"

"I disarmed it."

"I came to give you this." Roz handed him the card.

To her chagrin, Andy read the poem out loud.

There once was a fellow named Andy,
and I really thought he was dandy.
But I learned of his fame
and my pride is to blame
for taking the first exit handy.
But then Andy wrote me some poems,
and I realized I should get to know him. (better)

He had to prove himself to Gavin,
before more dates we could be havin'
now an apology is what I owe him.

Roz grimaced. "I probably should have spent more than five minutes writing that."

Andy laughed. "It's great. Very…um, rhymey."

"You should talk, Mr. Gnome Poem."

"So," he tapped the card against his palm. "Can I take you out to dinner now, without having to go through Gavin?"

"Yes," she dropped her gaze, "I'm so sorry, Andy. I don't know what was wrong with me. I haven't been myself the past few days." A burst of uncomfortable laughter escaped, followed by a partial confession. "I don't think I've ever met someone I like so much, and I was hurt that you didn't tell me who you were, and then you stood me up. Well, you stood Gavin up, I know, but it was actually me who came to meet you last night." She did a jazz-hands gesture. "Surprise!"

He wrapped his hand around her upper arm. His touch felt good: reassuring, comfortable, safe. "I got called out of town, I didn't mean to."

"I know. Olivia showed me the Lionel Lenord video."

Andy gaped. "You've spoken to Olivia?"

"It's a long story. Very." Bowie whined and tugged at the leash. "Should we walk a bit?" Andy made a 'lead on' gesture. They started down the sidewalk while Roz told Andy the story of her run in the woods and Olivia's rescue. "Andy, I'm so sorry I didn't speak to you directly. Please accept my apology." Roz wanted to tell him all about the Gavin Garrett ruse, too. He deserved to know. But it was all too humiliating. She deserved to enjoy a few minutes walking together before she risked ruining everything again.

As they reached the park, Andy stopped and reached out to

brush the hair back from her face, caressing her cheek with his thumb. "You don't need to apologize. If anything, I'm the one who should be sorry for not telling you more about myself before we spent the night together. So, can we start over?" He extended his hand. "Pleased to meet you. I'm Andy Arden, star of cable TV and tabloid divorces."

She giggled. "Hi Andy, I'm Roz."

They shook hands. Now was the time to say more, to tell Andy the whole story about Gavin. As soon as they ended their handshake, she would blurt it right out, get it over with. Instead of letting go, Andy pulled her closer, bending his head to hers while their clasped hands were sandwiched between their bodies. She responded by burying her free hand in his hair as their lips met.

The embrace lasted long enough for Bowie to give up on continuing the walk and flop down on the pavement with a sigh. Almost as soon as he settled, he jumped up again, hackles raised, rigid body pointed in the direction of the Blue Plate. He let out a single sharp bark. Bowie never barked. Startled, Roz broke the kiss. She sniffed. "Do you smell smoke?"

Andy lifted his chin to better catch the scent. "Yeah…I think it's coming from over there." He strained his eyes in the direction of the restaurant, but even with the park's lighting it was hard to see anything. They hurried toward the marina building. As they ran, Andy pulled out his phone.

As it became clearer that there was definitely a fire in the building, their jog turned to a run. When they were about a hundred yards from the Blue Plate, they saw flames through the back window.

Chapter Eighteen

Roz

"Roz, wait!" Andy was only a few steps behind her, but his voice was almost lost in the roar of adrenaline. "I called 911. Firefighters are on the way. It's not safe."

Roz looped Bowie's leash around a signpost at the edge of the parking lot. She couldn't just stand around waiting for help. Who knew how long it would take to arrive? She thought Erik was still at the house with Barry, safe, but she couldn't be sure. And if she could keep him from losing his business or sentimental belongings, she had to try. There was a fire extinguisher in the kitchen, she'd seen it at dinner and knew exactly where it was. Taking one last deep breath of clean night air, Roz pulled the back door open. The kitchen was full of billowing smoke that stung her eyes. She couldn't see any flames near the oven, stove, or grill. Trying to keep her head under the worst of it, she located the extinguisher and pulled the pin. Over the twin roars of the fire and her own pounding pulse, she heard sirens in the distance, faint.

She felt a series of frantic taps on her shoulder. Andy was right beside her, t-shirt pulled up over the lower half of his face. He pointed urgently toward the trash can in the corner of the kitchen. Roz aimed the nozzle into the can and sprayed. Flames licked their way up the wall above the can and she sprayed them, too, emptying the entire canister. She couldn't see fire anywhere else, only that thick gray smoke.

Roz couldn't hold her breath any longer and began to cough, the smoke overwhelming her. With an insistent arm around her waist, Andy dragged her outside.

"I think you got it," he coughed as the fire truck roared into the parking lot. Gear-clad firefighters burst through the door. Roz's lungs burned. Her throat was singed and dry. She couldn't control her coughing; it felt like the flames had scorched the inside of her chest. Andy guided her to a curb and sat next to her, rubbing her back slowly as she bent her head between her knees.

She took shallow breaths at first, allowing them to deepen as she felt ready. The soothing motion of Andy's hand on her back helped bring her breathing back to a normal rate, and the pounding in her head subsided. With each breath of fresh air, the burning in her chest eased.

Roz called Erik, her stomach a rock as she broke the news. Four minutes later, Celeste's car screeched into the parking lot. Erik, Barry, Celeste, and Olivia piled out. They all waited for the firefighters to emerge. Roz was quite certain the fire was gone, but they seemed to be taking forever to clear the building.

Erik was shell-shocked. "I don't understand," he said, "I always make sure everything is shut down and safe before I lock up, and I have a sprinkler system. Why didn't the sprinklers come on? Or the alarm?"

A police SUV pulled up, and a very tired-looking Sheriff Andersen climbed out. "Folks," he nodded, "this is getting to be a habit."

One of the firefighters appeared in the doorway, mask off, and beckoned the sheriff over. Roz could see them leaning in to examine the doorjamb.

Erik was pacing, one hand pressed to his mouth. Barry watched, anguish written on his face. Andy wrapped an arm around Roz to keep her warm, and she saw Olivia do the same for Celeste.

After what seemed like an eternity, Sheriff Andersen and the firefighters stepped out of the building. "Ms. Connolly," the sheriff said, "sir," he beckoned to Andy, "a word."

"Yes?" Andy helped Roz up from the curb.

"Can you tell us how you gained entry to the building this evening?"

"We smelled smoke and thought it was coming from here, and then we could see for sure that it was, so I went in through the back."

"Do you have a key? Did you have to break it open?"

"No." Right. She shouldn't have been able to open the door. "It wasn't locked, I just pulled it open."

"I see. We'll need you both to come in and give an official statement, but tomorrow will be fine."

Andy nodded. "Certainly, Sheriff. Anything we can do to help."

"Son," the sheriff waved Erik over. The others gathered around, and the sheriff hesitated.

"It's okay," Erik said. "My friends can hear whatever you have to say. This might have been much worse if Roz and Andy hadn't been here."

"That's true. Because the sprinklers failed, if this had been allowed to grow much more, the whole building could have gone up, likely spread to the marina or the ship supply." Roz shuddered, thinking of all the varnish, oil, and who knows what other flammable materials were on the shelves in Colin's shop, the gas pumps on the docks. It was possible Port Poulsen could have lost its whole waterfront tonight. "We'll need to get the county arson investigator in to do a full report, but it appears someone broke in, shut off your water main, and started the fire."

Celeste gasped. The color drained from Erik's face. Roz saw red. "Those bastards from the *Skua*."

"Possibly. The fire was in the garbage can; they think a cigarette on top of some motor oil-soaked rags."

"No one who's been in the kitchen today smokes, and I always empty the garbage before I go home."

"My deputy said the *Skua* cast off from the dock here at about midnight, but I'm sure they haven't gotten far. I'll get on the horn with the Coast Guard to see if we can get them in for questioning. You were lucky, Mr. Johansen. I don't think the damage is too extensive. You can get in a couple of days after the fire marshal finishes the investigation and clears the building, but I expect you'll be shut down for at least a few weeks."

Barry stepped between Erik and the sheriff. "Weeks? But he has things in there he needs tomorrow. Sheriff, I thought you would have a deputy patrolling this area tonight."

"Sir," the sheriff held an open palm toward Barry, "I do have a deputy patrolling, but it's a big area and if someone set this fire, they must have gotten around him. We don't know for certain that the *Skua* crew are responsible for this, but if they are, they'll be held accountable."

In contrast to Barry's anger, Erik was simply dejected. "All of the food we prepared for Nordic Fest was in the kitchen. Even if we could get into the fridge, they tell me they can't switch the power back on until the fire marshal clears the wiring. I guess in the big picture it's not that important. I'm just glad no one was hurt," he cast a grateful glance at Roz and Andy, "but I hate to let everyone down."

"Well," Olivia said, her tone brisk. "I haven't done a lot of Scandinavian cooking but I'm sure I can make a dent in it if you tell me what you need. And we have several pairs of hands here to pitch in. Andy is a competent sous chef, thanks to me. We can do a lot in the kitchen at your house."

Erik gave her a weak smile. "That's very kind of you, but I can't impose."

"Nonsense. It'll be great PR for me, which I could certainly use."

Erik opened his mouth to protest again, but Andy stopped him, clapping a hand on his back. "Just do what she says, Erik."

"We should get some sleep then, so we can get started bright and early. Sheriff, if you don't need us anymore…"

Sheriff Andersen waved them away. "Go on. We can do formal interviews tomorrow. I was looking forward to some meatballs and lefse, myself."

The group turned and walked up the street to Erik's house, Andy and Roz in the rear. He reached for her hand. His palm felt warm and strong, and interlacing their fingers felt like something natural they'd been doing for years. She squeezed. "Thanks for that."

"You performed the heroics. That was very brave, Roz."

"I just couldn't stand there and watch Erik's family business go up in smoke."

They reached the gate of Erik's house.

"Do you want to come in?" She let the question trail off, glancing through the open door to the stairs that led to her room.

Andy grimaced. "I would love to, but it seems a little awkward." He gestured toward Celeste and Olivia standing near the door. If there was something significant between them, they'd all have to get over the strangeness of the situation eventually, but for now, she was too overwhelmed.

"You've got a smudge." Andy brushed the soot from Roz's face, then bent his lips to hers. Maybe it was the excitement of the fire, or maybe it was Andy, but she couldn't get close enough to him. She pressed herself into his chest and dug her fingers into the small of his back, pulling herself as close as she could. Their bodies responded together until they had to come up for air.

Andy's voice was a hoarse whisper when he said, "Come home with me." He was looking straight into her eyes, his pupils blown wide by adrenaline and desire. She was sure hers looked the same way.

Roz had to break the tension, or she'd explode. She smiled and tried to put on a joking tone, but her reply was breathy. "Another night in a glamorous hotel with you? How can I resist?"

"Mrs. Muir's is not exactly the Four Seasons."

"I'm sure it's perfect."

They were all the way to his front door by the time Roz realized Bowie had run right along with them, his leash still in her shaking hand. They both burst out laughing.

Andy took the leash and replaced it with his own warm hand, then led her up the steps.

As soon as they shut the door to Andy's room behind them, they crashed into each other with all the frustrated wanting of the past several days, bodies falling into each other until they were both too exhausted to move.

Chapter Nineteen

Celeste

Celeste was awake as she sipped tea at the dining room table, but barely, when Olivia tapped on the front door just before dawn. She'd been so tired by the time they returned to Erik's house after the fire, she'd fallen right to sleep despite the excitement. Olivia had promised to come first thing in the morning to start working on festival banquet food. It was going to be a long day.

Erik was already awake and dressed. He let Olivia in, then tactfully retreated upstairs to give them a moment. "There's coffee on the counter," he said. "I'll be back down in a few minutes to get started."

In the light of the new day, Celeste was shy all over again.

They'd spent hours together on the porch last night, gone through the trauma of rushing to the fire, but now doubt crept in. It seemed too good to be true.

"Good morning," Olivia said, stepping in to kiss Celeste as if it were the most natural thing in the world. Like they'd been doing this for years.

Celeste gave herself a moment to enjoy the warmth of Olivia's body pressed against hers and inhale the spice of Olivia's shampoo. There was so much to explore, but it would have to wait.

As if she were reading Celeste's mind, Olivia broke the embrace and said, "We'd better get to work."

Olivia had already sketched out a plan for the day. Erik joined them in the kitchen to go over it, and they discussed cooking times, mise en place, streamlining the menu. As she was beginning to know Olivia, one of the things Celeste admired was her sense of responsibility and take-charge attitude.

Barry stumbled in a few minutes later, lured by the promising aroma of coffee. The bruise under his eye had turned deep purple overnight. He caught Celeste's worried stare and said, "It looks worse, but it feels much better."

"Do you feel confident about the decor, Celeste?" Erik asked. "Just do whatever you can. I want it to look nice, but people will understand the circumstances."

"I think so." At least most of the park was decorated; the table linens and centerpieces were a lost cause, but they'd be easier to pull together last minute. Her eye fell on a stack of platters on the kitchen table. The medley of bright colors and stylized floral designs gave her an idea. "Do you think more people have stuff like this in their houses, and would be willing to lend it?"

Erik considered. "Probably, although we don't have as many Scandinavian families in town as we used to. I only have this stuff because it belonged to my parents. What are you thinking?"

"The festival is Scandinavian because that heritage is part of the town history, right?"

He nodded.

"But there is a bigger variety of cultural backgrounds here now?"

"Right. We mostly stick to the Scandi theme because it's traditional. And fun; kids like the Viking stuff."

"Well, what if we open it up a little bit more? For the decor inside, we can ask people to contribute things from their own homes, make it more about the people who live here now."

"I like that," Erik said. "It reminds me of a quilt. I'll text the volunteers and ask them to see about gathering some things. What if I also ask folks to bring something for the dessert table? That would take a little pressure off of us," he said to Olivia.

"Fine with me," Olivia said. "I usually prefer a more cohesive menu but we have to work with the time we've got."

They started working, but Erik's kitchen was much too small for the four of them. Olivia needed space to spread out the ten enormous salmon filets she'd somehow managed to procure overnight, Erik needed the same counter space for cooling racks and to season potatoes.

They were all on top of each other. Barry tripped over Celeste, spilling half a container of cinnamon across a salmon filet. Olivia couldn't reach all the shelves and Erik frequently had to pause his own tasks to get something down for her. Erik finally said, "Let's divide and conquer. One of us should be able to get into the banquet hall soon to use the kitchen there. Volunteers will show up in a couple of hours."

Olivia agreed. "This is your kitchen."

"You'll probably be better than I am at giving instructions to the volunteers."

"I'll go to the hall, then." Olivia said, with a decisive nod.

"I'll go with you." Celeste was pleased. This way she could start putting the hall together, but it also meant she'd get to spend the whole day with Olivia

Roz

Roz squinted into the beam of morning sun making its way through the gap in the shabby-chic floral curtains and across her pillow. Her phone buzzed with a text from Celeste. "Olivia and Erik went to get supplies; we'll start cooking when they get back. Bring Andy over when you're awake."

Roz checked the clock. It was a few minutes past seven. She'd meant to get up much earlier. The festival banquet was supposed to start in the early evening, and with most of the food and decorations either ruined or inaccessible, everyone would have to scramble to make it happen. Roz tapped out a quick reply. "Due at police station to give formal statements. Will be there to help ASAP."

Next to her, Andy lay on his back with Bowie curled along his other side. Both snored softly. She nudged Andy, who shifted and mumbled something unintelligible. Bowie lifted his head and thumped his tail twice, and Andy blinked his eyes open. The promise of a lazy smile twinkled in the corner of his mouth. "Good morning."

"Morning." She showed him the texts. "I think we're about to be put to work. Are you okay with that? Did you have work stuff to do today?"

"Nah. The rest of the crew left this morning. Olivia and I were supposed to leave also, but" his grin broke through, "it looks like we both have reasons to stick around awhile."

Roz couldn't help but smile back. Andy's warmth was contagious. "I know everyone will be grateful for the help."

"Oh, it's not entirely altruistic," Andy said, a glint in his eye.

She clutched the sheet to her chest in counterfeit shock. "Golly, Mr. Arden. If I'm expected to provide certain favors in exchange for your assistance, we'd better define the terms."

He leaned up to kiss her lips, then dropped a peck on her shoulder. "We should probably, um…discuss that later. I believe we are presently required elsewhere."

Bowie whined at the door. Roz dropped her ingenue persona and rose to put on the sweats she'd traded her smoky pajamas for last night, saying, "All my stuff is at Erik's house. I think I'll go to the police station first, then back there to shower and change. Should we go to the station together?"

"Sounds good."

Roz opened the door to leave but slammed it shut again abruptly, having been treated to the spectacle of a scandalized-looking matron wearing the kind of old-fashioned dressing gown you only saw on spinsters in old movies (Mrs. Muir, she presumed), and two hissing calico cats, fluffy tails puffed up like bottlebrushes. She clutched her heart. This time the shocked gesture was genuine. "Oh my god. It's like *The Shining* out there." Roz looked around for Bowie and saw only the tip of a white tail poking out from under the bed.

Andy got out of bed and pulled on jeans and a t-shirt. "Let me see if I can do something about that. You two wait until the coast is clear."

Roz heard his voice at a low murmur in the hall, punctuated occasionally by Mrs. Muir's exclamations. Then she heard jovial laughter from Andy and a faint ladylike giggle from the innkeeper. While she waited, she idly checked the other notifications on her phone. She had two missed calls and a text from Margaret Olson, the NWC board chair, from yesterday afternoon. Between fighting with Celeste, getting lost, meeting Olivia, and then Andy and the fire, she had been so preoccupied she had missed this.

The text read, "Roz, I was hoping to speak with you, but heard you were out of town. Please call me when you can, there are some things we need to discuss. Margaret."

She'd known she might have to deal with the NWC board sooner or later. Roz wasn't sure if they knew about her work for Jackie yet or not, but the situation wasn't sustainable. If she wanted to keep working for the Gazette, she'd have to tell the board. Maybe she could retain her shares but become a silent partner. She made a mental note to call Margaret later if she got a free moment. She had a feeling it was going to be a rather hectic day, and surely discussing bureaucratic matters could wait until Monday.

She knelt to reach under the bed and gave Bowie a pat on the haunches. "Come on, buddy. It's okay." He whined and wagged the tip of his tail but didn't budge. She patted the floor by her knees and waved her fingers in a "come here" gesture, his hand signal for come. He crawled out uncertainly, belly close to the ground. She gave him a thumbs-up and a pat and then clipped his leash on, but when she tugged it, he planted his front paws and gave her a look that clearly said, "No way, lady."

There was a tap on the door and Andy came in. "I offered to pay a double occupancy fee and pet fee and she's fine with it. Even sent you breakfast." He handed Roz a scone and a mug of coffee, and brandished a peeled hard-boiled egg, which he tossed to Bowie. The egg landed on the floor with a light bounce. Bowie looked at it, then the open bedroom door, and let out a plaintive whine. "Did those big kitties scare you? Poor baby!" Andy closed the door, then sank to the floor, wrapped an arm around Bowie, and picked the egg up and tore it into small pieces, feeding him by hand. "Mrs. M. shut the cats in her bedroom, so he won't see them again."

Roz leaned on the dresser sipping her coffee, amused and

besotted. If she'd had a chance to see Andy in action like this sooner, she would never have had any question about what a good guy he was. With his bedhead and Bowie in his arms, he looked sexy as hell; someone really ought to turn this view into a calendar.

"He won't budge. I don't think he's going out there under his own steam, and I can lift him, but I don't think I can carry him down the stairs."

"Right." Andy brushed the egg yolk from his jeans. "Well, I didn't get to rescue anybody last night, so I guess this will have to do." He scooped Bowie up and carried him down the hall. Roz followed them down the stairs and opened the front door. As soon as Andy set him down, Bowie trotted over to the azalea.

Andy guffawed. "I think I'll offer Mrs. Muir a little extra cash for a new plant."

"Hey, it's free fertilizer," Roz said, but she caught the way Andy was taking responsibility for Bowie. It made her feel like they were a team, and she liked that feeling.

Chapter Twenty

Roz

The police station was a few blocks away from the quaint commercial core of town, but still walking distance from the B&B. The squat, industrial brick building didn't fit the storybook atmosphere of the rest of Port Poulsen. Still, it was bright and reasonably pleasant inside. The entry was lined with polished wooden benches facing a service window presided over by a desk sergeant. Roz gave her their names.

"Oh yes, our newest volunteer firefighters. Come on back, Sheriff Andersen is leaving shortly, but I know he wants to speak with you." The sergeant leaned down to scratch Bowie's head and gave him a biscuit from the jar on her desk.

The back of the building housed a few desks, a couple of rather flimsy looking holding cells, and the sheriff's office, a walled-off corner of the large, rectangular room. Judging by the decor, Sheriff Andersen was an avid fly fisherman, a proud soccer dad, and a hockey fan. Roz and Andy sat in the chairs facing his desk, and Bowie curled up on the carpet between them.

"Ms. Connolly, Mr. Arden, thanks for coming in this morning. I want to get your formal statements written down while the events of last night are still fresh in your minds." He turned on a digital recorder and placed it on the desk between them.

As a journalist, Roz was used to conducting interviews, but she had never been the subject of one. "How does this work? Do you ask us questions, or —"

"Just tell me what happened, in your own words."

"Shouldn't we be separated? To make sure our stories match?" Andy's tone was earnest and deferential, like a student trying to earn an A.

Roz saw amusement flicker in the sheriff's eyes. "You're not suspects, sir."

"We were in the park, all three of us." She nodded down at Bowie. "We smelled smoke, so we looked around and saw that it was coming from the Blue Plate."

"Did you see anyone exit the building?"

"No."

"Which direction were you looking in prior to smelling the smoke?"

Andy blushed. Roz had never seen anything quite so wholesome in her life. "My eyes were closed."

Roz responded to the sheriff's inquisitive glance. "Mine, too."

Sheriff Andersen leaned back in his chair, an eyebrow raised. "I see. I don't suppose you happened to hear anything?"

"No," Roz shook her head. "So, we went toward the building. Andy called 911." At this, the sheriff nodded approval at Andy.

"It didn't seem too dangerous to go in, so I did. I'd been there earlier in the evening and knew where the fire extinguisher was."

"Tell me about the entry. Which door did you go in through?"

"The back door, the one that leads into the kitchen."

"How did you get it open?"

She mentally walked herself through what she'd done, to be sure. "I pulled it right open. I guess it wasn't locked."

"I saw her pull the handle," Andy added, "and I was surprised it opened. I had been looking around for something to break the lock, and then we didn't need it."

"Ms. Connolly, you say you were there earlier in the evening. As far as you know, was anything out of place?"

It had been so smoky inside. "I don't think so, but it's hard to say. I couldn't see very clearly."

"And you'd never been there before, Mr. Arden?"

"That's correct. I'd been in the front as a customer, but never in the kitchen."

The sheriff made a "go on" motion at Roz.

She said, "Then I aimed the extinguisher at the bottom of the fire — Andy was the one to see that it was in the trash can — and started shooting foam at the flames. By then we could hear the sirens and we exited the building."

"Thank you," Sheriff Andersen said, leaning forward to turn off his recorder. "In this jurisdiction, fires such as this one are a joint investigation between the sheriff's department and the county fire marshal. She'll be in sometime in the next few days to make a final determination about the cause, but I think it is pretty clearly arson. In addition to the broken lock, the water main was shut off, which prevented the sprinkler system from extinguishing the flames, and the smoke alarms were ripped down. Whoever did this was counting on no one being in the vicinity that late at night."

Roz went cold. "Erik has been sleeping there almost every night. He could have been trapped upstairs."

"He's lucky he wasn't. Now, we do suspect crew members of the *Skua* based on the altercation they had with Mr. Johansen and Mr. Santos yesterday, and the fact that the boat seems to have left the harbor shortly after the fire started. I just got word from the Coast Guard that the *Skua*'s engine failed off Fidalgo Island, and they're being towed to Anacortes."

Roz said, "I was in Colin's shop when he was talking to the captain, and he seemed…disinclined to pay for thorough work."

"Yup, that sounds about right," the sheriff said. "I'll have Anacortes PD hold them, and I'm sending a deputy up there to interview crew members about the fire. Based on the fire department's quick and dirty analysis of the contents of that trash can, it sounds like it was full of rags with trace amounts of marine varnish, not typical restaurant garbage. We'll get a warrant to search the boat and see what we can find on board. Off the record, I'm pretty sure we'll be able to charge these guys with setting the fire."

"That will be a relief for Erik, I'm sure," Roz said. She checked her watch. "Did you get everything you needed from us, Sheriff? We promised to help with the festival preparations and there isn't much time—"

"Oh, I know. My wife and kids have been baking all morning, and they'll rope me in before too long, I'd wager. Go on."

Outside the station, Roz took Bowie's leash from Andy and kissed him. "See you in a bit."

All the way back to Erik's house, Bowie kept glancing behind them with a worried furrow in his brow, like he was asking why Andy wasn't coming. Her dog, it seemed, had decided Andy was part of his pack. "It's okay, buddy. We'll see him later." She leaned down to scratch him on the ribs, and he licked her cheek. "You like him, huh? Me too."

Roz was humming as she skipped up the steps of Erik's porch. The more time she spent with Andy, the deeper she fell. She should be grateful for the deafening car alarm on the Geography Channel's truck. Without it, she would have simply dropped off her terrible poem unnoticed, not expecting to hear from Andy again. And if Andy hadn't come outside and they hadn't taken a walk, they would not have stumbled upon the diner fire.

As she was coming up the porch stairs, Celeste and Olivia emerged from the front door, arms full of grocery bags and kitchen implements. "There's not enough counter space in this kitchen for all of us," Celeste said, shifting an oversized stock pot to her hip to rebalance the load she was carrying. "We're going to work at the community hall. Erik and Barry are doing the baking here."

Roz was surprised to find herself ill-at-ease around Olivia again. They were all mature adults, but the situation was strange, to say the least—she'd broken down in front of this woman yesterday and spent the night with her ex-husband. Not to mention, Roz was in Andy's sweats, hair messy, while Olivia looked polished in neat jeans and a checked shirt, sleeves rolled just so, not a single hair out of place. Self-conscious, she tucked the strands that had escaped from her ponytail behind her ears. Roz knew she cleaned up okay, but she hoped Andy didn't mind her being a bit rougher around the edges than his ex. She had a feeling Olivia perpetually looked like she'd stepped out of the pages of a Ralph Lauren catalog.

As they passed on the porch, Olivia gave her a brief smile and a wink. Roz had misjudged her based on that first column. Unfair, when she of all people knew how hard it was to stand up to Fred.

She would pop her head into the kitchen to say hello before

going upstairs to shower. The men had the counter covered in carbohydrates. Barry was piping custard into buns, and Erik was ricing potatoes for lefse. They both had flour in their hair, and Barry wore an apron emblazoned with the slogan "Norway or the Highway."

Across the kitchen island, they seemed to be in the midst of an intense conversation. "It would be a big change," Erik was saying.

"I know," Barry replied, "but it's not like we're getting engaged or anything, not now, anyway." Roz's eyebrows hit her hairline. She couldn't resist eavesdropping a little longer.

"We do make good partners," Erik agreed, "but living here is a lot different from living in the city. You'll miss out on lots of things."

Barry swatted at the air in front of him with a potholder. "I won't miss the city. I like it here. With you. Life is short, Erik. There's no good reason to postpone things that make us happy." On tiptoe, Barry took Erik's face between his hands and kissed him.

Roz gave them a moment before clearing her throat. They turned to look at her, Barry grinning, Erik blushing. "Sorry. Hi. I'm going to get cleaned up. Andy should be here soon."

"Great," Erik said. "We'll need some help rolling krumkake."

"Oh hey, I know how to do that! Those buttery cone cookies, right?" she exclaimed. "My mom used to make them at Christmas." Kate hadn't been one to spend a lot of time in the kitchen, but during the holidays she always set a day aside to make several kinds of cookies for friends and neighbors. The krumkake were a nod to her own Norwegian grandmother. One of Roz's earliest memories was standing at the counter on a step stool, using a wooden mold to roll the waffle-like cookies into their cone shapes while they were still warm and pliable. She hadn't thought about that in years, and she smiled to herself.

Roz waited for the wave of longing to come, as it always did when she thought about Kate, but it didn't materialize. The sorrow wasn't gone but it had subsided, tempered by fondness for her mother and gratitude for her happy childhood.

She knew she would always have these memories and the things that Kate had taught her. In one sense, she had lost her mother. In another, it was impossible to ever lose her. She'd spent so much of the past eight months reeling from the tragedy that she had forgotten how lucky she was. This was grief, too; feeling love for someone who wasn't there to receive it.

When she got out of the shower, Roz checked her phone and found a text from Jackie, "Heard what you did at the Blue Plate. Nice work. Can you get 250 words up by afternoon about the fire and alternate festival preparations? -JJ"

Jackie. Another person to whom she owed an apology. Roz typed back. "Absolutely. I also have some info about the fire from Sheriff A. Are you in the office this morning? I'd like to chat in person."

Jackie replied immediately, "At home, doing some festival stuff myself. Come on by."

Chapter Twenty-One

Roz

When she told him about Jackie's text, Erik ushered her out of the house. "Go. We can handle this, and you getting a story up online will help more than cookie rolling."

Jackie's house was a few sunny blocks away from downtown, past hundred-year-old houses. She was beginning to see why Jackie liked it here. This walk beat a crowded, smelly bus.

Roz rang the bell, but after a long moment with no answer, she opened the door and poked her head inside, calling, "Hello?" A string of muffled curses and the smell of burned sugar wafted from the back of the house. Good grief, if she had to put out another fire…

"Roz? Come on back. I'm having a little trouble here."

Roz found Jackie in the kitchen, trying to stir a large bowl of Rice Krispies and marshmallows. Wisps of smoke billowed from the bowl, and a charred lump of cereal smoldered in the sink. A dab of marshmallow was stuck to Jackie's forehead, and the kitchen counter was covered with stray cereal.

Roz blinked, trying to process the chaos in her boss's kitchen. Jackie clearly read the question on her face and answered. "So, Erik asked me to make some 'simple cookies' for the dessert table. Rosalind, I do not bake. But you know how persuasive Erik can be, so I said, 'Sure, how hard could it be?' I thought I'd make Rice Krispies treats. No bake, just melt everything together. So that's what I did. But when I put all this in the microwave, it started smoking."

"I don't bake much either," Roz said, "but we should be able to figure it out between the two of us. Want some help?"

"God, yes." Jackie gestured frenetically at the mess.

Roz searched her phone for a recipe. "Okay. This says you're supposed to melt all the gooey ingredients first and then stir the cereal in. Um," she evaluated the smoldering mess in Jackie's bowl, "I don't think this is salvageable."

Jackie said, "Toss it. We'll start over."

They worked for a few minutes in sticky silence, then Roz said, "Listen, Jackie. I need to apologize to you. I didn't mean to be so pushy. And I'm so sorry for your loss. I'm only beginning to realize how much losing Mom affected me, and that's much different from losing a spouse. I understand why your priorities changed."

Jackie waved her words away with a spatula. "You're forgiven. Maybe I could have been more forthcoming. I started to hate telling people who don't already know that my husband died. It's like as soon as I do, I've got 'widow' tattooed across my forehead and they don't see anything else. They mean well, but it's wearisome."

"Yeah. I've felt a bit of that, too." She hadn't realized it until now, but while Roz loved the opportunity to talk about her mom with people who had known and missed Kate, explaining what had happened to new people drained her. The disingenuous sympathy and the questions were exhausting, and there was sometimes a ghoulish degree of curiosity. "I get it."

They worked in silence for a while, pressing the treats into pans. Jackie covered them with plastic wrap, then said, "All right, let's get down to the work we're actually good at. I'd appreciate it if you could help me with the legwork, since I want to spend time with my son this weekend, but I will write the articles covering the arson angle. I'd like you to focus on the community pitching in to make the festival happen. I bet you can roll in some of the work you've already done."

"That's fine. Hey Jackie, I've been thinking a lot about Gavin. Monday, I'd like to get a lawyer to look at my NWC paperwork and see if there's any wiggle room in the shareholder agreement. I don't think I went about this the right way."

"I see." Jackie said. "I can't say I've been all that comfortable with it myself, but Gavin has brought us a lot of web traffic. We'd have to find a good way to transition if you're going to start writing under your own byline."

"Absolutely." Roz agreed. She'd been thinking about this, too. Done well, the revelation that she was Gavin could be a good story in itself. She needed to choose the right moment. While Jackie loaded her dishwasher, Roz settled onto a barstool, took out her notebook, and scrawled "Gavin Confession" at the top of a page. Below, she jotted down a few bullet points: the shareholder agreement and how rules like that shackle people to toxic family businesses, maybe something about continuing the family legacy, the different types of questions a male columnist might get.

She absolutely must have that embarrassing, overdue conversation with Andy before she came clean publicly. Thinking about it made her heart pound. She needed time to figure out the right spin. They'd have a nice evening together at the festival and then she could sit him down tomorrow morning and explain. She was beginning to trust that he understood her and would get why she'd done it, but she didn't trust that understanding enough to break the news carelessly.

"I'll figure something out," she said to Jackie. "In the meantime, I want to go down to the waterfront and get a good look at the Blue Plate in daylight so I can report better on the damage, then I'll swing by the hall to see how the preparations there are going. I'll put a short piece about the festival on the website this afternoon."

"That's fine." The doorbell rang. "Can you get that? I'm still sticky."

Roz opened the door to find Phoebe Sheppard-Shepherd, wearing yet another eyeball-assaulting Iris Indigo print, on Jackie's porch. This woman was inescapable.

"Hi! I'm looking for Jackie Jones. The festival chair is sending me around to ask members of the Chamber of Commerce if they have table linens we can borrow—all of the tablecloths that were supposed to be used for the banquet were ruined."

Celeste's beautiful hand-painted cloths. Such a shame.

"Sure." Roz ushered Phoebe toward the kitchen.

"Hey, I know you!" Phoebe chirped, "You're the admin for the paper. Do you live here?"

"I'm visiting on a…work matter." She realized too late that her notebook was open on Jackie's breakfast bar. Casually (she hoped), Roz flung a dish towel over the notes.

"Wow, on a Saturday?" Phoebe exclaimed. "I'm so glad I'm my own boss and can make my own hours!"

Roz did half an eye roll before she caught herself. "Hey Jackie,

Phoebe is looking for tablecloths they can use for the banquet. Do you have any?" She doubted Jackie did, she didn't seem much like the table-linens type.

"I have a whole bunch my mother-in-law gave me," Jackie pointed to a cabinet near the pantry. "Help yourself."

Phoebe pounced on the shelves of linens, heaping them on the counter to sort through. While she was busy with those, Roz said to Jackie, "I'm off to the waterfront to continue working on that project. I'll call you later with an update." She grabbed her bag and let herself out.

Andy

Andy didn't know whose borrowed pickup he was driving. Joe had left in the Geography Channel truck before dawn, so Erik had arranged a loaner. Someone just showed up at Mrs. Muir's with a truck and left the keys, along with several bags of potatoes. Mrs. Muir had already churned out gallons of lefse batter, which he was taking to the community hall next to the waterfront park.

In the hall, Andy found Olivia presiding over a squadron of Scandinavian matrons, chopping cucumbers and dill, and rolling meatballs. Among them was a shy teenage boy with a light brown complexion and dark curly hair. Andy asked him, "Where should I put this?"

"Over there by the griddles," the kid answered. "My gran is going to show everyone how to roll them out."

An older white woman with a cloud of snowy hair and a sweatshirt appliquéd with a Viking ship waved and placed her hand on the boy's shoulder. "I'm Alice. This is my grandson, Justin, and I've already taught him how to make perfect lefse today. If he can do it, you can, too." She showed Andy how to form the small doughy patties by hand, roll them flat, and then lay them on the griddle, flipping them when they bubbled. Once cooked, they were to be stacked in pans to warm for the banquet, but Alice insisted he try one fresh off the griddle, spread with butter. It was simple, warm, and delicious.

While he worked, Andy watched Olivia confer with Celeste about the buffet layout. She put a gentle hand on the small of Celeste's back, regarding her thoughtfully and listening attentively to whatever Celeste was saying about the arrangement of trays and serving bowls. Olivia caught his eye and gave him a self-conscious smile. Andy grinned back. They looked good together. He was happy to see Olivia moving on. It was none of his business with whom, but Celeste was great. Her connection with Roz might complicate things if both budding romances moved forward, but they'd all be able to navigate the situation cordially. Despite their arguments, he wanted to remain friends with Liv, but it seemed awkward — maybe this would actually help.

A pile of colorful linens burst through the door, the legs sticking out from under it clad in tight red pants patterned with tiny beer mugs. A muffled, girlish voice called from deep within the bundle, "Where can I put these down?" Andy guided her to a clean table, unsure how she'd seen over the pile of fabric to get into the building. The woman dumped the cloths, adjusted her ponytail, and turned triumphantly to Celeste. "I got tablecloths from most of the Chamber of Commerce members. None of them match the way the other linens would have, but I can make it look great."

Celeste examined the mix of patterns and colors. "I think it will be perfect, Phoebe. Thank you." They compared prints, placing complementary colors together to drape the tables and buffet.

Andy's phone buzzed with a video call. Charles. He almost didn't take it; technically he was off the clock forever and no longer obligated to talk to their producer. In case it was important, he sighed and picked up. "Hi, Charles."

"Andy! The network was crazy for the raw footage we showed them from yesterday. It was like your best early episodes, but even better! Loved Olivia coaching you on how to cook the meal again to impress a date. Golden! Do you know where she is now? I've been trying to reach her, but she isn't picking up her phone."

"She's pretty busy, Charles. There's been a bit of a mess here and we're trying to help sort it out." Andy explained about the festival and the fire, panning his phone around so Charles could see the bustling hall. "Hold on, I'll grab Liv." He walked the phone over to Olivia, who set aside the salmon she was seasoning, putting her face next to Andy's so that Charles could see them both.

"Olivia!" Charles gushed about the network's reaction to the new footage. "And, I have news," he added. "They want to sign you on for a fourth season at a twenty-five percent raise. They don't care whether you're married or not, they think you have a good rapport either way. We think the audience will follow. I'll get new contracts to your agents by Monday."

Andy exhaled. "I have to stop you there, Charles. I don't want to do another season, at any price. It's been great but I want to move on to other things." He glanced sideways at Olivia. "I'm sorry."

Olivia pressed her lips together, her I'm-disappointed-but-putting-on-a-brave-face tell. "It's all right, Andy. You only did the show in the first place because I wanted to. It wouldn't be fair of me to expect you to continue."

"This is certainly disappointing," Charles said. "But the execs were very specific about wanting both of you. They, ah, don't feel Olivia is relatable on her own."

Over the phone, Charles couldn't see the tears welling up in Olivia's eyes. She was so good at keeping them from falling down her cheeks. Andy had never known how she managed it. But he saw them; he always had.

Briskly, Olivia excused herself. "If that's all Charles, I've made a commitment to these people, and we have a lot of work to do." She stepped away and began hefting the pans of salmon into the oven, squaring her shoulders to lift the heavy trays.

"Hey Charles," Andy said. "Stay on. I want to show you something." Stepping discreetly into a corner, he turned the phone camera outward, toward the banquet preparations. Olivia was finished with the fish and was showing Justin and one of the grannies her trick for rolling even, consistently sized meatballs. She got them started and then listened as Alice showed her how to roll lefse out and drop it onto the sizzling griddle, then walked over to compliment Celeste and Phoebe's work on the buffet, now decorated with fall leaves and linens in a riot of bold colors and mixed patterns. He came back on camera to say, "You might call that...relatable?"

"Pretty good." Charles conceded. "Tell you what, send me some recorded footage of that kind of thing and I'll show it to the execs and see if they think there's anything there."

"You bet," said Andy. He'd get Olivia's permission first. The last thing she needed was to be filmed surreptitiously again, even if it was with honorable intentions.

Olivia was skeptical when he asked her. "You heard Charles, Andy. They don't want me by myself. It's okay, honestly. I'm sure I'll land somewhere. I could always think about opening a restaurant. People would come just to see if I'm really as beastly as they've heard."

"Liv," he looked her straight in the eye. "I know there's something here. Charles sees it, too. Give it a chance."

She sighed. "All right."

Olivia was understandably cautious with her optimism, but he detected a triumphant swagger in her step as she returned to the kitchen. If this worked, they'd both get what they wanted; Olivia could stay in front of the camera, and Andy could step away without worrying his reluctance was hurting her career.

Chapter Twenty-Two

Arson Suspects Apprehended
By: Jacqueline Jones, editor-in-chief

Crew members of the Skua, a vessel under contract with Case Oil, were detained this morning in Anacortes for questioning in a suspected arson at the Blue Plate diner in Port Poulsen. Sheriff Peter Andersen confirmed these individuals were involved in an altercation with the business owner earlier this week.

The Skua had been docked at the Port Poulsen Marina for maintenance work and was on its way to provide supply and transport support to Alaskan drilling camps when engine difficulties caused it to return to Anacortes.

While damage to the Blue Plate was minor, the restaurant will remain closed until further notice.

Celeste

The banquet hall was coming together beautifully. Celeste had replaced the decorations lost in the fire with borrowed items from homes around Port Poulsen. The effect was pleasingly eclectic. She had one last idea to tie the room together, bringing some of the outdoors in. She'd given a group of kids the task of gathering a few pinecones and the prettiest leaves from around the waterfront park. Celeste was headed to the beach to find some driftwood and seashells to represent the seaside aspect of the community.

As she passed the marina, she saw a familiar mast at the boat-yard dock. Her dad's sailboat was in the slip formerly occupied by the *Skua*. What would her father be doing here? She hadn't told him where she was or even spoken to him since the morning she quit NWC.

She didn't feel ready to see him, but if he was here, it would be better to get it over with than be surprised by him later. She approached the boat and rapped on the cabin window, but there was no response.

"Celeste?" Fred's voice came from behind her. She turned to find him standing on the dock, wearing his boating clothes: top-siders, cargo shorts, and a faded seersucker shirt. He held a latte from the café adjacent to the bookstore.

"Dad, what are you doing here?"

"I was looking for you. I guess you found me first. Your mom told me where you were, and I needed to get some work done on the *Grand Duchess*, so…" He shrugged, letting his voice trail off. "Can we talk? Let's get a cup of coffee."

"You have a cup of coffee." He never remembered that she only drank tea.

She didn't want this to be a long conversation. Under other circumstances, they might have gone into the Blue Plate, but that wasn't an option. She motioned to one of the benches along the dock. "Let's sit."

Celeste fought the urge to break the silence. It wasn't her responsibility to help this conversation go smoothly.

Finally, Fred spoke. "Listen, sweetheart. I'm sorry if you don't feel like I'm supportive of your life choices. Your mother says I need to be more 'affirmative,' whatever that means, if I want you to feel comfortable including me in your life."

"Okay." It didn't sound like he had made much progress. She didn't want to cut him out of her life entirely, but she needed a relationship where her identity and her choices were respected, especially if one of those choices was a relationship with Olivia.

"I've made a lot of mistakes," Fred continued, "and I'm going to take some time to sort myself out. I'm stepping away from NWC. Retiring early."

"Dad, really? I didn't know you were thinking about retirement." After Kate died, he'd become more invested in the magazine than ever.

"I wasn't." His sardonic smile was a shadow of its former self. "The board had some input. I think Rosalind will be happy."

"I'm sorry." She didn't know what else to say. Celeste wasn't sorry her former boss had been unseated, but she was sorry if her father was hurt.

"I am, too. But I'm going to make the best of it. You know I always wanted to do an extended sailing trip, and maybe the board did me a favor by pushing me into retirement while I'm still relatively young and healthy. I'm having the *Grand Duchess* checked out, then I'll leave from here."

"Dad, is that safe, to go all alone?"

He laughed, the old arrogance slipping back into his

demeanor. "Of course it's safe. I know what I'm doing, and the equipment on *Grand Duchess* is state of the art. You let me worry about me, and you focus on worrying about you."

This would have been the perfect opening to tell him about Olivia and her career plans, but Celeste wanted more time before she exposed those choices to her father. She remained silent.

"Well," Fred dusted his hands together. "It looks like there's going to be quite an event here tonight. Your mom said you'd been working on it. I don't suppose there's an extra ticket for your old man?" He was putting on the folksy tone he used when he wanted something; he didn't usually use it on Celeste. It made her feel like a stranger.

She couldn't imagine what the evening would be like with him sharing a table with Roz and Olivia. Neither of them would want him there. More importantly, she didn't want him there, either. It was going to take Celeste some time to reconcile the person who'd done all of these despicable things with the father who taught her how to tie a proper clove hitch knot. She'd work on it, probably with a therapist, but not tonight. Tonight was her night to keep getting to know Olivia and enjoy the payoff for all her hard work on the banquet.

"I'm sorry, but I think it would be best if you stayed on your boat tonight, Dad. I still need some space away from you, and I'm not willing to be the buffer between you and Roz again any time soon. If you want to turn over a new leaf, you can start by respecting my wishes."

"My goodness. I was only hoping for a free dinner. If you don't want me to come, I won't." He laughed, but it sounded fake; Celeste wasn't sure if he was covering genuinely hurt feelings, or if he was handling her. Probably a bit of both.

"Thank you."

They sat a while longer, chatting about nothing important;

memories of boat trips taken when Celeste was young, Fred's planned route for his sail. It was nice to simply be, without the conversation being tense or loaded. It was too bad her whole relationship with her dad couldn't be like this. She'd accepted that it never would, which made it feel more important to appreciate these short windows.

Roz

Caution tape and a notice from the fire marshal declaring the premises closed pending inspection marked the door of the Blue Plate. For Erik's sake, she hoped it wouldn't take too long to conclude the investigation. Roz cupped her hands around her eyes and peered in through the window. Thankfully, the dining room appeared to be untouched. Erik would need to do an inventory to be certain, but it didn't look like anything was broken or missing; the damage must be limited to the kitchen. That was lucky. The *Skua* crew had ruined one of Erik's paintings the other night and Roz hoped that would be the extent of any damage to irreplaceable items.

When she came around the corner of the building, Roz did a double take. Sitting on one of the benches at the top of the dock were Celeste and…Fred? Celeste had a piece of driftwood in her lap. Fred was looking down at his hands, but Celeste glanced up and caught Roz's eye. The two of them had an entire conversation via facial expressions; Roz raising her eyebrows to ask what was going on and if she should come over, Celeste shaking her head and waving her off, to say she'd fill her in later.

Roz retreated down the beach to give them some space and found a place to sit on a log near the high tide line, hidden from sight by some scrubby shrubs. She'd prefer to avoid a conversation with Fred. She took her laptop out to draft the article Jackie wanted to post about the festival, but her mind kept circling back to curiosity about what Fred was doing here and what he and Celeste were talking about. She hoped Celeste was okay; if Roz wasn't ready to talk to Fred yet she couldn't imagine Celeste was.

She had completed a draft and was proofreading it by the time Celeste walked down the beach. "Over here," Roz called.

Celeste joined her on the log and told her about Fred's retirement and sailing plans. "It's so strange," she said. "I didn't think he was even considering retirement. And sailing across the ocean all by himself… I know I wanted to put some distance between us, but I hope it's safe."

"I know the guy who runs the boatyard, we can ask him. I know he's your dad, Celly, and you want the best for him, but maybe this is better for everyone. And hey, I'll worry too. Fred and I sure have had our differences, but my mom saw something in him all those years ago. He did help raise me, after all."

Celeste laughed. "Mostly by grounding you."

"True. But I hope he finds something he needs on this trip. I have to give him credit for seeing that NWC needs a new direction and stepping down."

"I'm not sure it was his decision. You should talk to someone from the board."

"I did have a voicemail from Margaret. She didn't say what it was about. I'll call her back right now."

Puzzle pieces clicked into place. If Frederick had retired — or been pushed out — the editor-in-chief position was vacant. She dialed Margaret's home number, and her suspicions were confirmed.

"I owe you an apology, Roz. The board thought taking on a leadership role with your mom's death so new would be too much for you, but clearly, Frederick didn't handle being sole editor very well. We were recently made aware of some misconduct that told us it is time for a change."

"No hard feelings," Roz said. "I was disappointed, but I knew the board had their reasons."

"NWC needs fresh leadership," Margaret said. "I know you didn't leave on good terms, but with Frederick gone, we hope you'll come back to be editor-in-chief."

This was a dream come true; everything she could have wanted. While it was thrilling, it was also scary. Roz knew she would need to make some changes to the company — and herself. She took a deep breath and hoped her voice sounded calm when she gave Margaret her answer.

"I'll have to tie up some loose ends, but yes. I would love to come back. I have some ideas to freshen up the magazine while still honoring the original vision."

She didn't let herself make eye contact with Celeste until after she'd hung up.

"They're asking you back?" Celeste confirmed.

"They're asking me back *as editor*."

"Roz! That's amazing. You're going to do great."

"Oh god, I have to tell Jackie."

"I'll give you some privacy. I still have lots to do."

Jackie, thankfully, was thrilled for her. "I know this is what Kate would have wanted for you," Jackie said, "It was nice working with you, but frankly a lot more drama than I need in my life. We can phase out Gavin Garrett and no one will be the wiser."

"I may keep his social accounts open just for fun." Roz joked. "On another topic, Jackie, I have a proposal for you." Roz explained what she was thinking, and Jackie agreed to consider it.

Local Spirit Rising from the Ashes
Rosalind Connolly, guest reporter

In the wake of a Friday night fire that shut down Nordic Fest chairperson Erik Johansen's business, the Blue Plate, Port Poulsen residents banded together to ensure that Frigga's Feast, the annual festival banquet, will still go forward. Prepared foods and supplies were ruined or inaccessible due to the ongoing arson investigation, so friends of the festival opened their kitchens and rolled up their sleeves to keep the event on track. Locals were aided by celebrity chef Olivia Arden, who is in the area filming the final episode of her series, Ardent Life Adventures. Olivia's co-host, Andy Arden, also lent a hand.

Tickets for the banquet are available at the door. Mr. Johansen and Ms. Arden assure festival-goers that a good time and a fine meal will be had by all who attend, with local traditional favorites as well as contemporary dishes prepared by Ms. Arden. Tickets are $35 and profits benefit the Community Fund.

Chapter Twenty-Three

Roz

The community center was crowded by the time Roz arrived. The drab, industrial space had been livened with splashes of color on all the tables, and the banquet spread covered a full wall. Roz couldn't see the food past the line of people filling their plates, but the savory smell made her mouth water. The hall buzzed with chatter and the commotion of people greeting friends and finding seats. She made her way to a table in the back corner where Celeste was saving seats for their group. In the center of the table, an arrangement of driftwood, beach rocks, and wildflowers were set off by a cobalt blue tablecloth patterned with tiny red and yellow flowers.

"I made you a plate." Celeste said. "I was going to wait for

Olivia, but she said she wasn't sure when she'd get a chance to eat. And knowing you, you haven't eaten all day."

"You're the best. I'm starving." Roz dug in. The salmon was perfect; flaky without being dry, spiced just enough, and the salt-crusted skins of the potatoes gave way to fluffy interiors.

After a few bites, Roz filled Celeste in on what she'd learned. "I spoke to Colin at the boatyard about Fred's boat. He says *Grand Duchess* is sound for open-ocean sailing. Apparently, it's a good choice for a solo sail because the electronics for communications and navigation are top of the line, and it's a sturdy size but not too big to handle alone. I thought your dad was being pretentious when he traded his old boat in for it last year, but I guess it's a good thing he did." However Fred and Celeste had left things, Roz knew Celeste would worry.

"Thanks for checking. I have to trust he knows what he's doing. And I think it's best for us to have a break from each other."

Roz picked at the tablecloth. "Do you think you'll come back to work at NWC now that he's gone? I'm offering you and Barry your jobs back, of course. We can talk about what direction you'd want for your content."

Celeste exhaled slowly before answering in an even tone. She shook her head with a wistful smile. "Roz, no. I'm so happy for you, but I meant what I said about making a change. Olivia is going to put me in touch with some local caterers I can work with to do event design."

Roz was disappointed, but not surprised. It would have been perfect if everything could go back to normal, minus the head-aches from Fred, but she was proud of Celeste for looking out for her own interests. "I'll write you a glowing reference, of course."

Celeste laughed. "I'm not sure references from family count. But thank you."

Andy

Andy flexed his hands and rolled his wrists as he walked down the hill. While he was no stranger to intense physical activity, the hours he'd spent shaping latkes and meatballs had used tiny muscles in his fingers he hadn't known existed. He had prepared pan after pan of food with the other volunteers, taking short breaks to film Olivia at work. He'd turned Justin loose with a camera, too, and the kid had captured some great footage. It was no surprise that Jackie's son had a good journalistic instinct.

While they worked, Andy had taken video of Alice, Justin's grandmother, speaking about the programs the banquet proceeds would help fund. "We look forward to this all year, but it's more than a fun party," she'd said. "The money we raise this weekend helps fund the community center. It's an important resource, especially for seniors and young people. There are scholarships to the college in Bremerton, after school programs, and we run a small food bank and transportation service for seniors. Ms. Arden's help today is going to have a real impact on this community."

Andy made his way through the maze of vendor booths in the park to the hall, bought a ticket from the couple at the admission table, and stepped inside. The room was a beehive of color and activity; neighbors of all ages greeted and jested with each other, already piling plates with food. He was surprised to see many people helping themselves to lutefisk, even though Alice had assured him it would be eaten. "Most of us don't care for it," she'd confessed, "but eating it is a bit like accepting an ancestral dare." Andy would stick to the baked goods and leave the lye-pickled fish to the die-hard Scandinavians.

Olivia waved from the kitchen window. She was surrounded by a group of ladies who were watching her pull a salmon filet from the oven and anoint it with fresh lemon and a sprinkle of dill, and she was glowing. In fact, in the past twenty-four hours, she'd looked happier than he could remember seeing her since college. Others were noticing, too. Olivia exuded a gracious aura that the whole gathering seemed to bask in. Andy used his phone to get a few minutes of footage. Where were the tabloid photographers now? He hoped one day Liv would have the right vehicle to show the world her true strengths. In spite of the way she'd been treated in the press, she was at her best in the limelight.

He craned his neck and searched the crowd. Where was Roz? When they got up this morning, they'd intended to spend the day together, but responsibilities had drawn them in different directions and kept them separated. Andy hoped this would be the first of many days they would spend apart only to reunite in the evening to tell each other about their days.

He finally spotted her seated at a corner table with Celeste, but before he could weave through the crowd someone grabbed his elbow. It was Alice's husband, Henry, an avid fly fisherman who had a bone to pick with Andy about the Montana fly fishing episode of *Ardent Life Adventures*.

"Son," Henry's grip on his shoulder was firm. "You have to use the right fly for your locale. The green butted skunk is completely overrated. For steelhead, you want a spinner or a beadhead nymph."

"I'll keep that in mind, sir."

Andy was about to escape when Alice sidled up to ask what it had been like to go on the Lionel Lenord show, and before long he'd amassed a small audience. He caught Roz's eye and shrugged. They'd connect eventually but for now he rather liked communicating with her across a crowded room, looking forward to the time they'd spend together later, alone.

Roz

"Whew!" Barry landed in the chair next to Roz, trailed by Erik.

"This is wonderful, Erik," Roz said. "Well done."

"Thanks," he replied. "I couldn't have pulled it off without all the help. Speaking of which—" he nudged Barry with an elbow.

"We have some news," Barry said. "I'm staying on at the Blue Plate as manager."

"You're moving here?" Celeste asked.

"When my lease is up next month. Erik thinks it's 'too soon to cohabitate.'" Barry rolled his eyes. "So, I'll technically be living in the apartment above the restaurant as soon as the fire damage is repaired."

"But we plan to see a lot of each other outside of work." Erik covered Barry's hand with his.

"That is big news," Roz said. "I'm thrilled for you both." If someone had told her she, Celeste, and Barry would all meet someone special within a week, she would have laughed them out of the room. She couldn't explain it, but maybe they had sent something into the universe that morning they all left NWC, opening them up to new possibilities.

"I think that's great, Bear. We have some news ourselves." Celeste filled them in on her conversation with Fred, and Roz took over to tell them about her call with Margaret.

"Roz!" Barry said, "That's amazing. You are going to take NWC by storm. I'd come back in a heartbeat if I didn't have a better offer on the table." He beamed at Erik.

Roz laughed. "I get it."

"Well," Erik stood up and dusted his palms. "It's time for my speech. Roz, could you join me up front please?"

"What? Why?"

"Just go." Barry gave her a gentle shove toward the front of hall, where a PA system had been set up.

Jittery, Roz stood next to Erik at the front of the room. He tapped the microphone to get everyone's attention, and said, "Friends, welcome to the Seventy-Ninth Annual Frigga's Feast!" The crowd erupted into applause. "This is my first year chairing the festival. My father did it for many years and it meant the world to him. And so, it means the world to me to carry on the tradition. This year, we had a few bumps in the road, but pulled it off with help from all of you. I'd like to especially thank Olivia Arden, who donated and cooked the delicious salmon this year. Thanks to all of you, I am pleased to say that we've raised more than eleven thousand dollars for our community fund tonight!" The crowd clapped again, with several 'woo-hoos' thrown in. "As you know, a fire at my restaurant threw a wrench into some of our banquet preparations. But that fire would have been much worse without the help of Roz Connolly here, and her friend Andy Arden. Andy, can you come up here, please?"

Andy joined Roz at Erik's side, grabbing her hand for a moment to squeeze it. "Roz and Andy risked their own safety, and for that I can't thank them enough. But I can try. Andy, Roz, we'd like to bestow on you the great honor of being the first recipients of the Medal of Musphelheim." He chuckled. "For those of you not versed in Norse mythology, Musphelheim is the realm of the fire giants. It's a new honor, because we made it up this morning. But," Erik put on a mock-serious tone, "it's a very great honor, nonetheless. Please excuse the hasty construction of your medals."

Some of the younger kids jogged forward with aluminum foil medallions surrounded by red, orange, and yellow tissue-paper flames. Roz and Andy bent down so that the medals could be placed around their necks, then stood up and bowed to the cheering crowd.

As the applause died down, a voice called out from the side

of the room. "That woman is a fraud!"

Confused murmurs spread from table to table as Phoebe Sheppard-Shepherd marched to the front of the room. She was incandescent with rage and brandished Roz's notebook. The one she had left at Jackie's house.

Roz's stomach bottomed out. She couldn't be certain, but it looked like Phoebe had the book open to her page of notes about strategically revealing Gavin's identity.

"Phoebe, I'm sure there's been some mistake," Erik began, but Phoebe snatched the microphone from his hand. Roz waited patiently for the floorboards to open and swallow her, but no such luck. With a squeeze, Andy let go of her hand. She wiped her sweaty palms on her dress, unable to turn in Andy's direction and meet his eyes, while Phoebe continued her rant.

"I met this woman in the newspaper offices, and she claimed to be the administrative assistant! But I found this notebook, and…" Phoebe paused for dramatic impact, "she and Gavin Garrett are the same person. That's right! She's been providing advice under false pretenses!"

Phoebe was still holding her dramatic pause, as though she were expecting shocked exclamations from the crowd, but none came.

Roz sheepishly mustered her loudest voice.

"It's true. I was writing as Gavin Garrett. This wasn't how I envisioned telling everyone. But I guess… now you know?" She laughed nervously, the room still silent. "It was a pen name and well… it's complicated."

Phoebe continued, "She meddled with my marriage and my business —" There was some grumbling from the crowd and Roz felt the sting of a few dirty looks this time.

"Phoebe, I am truly sorry. I only to wanted help."

Phoebe sputtered at the audience, "Don't believe her. She

lied to us!"

Erik shifted nervously on his feet and gingerly acquired the microphone back from Phoebe.

"Ok, so on that note…"

"Doesn't anyone else care?" Phoebe shouted out to the crowd.

A few people muttered exclamations along the lines of "Not really…" and "She saved the waterfront."

From the back of the hall, a studious looking woman piped up to say, "Actually, Ann Landers and Dear Abby both wrote under pen names," which prompted another woman at her table to say, "I'm pretty sure Miss Manners is an alias, too."

This elicited laughter from the room, and Phoebe's triumph melted from her face. Steve came to her side and put his arm around her. Her righteous anger dissolved. Phoebe's posture collapsed, her lower lip protruded, and her wide blue eyes brimmed with tears.

Steve gently walked Phoebe to the side of the stage. "Babe," he said quietly, "a week ago I thought you cared more about your hustle than me, and I didn't know how to talk to you about it. This woman helped me understand that you were trying to do something for our family, and make sure we have a plan to pay for whatever we might need to do to help it grow. I don't know if that would have happened without this person, no matter what her name is."

"I guess," Phoebe shot a reproachful glance at Roz, "but I don't think what she did was right."

"You know what, Phoebe?" Roz turned to face Phoebe and Steve instead of the crowd, reaching out a hand to pat Phoebe awkwardly on the upper arm. "It wasn't. I owe you an apology. I wish both of you the best, and I want you to know that I'll be making some changes, starting with retiring my pen name."

"Thank you," said Steve. He guided Phoebe, who was still

tomato-red, back to their table.

"Well," Erik said slowly into the microphone, "I don't have anything to follow that." The crowd laughed. "Enjoy your meals, everyone, and join us in the beer garden later for dancing."

Roz needed to know how Andy was taking all of this. She turned to where she'd left him standing at the back of the stage, but he was gone.

Celeste

When Phoebe took the microphone, Olivia had murmured in her ear, "I could use a drink. How about you?"

Celeste nodded, unable to tear her eyes away from the scene playing out up front. She was torn between satisfaction that Roz was seeing the natural consequences of her actions and worry that she'd be hurt. The worry crystallized when Andy stepped away. Her gaze followed his path across the room; if he stormed out, she'd follow him, try to talk him into coming back to at least hear Roz out.

But Andy didn't go out the door, he headed for the bar, where Olivia was in a heated conversation with — *Oh no*. Her father.

Celeste was out of her chair before she even thought about what she was going to do, bumping into the backs of several chairs as she hurried to them.

She arrived in time to hear the last words Olivia spat at Fred. " — would break Celeste's heart."

"Dad. You said you'd keep your distance tonight."

"I didn't want to miss a good time," he said. "I just came for a quick drink." He'd clearly already had several. His face was flushed and there was a sway in his stance.

Fred turned to Olivia. "I only want what's best for my daughter."

Olivia said, "I don't know Celeste well yet, but I do know that she asked you to give her some space and the first thing you did was show up here, uninvited. I don't think you have any idea what's best for her." Her tone was fierce, and her words made Celeste feel seen and protected.

"She's right, Dad. You need to go." Celeste made eye contact and held it. She registered shock and betrayal in his expression, but she wasn't going to back down. This was her boundary to hold.

"Mr. George," Andy said. "Why don't I walk you back to your boat and let everyone enjoy their evening."

With an arm around his shoulders that was half support, half firm guidance, Andy moved Fred out the door.

"What would break my heart?" Celeste asked, although she wasn't sure she wanted to know.

"My experience working with your father was pretty—" Olivia paused, clearly searching for the right words " —unpleasant. I don't want to have secrets between us, but are you sure you want to hear the details?"

"Let's sit down." As they walked, Celeste thought about Olivia's question. She could read between the lines of Olivia's reaction and Fred's forced resignation well enough to know that whatever Olivia told her would be painful for both of them. Maybe she needed to know, but it would keep.

"No. Not tonight, at least. Let's just try to enjoy the rest of the party." Olivia would be leaving for California in the morning, and she didn't want an ugly conversation to mar the rest of their night together. There would be plenty of time later for that conversation, and more, in the months to come.

Chapter Twenty-Four

Roz

Although the crowd's nonchalant reaction to Phoebe's revelation was gratifying, it didn't matter as much as Andy's. Roz's opportunity to talk to him and explain everything was gone now, and she couldn't blame him for not taking the truth in stride. His interactions with Gavin had been direct and personal, and the anonymity had been one-sided. She scanned the room, hoping he hadn't left, but didn't see him anywhere.

That was that, then. He knew what she'd done and didn't want anything to do with her. The old Roz might have cut and run to maintain her pride, but that wasn't an option. She cared too much. Not just about preserving his good opinion of her, but about giving him the apology he deserved — even if he still rejected her. He couldn't have gotten far. She had to find him.

As she passed the bar, Jackie stopped Roz and handed her a drink.

"You look like you need this," Jackie said. She continued with a wry chuckle, "That was awkward, although I suppose it solves the problem of whether to make an announcement about ending Gavin Garrett's column."

"I'm sorry about that. And the mess I've made of everything this week. I'm doing my best to make everything right."

"Do a good job with NWC, and I'll consider us even."

"Deal." They clinked their plastic cups. "If only Phoebe was as gracious as you are. What a piece of work."

"Yeah." A devilish grin spread over Jackie's face. "I'm going to hire her."

Roz choked on her drink. "What?"

"I'm about to be down a staff member, she's a decent writer, and," Jackie smirked, "a tenacious investigator. I could also use some help with marketing, and she has skills — she can get just about anyone to buy those damn leggings. Ad space and subscriptions should be a piece of cake for her. Plus, the paper's in a co-op for a health plan that has good coverage for fertility medicine."

"Jackie, you're a sucker for a hot mess."

Jackie gave her a pointed look, clearly aware Roz was referring to herself as well as Phoebe. She said, "Family is important. This is something I can do to make someone's life better, and it happens to be a smart business decision in the bargain."

"I hope you don't end up with a wardrobe full of leggings with tiny typewriters and newspapers all over them."

Jackie arched a brow. "One does hope that, yes. I think perhaps once she has a new career to pour her energy into, the clothing will take a back seat."

"I hope you're right." This conversation was riveting, but Roz had been distracted from her search for too long. "Listen, do you know where Andy went?"

"I saw him head outside a few minutes ago."

"Thanks." Roz shrugged into her jacket and made her way to the door.

The troll garden Celeste created in the picnic shelters had looked adequately charming in daylight, but with the over-sized cardboard cutout mushrooms and plants lit by fairy lights, and the gentle illumination from the park's lamp posts, it had taken on a fantasy quality. A few couples were already linger-ing in the dappled glow, and the DJ had started playing. Roz scanned the half-light for Andy but didn't see him in the party area. Expanding her search, she found herself on the path leading toward the marina.

In the distance, she made out the silhouette of a man walking up the ramp connecting the dock to the shoreline. As he drew closer, she recognized Andy's sure stride.

Roz rushed forward to meet him. "Andy, I've been looking everywhere for you. Listen, I can explain everything. You don't have to forgive me, but please hear me out."

Andy gave his head a confused shake. "I'm all ears, but I don't think you have anything to explain to me."

"I mean about what Phoebe said, after the medals were handed out. I know what I did wasn't right, and you're the one who was most wronged. I'm so sorry. But I didn't set out to lie to you or hurt you, I promise."

"Roz," Andy guided her to a bench and sat angled toward her, taking her hand in his. "*I'm* sorry. When we were getting our medals, I looked out and saw Olivia arguing with Fred, and I thought I was needed. If I was wrong about that, I apologize. I didn't mean to leave you in the hot seat alone."

Roz's mind whirled away from her apology. "Fred was there? Celeste asked him not to come."

"He'd had a few drinks. Quite a few. I'm not sure he was thinking all that rationally."

"Oh no." Roz hoped Celeste and Olivia were okay.

"I took Fred back to his boat and I don't think he'll be coming near either of them uninvited again. Celeste made herself quite clear."

"Good." Fred didn't drink to excess often, but when he did, he could be vicious.

"Roz, I want to make sure you understand. Olivia has been a big part of my life and she'll always be a friend I care about," Andy took her hand, "but I'm ready for this new love, and in the future my friendships won't prevent me from being there for you. You needed me too and I see that now."

She thought about it for a second, then smiled, "I don't mind." She meant it. Some people might say she had reason to be jealous — this was the second time since she'd known him that Andy had disappeared in order to help Olivia — but she admired the way he was tuned in to the people he cared about and helped when needed. Andy's steadfast support for his ex spoke volumes about him.

She gave her nervous energy free rein and blurted, "I had everything under control. I'm not sure what you could have done and I'm glad you were able to help Celeste and Olivia. Fred can be a stubborn ass and he doesn't always listen to—" Andy's words registered belatedly, warm and welcome. Roz stopped speaking abruptly and looked into Andy's eyes. "Did you say, 'love'?"

"Maybe." Andy grinned with a hint of roguishness, replaced by sincerity before he spoke again. "This is so new for both of us, but I feel at home with you. Like I've known you forever. At the same time, I feel like getting to know you better, every part of you, is a great adventure I'm only beginning."

"Me too." It was exactly the same for her. Despite their stops and starts, she felt like she was on the precipice of something wonderful. But the glow inside her dimmed…did he truly know her, or did he still not know what she'd done? "Did you hear what Phoebe said?"

He shook his head, "I was preoccupied with Fred, I'm sorry. But what could she possibly have to say that would change how I feel about you?"

He started to lean in for a kiss, but Roz stopped him with a hand on his chest. "Well," she began. This was ridiculous, how could she explain it? They couldn't move forward until he knew the full truth. Best to just say it. "She found my notebook and figured out that there is no Gavin Garrett. It's been me all along."

She scooted a bit away from him on the bench, bracing herself for the hurt, angry reaction she assumed to be forthcoming.

Andy's guffaw broke the stillness of the evening. Roz watched, confused, as he wiped tears of laughter from the corners of his eyes. "Oh, Roz. I'm sorry—really sorry. It's sweet of you to apologize, but I knew you were Gavin the whole time."

Roz was speechless. She'd been agonizing over this, and he already knew?

He moved closer to her, and the solid warmth of his body was comforting. She hadn't noticed how chilly the night had turned, or that she had her arms firmly crossed until he gently disengaged one hand, lacing his fingers through it. "I thought you knew I knew." She blinked at him, and he took her face in both hands and kissed her on the forehead.

Roz struggled to understand. "But I lied to you. I wrote to you as him. It was totally manipulative and deceitful. Aren't you mad?"

"I was annoyed, for a while," he admitted. "I felt conde-scended to, and I thought it was a bit…childish?"

Ouch. She deserved that, but still.

He squeezed her hand. "Sorry. But I screwed up, too. If any-thing, I'm the one who should be sorry for not telling you more about myself before we spent the night together."

She smacked him on the shoulder. "But how could you possi-bly have known for sure?"

"Roz, you're wearing my jacket in your profile picture. Come on." He held out his phone to show her, pointing out the blackberry stain on the collar of Gavin's jacket in his profile pic-ture, and its twin on the one he was currently wearing. "Even if I wasn't sure from the things Gavin wrote to me, I knew that stain was there."

Roz hadn't known it was possible to feel this embarrassed. Of course. Barry borrowed Andy's jacket for her photo shoot as Gavin. Otherwise, they wouldn't even have met. She buried her face in her hands and groaned. "You must think I'm such a buffoon."

Andy stroked her back. "I don't. I was having fun. I found it charming, the lengths you were willing to go to. Also…I knew I'd put you off at the hotel. I wasn't as forthcoming as I should have been either. I wanted a chance to win some of your trust back and get close to you."

"Oh." Roz said, sitting up to look him in the eye.

"Yeah." Andy took her face between his hands and kissed her on the lips. She answered it, sliding her arm up his back to tangle her fingers in his hair.

They broke the kiss when the disco beat from the beer garden told them the dancing was in full swing.

Reluctantly, Roz said, "We should go back. Our friends are waiting."

"Yeah, we probably should," Andy replied, putting his arm around her.

"It would be unconscionable to leave the banquet without saying goodbye," Roz leaned her head against Andy's shoulder.

"Mm-hmm," Andy replied, leaning over to kiss her neck. "Egregious."

"People will be looking for us."

"Quite likely." He slipped his arm around her waist. His thumb moved in slow circles over the thin fabric of her dress.

"Twenty-four hours ago, I was wondering how I could get you to forgive me for deceiving you," she told him.

"Twenty-four hours ago, I was wondering how I was going to ever get you to talk to me again as yourself," he replied. "Since then, we've put out a fire, helped put on a banquet, you've been given your dream job, and I've become unemployed."

"And we got medals!" Roz added, holding hers up to admire it.

"And we got medals."

"About that unemployed thing…do you know what your next move is?"

"Joe and I are going to work on a photography book. You should see his pictures, they're amazing — but that won't take all of my time. Plenty of time to travel to Seattle to see you." He kissed her.

"You can write anywhere, right? I know Bowie would love to have you around."

"Oh, Bowie," he laughed, "you're going to pin this on the dog."

"No." She dropped the playful tone. "I'd like it, too. I don't want to freak you out, but I think you might be my person."

Andy pulled away from her and took both of her hands in his. He looked deep into her eyes and said, "I think you're mine, too. And I want to spend as much time with you as it takes for us both to be sure."

"You do?" There was still a tiny voice inside Roz, asking her if they were moving too fast. The tiny voice could shove it.

"I do." He slid his arm around her waist and drew her to him for a kiss. Together, they stood and strolled away from the party, hand in hand.

Chapter Twenty-Five

Eight Weeks Later

A letter from the new editor-in-chief,

As I sit down to write this, I feel like I'm greeting old friends. I grew up at NWC. Some of my earliest memories involve my mother sitting down to write her letters from the editor, way back when this was a print magazine. I have some very big shoes to fill. To tell you the truth, they might be a bit too big for me. But I have the example my mom left me, and the things she taught me for guidance, and I know I will grow into it. I hope you will join me on that journey.

With new leadership comes change, and I have some content

notes to share with you. First of all, I will no longer be answering "Kate Knows Best" letters. My mother was extremely proud of this column. I've realized recently that I do not yet have her expertise, nor do I have the appropriate experience to provide the advice our readers deserve. I've learned that to truly be of service to people, you have to make a genuine effort to understand their perspective. I've spent too much time telling people what I would do in their shoes instead of walking a mile with them.

I'm keenly aware that for every person who writes in, there are hundreds more in similar situations who will read the answer. It is a tremendous responsibility. I asked myself what my mother would have told me to do. Kate Connolly would have said, "Why don't you ask someone?" So, that's what we are going to do.

I'm changing the name of the column to "Our Best Advice," and am excited to tell you that we will be consulting a team of experts to answer your questions, including Jacqueline Jones answering parenting and career questions, and Olivia Arden (who gamely served as a guest columnist during my absence) answering questions about kitchen dilemmas and modern etiquette. Celeste George has left her design column to pursue other avenues, but I'm thrilled to announce that she will be on our panel for questions about LGBTQIA+ matters. We'll be bringing other expert "Kates" on board as well. I hope you love the new format.

In the meantime, I will focus on guiding the magazine and writing human interest pieces. I've missed getting out into the community, interviewing people, and digging into a subject to bring you stories about the world we live in.

I can't wait to show you what we've been working on.

All my best,

Rosalind Connolly

Roz

Roz saved the file and stood, turning toward the window. She joined her hands above her head and leaned into a stretch, grateful for the leggings that made the deep bend possible. To her chagrin, she'd purchased several pairs from the last of Phoebe's stock, and they really were comfortable. These were dark gray with a subtle black stripe that matched her oversized sweater, but she had a pair at home covered with rainbow paw prints. The south-facing window of her corner office framed Mount Rainier perfectly, and the late afternoon light made the celadon walls glow golden. This was Kate's old office. Roz had been tempted to keep Kate's furniture and earth-toned paint, but decided to make a fresh start, choosing her own soothing colors and modern, comfortable furniture. Celeste helped her pick the art for the walls, including a newly finished painting by Erik, a sharply detailed close-up of Kate's glasses balanced on a stack of her favorite books. It was a more fitting portrait of her mother than any likeness of her face could ever have been.

Roz had made changes at home, too. With Celeste's help, she cleared Kate's belongings out of the master bedroom, redecorating and making space for her own things and some of Andy's, since he was there most of the time now. She'd kept the cherrywood furniture which she had always loved, but exchanged Kate's floral quilt for a duvet with stripes in various shades of dusty blue, Andy's favorite color.

Roz's new assistant, Hailey, tapped on the open door. "I need your signature on a couple of things, and Rob from sports is here to talk about his Seahawks piece."

"Great." Roz glanced quickly at the sheaf of papers Hailey handed her: a couple of expense reports and the offer letter for

Celeste's replacement, and added her signature. "Send Rob in."

Halfway through an excruciating conversation about playoff odds and rival team coverage, Roz's phone buzzed with a text from Andy, "Just landed, picking up Thai on the way home. You want the red curry with prawns?"

She typed back, "Yes please! See you later, XO."

Roz felt a thrill at the prospect of seeing Andy even though he had only been gone a week, meeting with Joe and their publisher. Their book, combining Joe's vibrant photographs and Andy's expressive prose about each location, would be published in the spring in time for Father's Day and graduation gifts.

Roz finished her meeting and double checked her shopping list. She and Andy would be taking the ferry to Port Poulsen in the morning to spend Thanksgiving week with Barry and Erik. She couldn't wait to curl up in Erik's cozy house, sharing a meal with their friends.

She'd miss Celeste. Olivia was in the middle of shooting a Christmas special for the House & Garden Network and couldn't take time away from LA. Celeste was spending much of her time in California these days.

Roz shrugged her coat on over her sweater and tapped her thigh, signaling to Bowie that it was time to go. Making the office dog-friendly might not have been the most important change she had made but along with the relaxed dress code, it was one of her favorites. She clipped the leash on, and he trotted behind her to the elevator.

They walked home the long way. Roz would always miss her mom; facing the holidays was especially hard, and she would always feel deeply sad that Kate never got a chance to know Andy, whom she would have loved. Knowing how happy and proud Kate would have been was the next best thing.

The sidewalks were crowded, buzzing with pre-holiday

energy. A thousand tiny dramas played out all around her, but Roz was too engaged in her own story to register a single over-heard conversation.

Read Next

How to Align the Stars
by Amy Dressler

She's an astronomy professor at a small college in wine country. He's the annoying librarian she loves to hate… **How to Align the Stars** spins the original Shakespeare tale of *Much Ado About Nothing* into a smart romance, ending with a surprising twist.

Learn More: **www.egretlakebooks.com**

Book Club Guide

1. Who was your favorite character, and why?

2. Roz makes several rash decisions in this book because she is acting on feelings. What is a time you made an irrational choice during an emotionally fraught situation?

3. Do you think Roz and Celeste would be friends if they had never been stepsisters? Why or why not?

4. If you were the host of a show like *Ardent Life Adventures,* where would you go? What would you do and eat there?

5. Which character did you relate to the most? The least? Why?

6. How did your opinion of Olivia change over the course of the book?

7. Erik mentions that, like Roz, his mother has recently passed away. Jackie is widowed. How do each of the three handle grief differently?

8. Have you ever written a letter to an advice column? What was it about? Did it get published?

9. Bowie has some quirks that get Roz into awkward situations. Have you ever had a pet like that?

10. Do you think Roz should have faced harsher consequences for her deception?

11. What do you think Celeste's relationship with her father will look like in the future?

12. Do you think Roz and Andy will stay together? What about Olivia and Celeste? Barry and Erik?

Shakespeare Reader Guide

1. Which characters from the book are most similar or different from Shakespeare's *As You Like It* play, and why?

2. In Shakespeare's *As You Like It*, characters leave the French court for the forest, where they connect more deeply with their romantic desires. Here, characters leave the city for a small town. What similarities do you see in other modern romantic comedies?

3. What cultural norms around marriage have changed between the time the Shakespeare play was written and modern day? What cultural norms have remained the same?

4. *As You Like It* ends with four weddings, but *The Best Advice* doesn't have any weddings or engagements; instead, there are three new couples and one existing marriage made stronger. Do you think the romantic spirit of the original is effectively preserved and modernized?

5. "All the world's a stage, and all the men and women merely players," is one of Shakespeare's most famous lines. How are the characters in *The Best Advice* performing "roles?"

6. In *The Best Advice*, Olivia is Andy's ex-wife, but in *As You Like It*, Oliver is Orlando's estranged brother. How does changing the gender of this character and the nature of their relationship impact the story?

7. Why do you think author Amy Dressler chose to make the Rosalind character an advice columnist?

8. What themes are shared by *The Best Advice* and *As You Like It*?

Acknowledgments

This book would not be ending its long road to publication in your hands without a number of people who believed in it from the beginning. Most of all, S and Karen, who encouraged me to get back to writing and stick with it and helped me get the time and space to do so. I have been so touched by my friends and family who have championed my writing. Among them (but not limited to!) Karen Grande, Harriet Plucker, Alan and Cheryl Kane, Nancy Robison, Lea Webb, Jessica Robertson, Maureen Hayes, Joelle Davis, and Misti Ernsberger.

My very earliest readers, who are too many to list accurately (I needed a lot of pep talks) include Melissa Snider, Devon McCollum and Natasha Hall, Beth Heins, Todd Grooten, Peter Amos, Sarah Hawkins, and Megan Elba. Meghan Brawley, Olivia Allison, and Nicole Roth provided input through the whole journey and I can't thank them enough for their wisdom and patience. My husband once again used his nearly-supernatural eye for detail to assist with proofreading. Huge thanks to Tess Jones, who saw the potential in this book and helped me make it shine.

My deep dive into advice columns was invaluably informed

by the HAMKIAs, many of whom also provided helpful input and encouragement on this project.

I wouldn't be a writer without a mom who helped me grow up loving books. I miss her every single day but am so grateful to have had her.

About the Author

As a literature major, theater nerd, and believer in the cathartic power of humor, Amy Dressler has always gravitated toward Shakespeare's comedies. Finding ways to transpose those stories into contemporary settings that highlight the heroines' emotional arcs is a fun — albeit emotionally fraught — puzzle. She lives in the Seattle area and has worked as a librarian, freelance pop culture writer, and in local government.

FOLLOW AUTHOR AMY DRESSLER
www.AmyDressler.com

EXPLORE MORE BOOKS
www.EgretLakeBooks.com

If you like this book please leave a review on the
platform where you purchased it. We appreciate our
readers, thank you!

Instagram: **@egretlakebooks**
Newsletter: **www.egretlakebooks.com**

www.ingramcontent.com/pod-product-compliance
Lightning Source LLC
Chambersburg PA
CBHW030642020726
47493CB00006B/1834